THE NECESSITY
OF
RAIN

SARAH CHORN

Cover art by Pen Astridge

Edited by Nathan Hall

Proofread by Isabelle Wagner

Chapter headers by Allegra Pescatore

To everyone
Who has
Loved and lost.

There will be better days than this.

— DIVINE AETHER, GOD OF CREATION

AUTHOR'S NOTE

"There is nothing to writing. All you do is sit down at a typewriter and bleed." - Ernest Hemingway

I am the youngest of six kids, born to parents who were older when they had me. The age gap between me and my siblings ranges from eight to seventeen years. I have always been at a different cycle of life than the rest of my family. My parents have always been older. So have my brothers and sisters.

None of that mattered until recently.

I think it happened both slowly and all at once. The first time I showed up at my parents' house and realized my mom had stopped dying her hair and it was white now. Or when my niece had her first child. Or when my dad's twin brother died. Or...

And then there are moments that happen like a flash in the pan and suddenly I realize everything is different now, and yet it still feels the same. The discord is... acute. Part of me is still young and just learning the pain and pleasure of the world. The other part is listening to my sister talk about retirement.

I have a locked room in my soul, a place where I keep moments in amber. I will always be holding my kids for the first time, new and pink and full of life. I will always be watching them explore all those first experiences. I will always remember when that was me. I will always savor my own firsts, each one sweeter than the last.

Time passes faster when you start paying attention to it.

I wrote this book while I was gardening. In fact, it was gardening that told me what this story was really about. To garden, you must be aware of the cycles of life, the seasons, how endings are necessary for beginnings to exist.

This is the third incarnation of *The Necessity of Rain.*

It has taken me three tries to find my way through this story. It's required me to open myself in ways I didn't anticipate. More than a few times I've had to pause and collect myself before working on another section. Writing this was an act of delicate shattering. An exploration filled with both beauty and pain.

I turned forty this year. It was a strange experience. It's like one day you wake up and you're middle aged. Poised halfway between yesterday and tomorrow. Everyone around you is older. You go to school pickup and remember when you were in sixth grade and your friends' parents were as old as you are now. It's weird. And it's also liberating. There's freedom that comes with being where I'm at. I finally, in some measure, know myself.

I suppose this book has turned into my midlife crisis, my exploration of being poised in that moment, frozen halfway between the beginning and the end.

Dear reader, thank you so much for coming on this journey with me. This book explores topics such as end of life care, grief, and death of loved ones, and thus, may not be suitable for every reader.

I suppose what I am really saying is, keep tissues handy.

Sarah Chorn

May 18, 2023

Isra - Three Years Ago

Everything is burning. A bomb explodes. Too close. The halls of the World Tree tremble and groan.

It is just the three of us now: me and my two brothers, Manab and Atheed. We are all that is left of our monarch swarm. The war is picking us off one by one and I cannot help but feel I am next.

Before me, the goddess we serve sleeps, the life leaving her a bit more with each breath. I feel the loss of her Divinity like the severing of a limb. Where she once filled so much of me, now only emptiness remains.

Suddenly, I am hollow. I lack purpose. I am alone within the ocean of myself.

"The age of the Divine ends," Atheed says. His wings are closed tight, his body clenched, a bowstring the moment before an arrow is loosed. "She is mortal."

I wonder what it costs him to give voice to our new reality.

Divine Falcon lays before us on a bed we crafted of her favorite flowers, gathered fresh from the verdant forest of her Creation. A day ago, she settled herself upon them, her old crone's body rattling with every movement. The feathers around her face have fallen out and what wisps of hair remained were gray as storm clouds.

We have borne painful witness as the World Tree grew around her, first like a hug, and then a coffin. All I can see now are her eyes through the branches holding her close. They are closed and lined with wrinkles.

She had not recognized us, in the last. She had thought us dreams. Fantasy. Figments of her imagination.

Her final words were to her father.

Mortality is a blessing, she often told me as a child. Now, I see her wrapped in it and I shudder. It does not look like a blessing, but rather a cage.

"May she forgive us for what we do to her Creation." Manab's voice trembles.

I listen to the violence beyond our walls and feel cold.

Change is never bloodless, and Dawnland is hemorrhaging. Every day we are reduced. No one, it seems, has taken time to mourn what we have lost. And that... that feels like another kind of loss.

Another explosion rattles the World Tree, followed by the deafening roar of shattering. A glass bomb, then. Strange how easy it is for me to identify weapons based on the sounds of their destruction.

Manab's wings flutter and he runs a finger along his antenna, a nervous gesture I recognize from childhood. The three white spots on his left cheek shine, wet with tears.

None of us speak. This is a moment for which there are no words.

The World Tree vibrates again. Dust rains down from a fractured ceiling. Through a gap in the branches, I see Dawnland beyond. Where once was the sprawling Sacred Milkweed Grove, I now see a field of ash. Further, the charred husks of Dawnland Imperial University line the horizon like teeth. Further still are the blasted remains of the Imperial Hospital and Imperial Library.

The rainforest's canopy is damaged, exposing us to the merciless sun.

The Dawnland of my childhood was green and flourishing. I do not recognize this wasteland it has become, all smoke and blood and pain.

This is my home, and yet I am a stranger here.

There is a sorrow that lives beyond tears.

The World Tree trembles again. Dawnland is coming undone, tearing itself apart. I want to scream. I want to weep. I want to run or fight or flee. I want to do anything but stand here, impotent, useless, waiting for the next bomb to fall, and I its target.

I am so tired of being afraid.

I shift and my wings flare for balance.

There is motion in my periphery and I turn to see Divine Belladonna standing in the doorway, bright as the sun on a summer afternoon.

The words burst from me: "Why are you here? I thought you'd left days ago."

It is a certain kind of agony, thinking her gone. Yet it is time. She has spent years here, collecting wares. Now, the danger is too great, no matter how much she might make off trading wartime artifacts.

Her home of Meadowsweet is eager to welcome her back.

Belladonna makes her way to me. The closer she draws, the more I see her fear. "It must be now," she says to me. "There is still time to leave, but the window is closing."

Realization stabs deep. She is here because...

"Manab. Atheed." My eyes dart between them, wide and wild. Not three nights back we had sat together in Atheed's dark bedroom. *It is time to decide,* Manab had said, *if we die in Dawnland or flee.* "We discussed this. We agreed that we would stay. This is..."

Home.

"Isra—" Manab says.

"We agreed, brother. We would stay to the bitter end. All of us. Together."

"You said she knew, Manab. You said she agreed to go." Belladonna's voice is sharp. A knife could not slice half so well. "We risked all of this because you said Isra agreed. You said she wanted to leave."

Oh, these bombs. They keep falling. So many different kinds of them.

I feel faint.

"Zahia," Manab whispers, his eyes fixed on me. "Our sister is not two weeks cold. Taken by one of these cursed bomb blasts. Have you forgotten?"

How that question wounds.

How could I have forgotten? Zahia was my best friend as well as my sister. Losing her was like losing part of myself.

Another glass bomb shatters. This one so close my ears ring from it, and I cower, flaring my wings wide as though that might protect me. Bits of wood, dirt, and moss rain on me. I cannot help the mew of panic that is born in my throat.

The silence that follows is profound, so heavy, I feel it in my soul.

I am riven.

Zahia.

I remember a time, years ago. We were children laying on our backs amongst towering sacred milkweed stalks. Overhead, a wounded sky bled light.

"Did the moon hold its breath when it first witnessed the glory of the stars?" Zahia's voice pierced the silence, a knife forged of dreams.

"Zahia—"

"Does a warrior hold their breath as they charge into battle?"

"Sister, hush. If the luna moths hear us—"

"There are so many reasons to become breathless." Zahia sighed and even I, at such a tender age, could hear her longing, the girl already chafing at the bars of her ornate cage. "I wish to experience all of them."

Manab's hand clasps my shoulder, pulling me back into the present. "Do not ask me to lose you too."

"I can't stay here long," Belladonna says. "Isra, are you coming?"

It must be now or it will be never.

"You can't expect me to leave you," I whisper, my eyes flashing between Manab and Atheed. My heart is a wound, all ragged edges and pain. "Not now. You're all I have left."

I look at Atheed. He shakes his head and glances in the direction of the populist soldiers. "You know I can't, Isra. I won't leave him."

Even now. Especially now.

"Manab..." Belladonna says, tentative. Her hand is resting over her womb.

Manab turns his attention to her fully for the first time. "Are you well?"

I remember, suddenly, her fertility treatments. She shouldn't be here. Not with this danger all around. Why did she risk this? Why all this for... me?

"I'm fine," Belladonna answers, but her face is pinched and her words hard.

"Do you know—"

"Not yet," she says. "But I have not bled."

Manab's nostrils flare and some tension releases from him.

I am dizzy, spinning though I stand still, in the center of a world on fire.

This isn't just about me. It has never been just about me.

"Do you see, Isra? Belladonna underwent fertility treatments. She may even now be pregnant. It isn't just about the past or about all the siblings we've lost, but about the future." He pauses. "Atheed insists on running head-first into danger and I... I cannot leave. Sister, I am weak." A sob chokes him. "I cannot... I am not strong. But you... you are. You have always been the survivor."

I realize then, that neither of my brothers expects to live through this.

This... this is goodbye.

Manab leans forward and whispers low in my ear. "I need to know one of us had the chance to survive."

I feel the prick in my arm too late. Atheed sniffles behind me. Manab's hard face is carved with guilt.

"What have you done?" I ask.

"I'm sorry, Isra." His voice wavers.

"Manab, you can't— I can't— Did you drug her?" Belladonna's voice raises in pitch with each word until she is shrieking.

"I'm sorry." It seems all he is capable of saying. His eyes are wide. Madness lurks in that gaze.

I stagger. Already, the world grows soft around the edges.

"You've drugged her, Manab. What were you thinking? I can't take her like this! It's... it's..."

The world tilts. Goes sideways. Dark... So dark.

"You've... drugged..." I say, but the words stick on my tongue, pooling like molasses.

"It's safe," Manab says, helping ease me to the ground. "You will wake on Belladonna's ferry, and soon you will dine with the Most High in Meadowsweet. You will be safe."

I want to rage.

You are a fool, I want to shout.

There is no guarantee I will survive Chaos. No mortal yet has. Why would I be any different?

This will not work.

What have you done to me?

He lays me on the floor worn smooth by all the monarchs who came before. From the corner of my eye, I can see where Divine Falcon is cradled by the roots of the tree. How I envy her slumber. How I hate her for it.

The tears in Manab's eyes shimmer like starlight. "Forgive me," he whispers.

Atheed says something frantic, his panic acute.

"She will hate me for this," Manab whispers. His hand trails through my hair, and I memorize that touch. Will I ever feel it again?

Home is so many different things, and I am losing all of them at once.

"Manab," Belladonna shouts, "you lied to me. You manipulated all of us. She never agreed to this and now... you've drugged her. Why?"

"If she stays here, she will die." He hesitates. A sob claws its way up his throat. "I can't... I can't lose more siblings, Belladonna. One of us has to have a chance to see tomorrow."

"She likely won't survive Chaos, you know that. This was always the risk."

Manab goes still and hard. "I see how you look at her, Belladonna. You will not leave her. I... I am counting on that."

My eyes grow heavy. The world goes dark. I feel as though I am watching my life unfold through the far end of a tunnel.

"I love you, Isra," Atheed whispers into my ear.

Reality throbs like a pulse.

I see Divine Falcon, all those years ago, spinning with me in the Sacred Milkweed Grove. "Nothing ever ends," she'd singsonged. "It only changes shape."

A bomb explodes. Glass shatters.

"Damn you, Manab," Belladonna hisses.

And I know no more.

THEN
ROSEMARY

What I remember first is my mother's sorrow. When I was very young, she was able to hide it. Occasionally, I would catch her staring out our window, eyes pinned on the night sky as if she could but look hard enough and be there. However, as quickly caught, her mood would vanish, and she would turn bright eyes on me with a smile that could wake winter.

As I grew older, her dark moments lasted longer and were harder to hide. It started with a tear here and a trembling lip there. Then, she began forgetting.

I learned to subsist for both of us, begging on the corner and doing what odd jobs I was capable of down on the docks. It was a simple enough life, though I suppose I worked too hard and worried too much for a child my age. It was all I knew. And if we were turned out from tenements and had to work in the workhouses now and again, that was fine, for that was what most the residents of the Narrows had to do to survive. We were, in every way, average.

When my first vines grew long as locks of hair, and flowers bloomed along them, no one in the Narrows said a word, for our lives were surrounded by the strange, the tarnished, the wonderful. I knew myself to be odd, yes, but those in the Narrows are split evenly between criminals, cons, and castoffs. Why would I be any different?

Down there, in my own terrible way, I truly fit in.

So it was when my mother first took ill. I was twelve, or nearly so. I found myself rapping a fist on Landlady's door. I handed her the prayers for that week's rent and told her that my mother had begun coughing and her lungs rattled like a canvas sack with a hole in the bottom.

Landlady's apartment was small and cramped, yet nicer than mine, with a full stove and a fireplace, and a window that was not cracked. She had a bowl in her hands, which she set on a table next to a knife and small squares of cigarette paper. Next to her rocking chair was a bucket of sawdust. A prayer she'd been shaving was clutched between her thumb and index finger.

She looked at me then, blew ichor-laced smoke in my face, and said, "Get you to the Hall of the Gods. What with your flower hair, you'll be one of their get."

When I woke in the morning, however, Mother had a wet rag pressed to her face, her lungs whistled, and her lips trembled. She was getting worse by the day and winter was coming. Our tenement had no protection against it. I knew if I did not act soon, when chill weather hit, Mother would get worse.

"Nanny," Mother said, and my heart sank for when she called me that, I knew she was drifting and considered me a character from her childhood.

"Yes?" I asked around the lump in my throat. Outside our cracked window, the docks were filled with people. A few ferriers had arrived from points unknown, and workers were lined up eager to earn prayers for unloading cargo.

"May I have some porridge?"

I thought over our situation while I fixed Mother breakfast, and decided to call Landlady, who was kindly when it suited her. She helped Mother settle into the chair beside her stove, still hot from the morning's baking. I would pay her for this favor later, but Mother seemed happier, blooming like a flower in spring next to that heat, and I knew I'd give anything to see her whole, and safe, and warm always.

Taking great care, I prepared myself for the day. I wore my finest dress, which I knew would never be nearly fine enough for all it still had a torn hem, stains, and did not fit me right. Taking care to shine my tattered, too-small shoes as best I could, I studied myself in our cracked looking glass. The nebulas in my eyes danced, pink and full and bright and my hair had bloomed a chaotic mixture of foxglove, calendula, and agrimony, betraying my tangled mess of emotions. Last, I gathered my gloves—thin kidskin, the most expensive items we owned—and drew them on.

I hesitated on my cane, the carved wood walking stick that was so much a part of me I hardly thought about it anymore. Now, suddenly, it was all I could think about.

How could they take me seriously? This girl wearing rags with flower hair and a bad leg? Why was I wasting my time? How could one such as I hope to dally with the Divine?

Would they see me?

Or would they only see what I lack?

But my mother could not wait, and so I grabbed my cane and begged my leg to behave today. Our tenement was quiet as I left, a few of the residents just returning after a long night spent working the streets. The walls were thin, and I heard the thud of flesh hitting flesh, the roar of voices, behind one of the clapboard doors I passed on the way out of our rickety building.

Then, I set myself to the streets, mud up to my ankles after last night's storm, all my careful work undone within a block. Within two, my right hip was a knot of agony, and I knew I would be unable to make my way back home unless I rested for some time first.

The Narrows unfolded around me. Tumbledown buildings drunkenly shrugged exhausted shoulders. Children ran wild around streets full of refuse and waste. A few beggars stood on each corner and Landlady's boys could be seen about, selling her ichor-laced cigarettes. The stench of rotting fish and ocean mixed with that of unwashed bodies creating an unforgettable miasma that turned my stomach.

Still I went, even knowing I would be tracking the mud of the Narrows into those hallowed halls. Even knowing I would be a limping, pain-shriveled mess when this was over. Even knowing there could very well be nothing for me on the other end of this journey... I went.

Finally, after an eternity, I reached the edge of my arbor, that uninhabited no-man's land where the Narrows began fading, the buildings ghostly outlines propped against the border of Divine Rain's neighboring arbor. I never liked coming to this part of the city. It chilled me, to see how easily things could disappear, all these empty streets, buildings that seemed only half present, the edges of things undefined, hinting at what had once been and showing the wreckage of what was. This is where the Narrows and it's un-creation truly began, the slow, insidious creeping of it.

Divine Rain's arbor was a wild place, full of life and vital with it. No fading buildings or ghostly shadows here. Created with riverways instead of roads, and houses on stilts, entering this arbor was like entering a different world, and I took it all in with wide, wonder-filled eyes. I paid the bargeman one hard-earned prayer to ferry me across the arbor. We waited while the barge filled with people, and all of them with wings: dragonfly, bee, and moth. Flowers bloomed from between the trunks of mushroom-laden trees. Crocodiles swam through the waterway beside us. On the banks, I passed children picking coconuts and playing games, laughing so easily.

No one in the Narrows laughed easily.

It began to rain nearly as soon as the barge poled its way to the edge of Divine Muse's neighboring arbor, a place that was both as strange, and not so strange as Divine Rain's had been. Here, the city fell into more normal patterns, with roads and buildings lining them. Each one was a work of art and the cobblestone streets gleamed. Music filled the air and the sidewalks were strewn with colorful crafts.

My hair bloomed a riot, vines growing down to my lower back, flowers opening wide. I started to attract attention, for what was I if not strange? Down in the Narrows, it did not so much matter. Here, higher in the city, I began to gather a crowd around me. By the time I reached the Hall of the Gods, I was so bedraggled and overwrought, I scarce took in its magnificence, but still, how could I not?

The Hall of the Gods was a sprawling edifice, part temple, part office building, part residence. It was the seat of power for the Most High, the three gods of Creation and the children they Created. The second my foot touched that sacred soil, I felt part of me that had always been slumbering wake and stretch. The world seemed brighter, the city less ominous and frightening.

Sprawling and palatial, it was made from what looked to be one seamless, impossibly large hunk of pure, white marble. Every inch of it gleamed. Large stairs lead to an entryway, an open wall with no doors, an invitation of welcome.

Somehow, I managed to drag myself through Father Terra's Sacred Garden, a place I longed to spend more time examining, up the marble steps—each one an agony—and into the main hall.

The sudden brightness of the indoors after the slate clouds and rain was startling, and I felt my flowers recoil in horror, my vines shrink against my scalp. The lights became less an assault as my eyes adjusted and my vines uncoiled, loosening as a result. One wrapped around my arm. Flowers began to bud, but in my anxiety, refused to bloom.

Then, I became aware of the voices, hushed whispers all around.

"What manner of creature is this?" someone asked; a woman, I belatedly realized. I blinked and beheld the audience around me.

Elemental and surreal, they were. Human, but only just. The idea of mortality rested about them, but not much more. Their eyes blazed with stars, planets, moons, and their bodies were impossible to describe. Recognizable, and yet not, each of them defined somehow by their unique Divinity. There, a woman with doe ears. There, a man-shaped tree. There, another carved from a ray of moonlight.

It was quite a thing to behold. From the distant echoes of footsteps, I knew more were rushing in. I wanted nothing more than to cover myself in vines and hide. Yet I remembered my mother. I remembered the wet rag pressed to her face and the chill in our small, rented room. I thought of winter and I remained firm on my path.

I cleared my throat and the whispers quieted as those encircling me drew close. "I came here," I began, marshaling all the solemnity my childlike form could, "to ask for a job."

Silence then, followed by a startle guffaw.

What had they expected? I come here with open hands and ask for something not freely given? Perhaps it was my pride, or perhaps the thought of owing these creatures any part of me was too terrifying to behold, but I did not want their handouts, nor did I want their favor.

A lowly kitchen job, or a broom so I might sweep hallways was all I required, something that paid regularly. It would let me put my mother in a better room, with a fireplace, and give us access to a doctor.

I could keep begging, but whatever the Divine paid, I knew it would be a grand sight more than what I earned standing on a street corner with a bowl held aloft.

"What?" someone asked. "Why is she here?"

"She wants a"—a snort—"a job."

"Child," a deep-throated woman said. She smelled, somehow, like summer. "The door for servants is around back."

The crowd began to disburse, and I blew out a lungful of air. Only two remained, a man and a woman, and both dressed in clothes so fine I had never before seen their like. The woman looked to have been crafted from the sun itself, while the man had been birthed from night.

"Divine Muse," the woman said, "do you not see what is before you? Some god, and a rather mighty one at that, has a child, unaccounted for. Who do you think it might be?"

My cheeks burned. I hung my head, my vines drooping to hide me in their shadows.

"Be kind to her," Divine Muse replied, "She has done nothing wrong. I know we are looking for more hands to help. I see no reason she should not be among them."

"She has a limp, Muse."

"And so that does not make her worthy? She climbed all the way here from the Narrows, I'd guess, and she did it with that limp. Do not be so ready to write her off." He bent before me. He was dark and lean, and the moon in his eyes spun through an endless churn of cycles, dizzying and surreal. "She is made for grander things."

His smile, when it came, was gentle, and I loved him then.

"Come with me, child. I will take you to my office and see you fed and given dry clothes. You will tell me your tragic story, and I will see how I can help."

He grabbed my hand and squeezed it once. I trusted him instantly.

Perhaps what I loved most about Divine Muse, at least at first, was that he took me seriously. He looked upon my small frame and my slight build, my vines and flower hair, my leg, and realized I must have lived far more than my years let on and determined to treat me as an adult.

There are small kindnesses about us every day, if we choose to see them.

He led me down a hallway, and then hesitated at a flight of stairs before deciding not to take them, guiding me to a small office finely appointed in different shades of blue.

He kept the door open for my comfort, and then slipped away. A moment later, a woman appeared, this one with glowing silver eyes and long, raven-dark hair. She was not as Divine as Muse. This woman, whoever she was, had some mortal blood in her. Strange, how easy it was for me to sense these things, even then.

Her eyes widened when they found me, and then she set to work. When Muse reappeared, she pushed him out of the way. "Come back later, uncle. Let me see to my cousin."

She twisted that last word, though not unkindly.

Things were happening here. Things I did not understand.

NOW
BELLADONNA

When I was very young, my father told my mother that he had been hired to ferry goods between Meadowsweet and some other far-flung Creation.

I remember that day well. We broke our fast on berries brought from Father Terra's garden. Mother bid our lady, Marigold, to make fresh cream, and we heaped both upon lemon pancakes and ate them beneath a dandelion sky.

Mother's hair had been perfect and her dress pressed. I remember how white her lace gloves were. She smiled at all the right moments, but her lips trembled and her eyes were red from crying.

So we bid him goodbye. It was a sorrowful affair, for who knew how long such a journey would take? The way through Chaos was ever unpredictable. He might be gone weeks or lifetimes.

Father was a towering man, and he shined so bright it often hurt to look upon him. His hair was spun sunlight, and when he smiled, the world would somehow feel less hard.

He knelt and stared deep into my eyes before holding me so my ear was pressed against his throbbing heart. He did not speak, but he rarely spoke to me. My father's greatest gift was his silence, for that is my Divinity, and this world is so very loud.

Then he left, and he took his silence with him, and has not yet returned.

And that is why my mother hates the Divine. For if it was not for the Divinity in his blood, leaving would not have been an option.

I stand before her now, in this kitchen that reminds me of my childhood, and feel like a girl again. There is a new lady working here, and she goes by Daisy. She is younger than I remember Marigold being, and my mother is far older. How long have I been gone? Years, and a lot of them. Mother's hair is shot through with gray and her face is far more wrinkled than I remember. Though there are no laugh lines around her mouth.

That pains me. As hard as it was for me to leave Meadowsweet all those years ago, it must have been so much harder for her to stay behind, not knowing if she'd ever see me again. Has she spent her life in mourning?

"Belladonna?" she whispers. Her face loses color and she swoons as though she might faint. She reaches out to touch me but then stops herself, and I am grateful for it. After all these years, she still remembers how much touch pains me. "You returned. I thought... I thought your Divinity would drive you from me as well."

This... this barb hits too close to home.

I smile. She pulls a kerchief from somewhere and dabs at her eyes. Then, her glance darts over my shoulder and I know she is looking for him. For my father. Despite myself, I feel like I have failed her when he does not appear. It is as though she had hoped I left for the sole purpose of bringing him home.

His absence is a shadow hovering over my life, ever darkening it.

"It has been seventeen years," Mother says, motioning toward a table. A moment later, Daisy appears with tea in porcelain cups so fine I can see through them. A pink stenciled rose adorns the side. I sip, my delicate manners returning to me without a hitch. Mother smiles, as though I've passed some test, and for a moment, she looks younger. I keenly miss the years we spent apart. The times that might have been, if I'd but stayed.

"I cannot believe you're here," she says, and her eyes gleam with curiosity. She leans across the table, closer to me.

I have missed her powerfully. For all we have disagreed, she is still my mother and I have spent much of my life hungering for her insight and guidance. I have even longed for our arguments. It was... painful, leaving. To suddenly be alone after spending a life surrounded.

It takes a moment for me to gather the words I need to speak and I watch Mother's expression cloud. My aversion to touch she can deal with, but the slow speed with which I find my words is what she cannot abide.

"Still, Belladonna? Still you let your Divinity influence you? I had thought years and maturity would help you grow out of these... habits."

She clasps her hands in her lap and goes quiet and still.

Silence, however, is a language all its own—one I speak fluently —and hers is brittle and sharp, as much weapon as defense. I watch her lose herself in it.

My quiet serves as a reminder that I will always be connected, by blood and bone, to those who offered my father his last ferrying job. To those who gave him the opportunity to leave.

I try not to let this hurt me. I knew what I was returning to.

"We ferried goods to Dawnland," I tell her. "It is Divine Falcon's creation." I suppress a shudder. Those last months were torturous. I still hear bombs exploding. I still hear screaming. My sleep is troubled.

"Divine Falcon..." Her eyes grow distant.

"Father Terra's daughter."

"Yes, of course." She pauses. "How many prayers did you earn?"

It is striking that this is her first question about my journey. Not about what I experienced nor what Dawnland was like or what I did there. Not even how long I stayed.

No.

How many prayers did you earn?

Those words crash on me like winter runoff, and suddenly I am drowning. The light that is part of me dims, and exhaustion presses on my shoulders.

"I have already given our tithe to our arbor's goddess and paid my crew. I put the rest of our earnings in our temple for safekeeping. I'll save enough to keep the company afloat. Repairs on the ferry and such."

Though I will not be ferrying again for some time, I like keeping the option open. The freedom of being able to leave if the noise of Meadowsweet ever again becomes too much is what I need to be able to stay.

"Good." Mother's eyes look over my shoulder, where a picture of my father hangs in an ornate frame. His likeness is in every room of this house. As a child, I felt like he haunted this place. "Well, are you moving back in? I can have your old room refreshed."

"No," I say, and stand. My mother is studying me, as though I am a stranger to her.

I suddenly long to be anywhere but here, facing anyone but her.

"Where—"

"The Hall of the Gods," I say. "I am roomed in Mother Sol's wing. I have brought someone with me from Dawnland, and the Most High have asked me to stay and help her adjust."

Mother snorts. "You should not dally so with the Divine. The bound ones are all ill, you know. How good can they be if they cannot even manage to keep their Divinity about them?"

"It is my Great Grandmother you insult," I say. "And my father. And me."

And my daughter.

But I do not say this, for I see now that I cannot trust my mother's reaction to my daughter. She will not see Flora as a child seeking love, but rather a strange creature. She will see the odd about her and the divinity that makes it so.

Oh, my child. I ache to be with her. To hold her in my arms and feel her small body pressed close to mine. She is the only creature in this world whose touch does not hurt.

She had been born well into our journey through Chaos, on the deck of our ferry. The quiet of the between is all she's known. Until now. And I left her...

"I have to go," I say, and stalk to the door.

"Belladonna, you just—"

"There is something I must do, but I will be back tomorrow. We can have lunch, perhaps get to know each other after all these years."

"I..." Mother looks almost relieved to see my hand on the door, as though this was as awkward for her as it was me. I wonder if she has made a life for herself as a widow and a mourning mother. I wonder if my return has upset her routine.

She hates my father for leaving. Will she hate me for returning?

"Lunch sounds good, Belladonna," Mother finally says. Her eyes soften and I know we both need time apart to adjust to being together again. "I will have my lady fix us something refreshing."

"Lovely," I say.

"Please wear a dress," she replies, nodding at my trousers. "Proper lunching attire, Belladonna. Really, you have not grown so lax in your time away, have you?"

Enough of this. I lean forward, brace myself, and press my lips against her cheek. The quiet that surrounds me shatters and suddenly the world roars to life. Every sound is sharp enough to make my ears ring. The rasp of her breath, the press of her skin against mine, the trolly outside and its chiming bell.

It's all too much.

Too much.

"I have missed you," she whispers. And then I push back, put space between us, try not to look as sick as I feel while I wrap myself in quiet once more, a layer of it, to keep the world at bay. It is agony, to do this. Every part of me is tender and my silence shreds. Piece by painful piece, I slice my soul to ribbons as I shut the world out.

Outside, the day is bright and warm. The sun is closer here, yet it somehow feels less scalding, more welcoming. Perhaps it is Mother Sol's proximity that makes it so. Or perhaps I am home, a place my Divinity is tied to, and so Meadowsweet welcomes me the way it would any of its daughters.

I am drunk on the newness of this familiar Creation.

Up the hill I go, the four blocks to the Hall of the Gods. I ache for my daughter. For as long as she has been alive, we have never been apart, always as close as the ferry required. I want nothing more than to be near her, just the two of us, with the world so far away.

I don't truly see the city around me, nor the Hall of the Gods when I enter, so set I am on getting to Flora. Worry fuels wild imaginings of her crying, screaming for me, being confused and terrified. She will think I have abandoned her. Panic wraps a hand around my throat. Squeezes.

She is alone.

Alone in a strange world.

I am running to her. My heart is a thunderstorm.

Flora, Flora, I'm sorry...

After an eternity, I reach my door. It is her laughter I hear first. So high and innocent, piercing the wood that divides us. My soul clenches and then releases.

I enter the room slowly, as though afraid of what I will see.

But Flora is there, in the center of this soft space. The room is pale yellow with thick golden carpet and matching furnishings. Doors are flung open to the wide patio beyond, where baskets of flowers grow along a thick stone ledge. Sunlight clings to my daughter as though there is nowhere it would rather be. She is sitting with Isra, tugging on her antenna.

"Flora is happy, Belladonna. Meadowsweet will be good for her. Having more space, more things to do, more people to see... it will be good for her," Isra says with a wince when the child pulls too hard.

Yes, Meadowsweet will be good for Flora but it will change things. No matter how I long to keep her to myself, she cannot always be mine.

"Mama!" She grins at me and I melt.

I run to her, cradle her in my arms.

She is summer and air, and all things good. The monarch in her is strong, and yet I see myself in her as well, in the silence that binds us.

She is the only thing in this world I can touch without feeling pain.

NOW

ISRA

It is the waking that betrays me.

For if I am waking, it means I survived, and that means...

Wind plays like fingers over the fine chitin of my wings and I *know* I am not home. I know what has happened and oh, therein lies the knife. It stabs deep. Twists. My gasp of pain is swallowed by a gust off a nearby strange sea.

I open my eyes. The sky is so similar to the one I know, but it is too blue. The sun is both too close and too soft.

No, I am not home. Must I go through this process—this painful awareness—each time I rise in Meadowsweet? It is exhausting. Almost, I wish for Manab's medicine again, for the sweet surrender that sleep offers.

Air suffuses my lungs and my antennae shift, scenting for flowers. I curl on my side, keep my wings closed tight. For a moment, I feel the way I did as a child, watching my siblings all succumb to pupation before me. Watching them disappear, one by one, into rooms where I could not go, to experience things I could not understand.

I had not realized until that day how well the halls of the World Tree echoed. I was so small, and for the first time, truly alone.

That is how I feel now. I am alone and full of echoes.

Adrift.

I gasp again and my lungs squeeze, squeeze.

I am a butterfly, not a fish. I was not created for these depths.

It is my heart that shatters first, creating a tidal wave in the ocean of my soul.

This pain. Will it ever end?

I think of Dawnland, of what I would be doing right now if I had woken in the World Tree. I would press my hands against the wooden walls of my room, feel the presence of generations of monarchs just like me. One of the nymphs would bring me nectar and pomegranate seeds to break my fast, and I would eat both while sitting beside hyssop and zinnia, their sweet scent clinging to me like perfume.

Atheed would find me first, and then we would discover Manab in his laboratory, pondering his vials, wings drooping and antennae low. Likely, he'd have forgotten to sleep again...

I think of the prick of the needle and my memories gain an edge.

I miss my home. I miss the familiar walls of the World Tree and the forest itself. Mostly, I miss belonging somewhere. Being where I am understood.

Still, I cannot think—cannot feel—this now. I will never be able to survive the present if I am so lost in the past.

The door to my room opens, and Belladonna is there with Flora in her arms, a woman is behind them, carrying a tray laden with food, a spread fit for three. She shuffles past us and sets her burden on the small iron table on my patio. The woman, I note, is golden as a new day. One of Mother Sol's daughters, I assume, for she looks like a beam of purest sunlight. The smile she flashes at me is kind, and her eyes are full of wonder. Her gaze clings to my wings a beat too long. I flutter them, self-conscious.

In Dawnland, I am not so strange. Here, it is my differences that people fixate on: my wings and antenna, my strange speech, my odd mannerisms.

I do not like being so seen.

My wings draw tight. My antennae pick up the scent of nearby flowers, strange to me but no less delightful for it. They are close. If I but turned to my left, they would be right there, near the railing. The wind shifts, carrying with it the smell of salt and ocean. Vast, unexplored, strange places.

"Tanta!" Flora cries, using the Dawnland word for *aunt*. She reaches for me, and I cannot help the smile that lights my face. I see so much of Manab in her, and it fills me with the sweetest ache. It is her smile that undoes me, for when Flora smiles, I feel as though my brother is beside me again. Belladonna offers the child to me, and I take her solid weight in my arms. Peace fills me the moment I touch her.

What a gift Flora is.

Belladonna makes her quiet way to the table, a small smile curling the edges of her lips. I have learned, over the years, to accept her quiet. She looks content here in a way she never did in Dawnland. Like she belongs. It is as though this place is part of her the way the World Tree is part of me. I wonder if she feels like she's coming home to roost after too long away. If this moment is as sweet to her as returning would be to me?

I hope it is.

Everyone deserves to be welcomed.

I flare my wings wide and take a seat opposite Belladonna, settling Flora on my lap. The child reaches toward a bowl of strawberries with chubby fists. I take one and peel off the green stem, then help her with it, careful to make sure she doesn't choke. "Have you spoken with anyone about getting her milkweed?" I ask, without taking my eyes off my niece.

If nothing else, Flora will give me purpose and root me in this place. As long as I keep myself focused on her, perhaps this will not be so hard.

Belladonna's eyes cloud. "I have not yet."

We had a small supply on the ferry to Meadowsweet, but Flora is getting bigger now and she will need more. She has been living off of what we grew on our journey but soon, she will eat her way through our supply. I wish she had a milkweed grove like the one in Dawnland, used as a nursery for my siblings and I until our pupation. How nice it would be to have an entire grove for her to exist in, with milkweed as tall as trees Divinely guided in their growth like they were back home.

I used to spend time there, every afternoon, even after the populist soldiers burnt it down. Remembering those blissful days of childhood before I knew that even the sky could bleed fills me with a certain, unavoidable longing.

Sunlight spills like honey through the leaves of a nearby apple tree, illuminating a jar in the center of our breakfast spread on my patio table. It is clear, this jar, with a cork keeping the amber liquid within from spilling. "Is that—"

"Nectar," Belladonna says, smiling again. "Father Terra collected it for you himself."

I should be grateful for this kindness, but instead a wave of anxiety crashes upon me, and I am drowning. I stand and set Flora on my chair and pace across the patio, my wings flaring with each step.

I cannot predict myself. The simplest thing sets off waves of emotion so strong I feel as though I am lost to them. I ache and I yearn and I miss and I am terrified.

How do I find all of that in an innocent jar of nectar?

"What is it?" Belladonna asks. "Isra, what is wrong?"

"I will have to thank him now," I say, my thoughts focusing on the man who offered me such a gift. I spin and my wings flare, steadying me. I am across the patio now, and my antennae pick up the scent of hyssop, pregnant with delectable nectar. It is one of my favorite flowers. "I will have to face him, Belladonna."

I pause, and Belladonna studies me. She understands more from this beat of quiet than I can fathom, but still I feel I must say the words to make them real.

"I will have to tell Most High Father Terra of his daughter."

Belladonna makes to stand, but focuses on Flora, making sure the child stays perched safely on her chair. Flora's face is smeared red with strawberry. Sometimes, I wonder what to make of this child. She is so different from me, and yet so similar. She requires milkweed to thrive, her hair is striped black, yellow, and white, like any other monarch. Yet a creature like her has never existed.

I hatched from an egg my mother pressed into the leaf of a Sacred Milkweed plant in our nursery, one of hundreds. Flora was born from her mother's womb. She eats food as well as milkweed. I did not need food until after I'd survived pupation. The yellow and white of her hair glows, caressed by light.

I do not know what will become of her, but she will be a glorious creature to behold.

"Father Terra knows his daughter sleeps, Isra," Belladonna says, bringing me back to the moment. "She is part of him."

I understand she means well, reminding me that I will not be telling him anything he does not already know, but it does not ease me. I have never dreamed of meeting one of the Most High, for I knew they never left their Sacred Space. In Dawnland, Divine Falcon was our Most High, and her father was but another star in the night sky. Now I am here, and the thought of meeting Father Terra and then telling him...

"I cannot do it, Belladonna. I am not so strong as that."

She hesitates and then makes her way to me, while keeping Flora well under her watchful eye.

Belladonna draws in a deep breath before resting a hand on my shoulder. It must cost her, for her fingers clench there, nails digging into my skin. Then, she eases her grip. Her touch is warm and strong and it brings me back down to the world from where my panic has spun me.

She doesn't speak, but this is no surprise. Belladonna is one of few words. Instead, she eyes me and I feel laid bare before her, like she can see the parts of me I try to hide. Finally, she holds me in an embrace. Simple and silent is this act, but she says so much with it.

You are strong.

You have faced harder things and survived.

You are not alone.

A moment later, a small hand grasps my knee and peace stills the storm in my soul. Oh, Flora. To be able to bestow serenity with a touch...

"Tanta," Flora says, and I bend to lift her. She clutches my shoulder and runs a finger along the soft tip of my wing. I open them wide so she can have better access. My wings are sensitive, and the glide of her fingertips shivers through me.

"I don't know how to do this," I finally say. "How am I to break a god's heart, Belladonna, and survive?"

"You have done nothing wrong," Belladonna whispers. Flora grabs my wing too tight and I flinch. Belladonna takes her from me and settles the toddler on her hip. "Father Terra has the kindest soul."

But it isn't just Father Terra anymore. The weight of everything that has happened settles on me, and my legs tremble from the magnitude of it. My home, so far away. My brothers... are they alive? Will I ever see them again? Here I am, in a Creation I do not understand, populated by beings who are so strange to me, speaking a language I only just understand...

I should not be here.

The walls are closing in. The sun dims and the world is all sharp edges poised to wound.

I should not be here.

My breath comes out in razor-edged gasps while sweat beads my brow.

I should not be here.

Panic such as I have never known stirs up winter in my soul.

I should not be here.

I should not be here.

I should not be here.

I want Atheed. I want Manab. I want the World Tree and its memories. I want something to cleave to. My old life feels so small and far away.

This is all too much. Too much.

I do not realize I am crying until Belladonna leans forward and brushes a tear off my cheek. Gentle is that touch, painfully so.

All I have here is Belladonna. She is my only constant.

I think of the prick of a needle in my arm. Of my brothers, whom I had always thought would stand beside me, watching the drug take hold.

People are unpredictable.

"Look at me," Belladonna says as though sensing the path of my thoughts and I do. Her golden eyes are full of worry and guilt pierces me that I was the one to cause it. "I accept all of you, Isra. Even your storms. I will not leave you."

Had I spoken out loud? It doesn't matter.

I nod, and Belladonna and Flora hug me again. I sink into their embrace. How desperately I have needed this.

"You are so silent, but your pain is loud," the goddess whispers so softly I can barely hear it. "You can break now. No one is watching. It does not have to be beautiful."

And so...

I do.

NOW
ROSEMARY

In the right light, my father's hair shines silver.

Fear, deep and abiding, wraps cold hands around my throat. Squeezes. For a moment, I cannot breathe.

"How is she tonight?" I ask.

Anything. Anything to not think about that. To not think about what those strands of gray mean. I am not strong enough. Not yet.

So I force my thoughts away. From one pain to another.

Mother is perched on the window seat, staring at the rose garden beyond. Tears hover on her lashes. Outside, the world is cast in shades of soft light.

"She drifts," my father says. Simple are those words, and yet I can hear the pain etched in each of them.

I take a moment to park my wheelchair, next to where I keep my spare cane, and stand. My bones grind and my hip is unsteady, but I make my way to her, each step an effort of will. The weather is changing, a new chill is in the air, and I feel it in my bones, in the way my muscles knot and coil.

Mother does not look at me when I reach her. She's whispering something so low I cannot hear the words. "Mother?"

I ease onto the padded cushion, groan as my leg slips and I land in an ungainly heap.

She reaches out to touch me, but stops herself, her fingers hovering a breath from my cheek. "Sometimes I look at you and think you are real, but I know you are not. Why do my dreams haunt me so?"

Father chokes on a sob. Sorrow fills the room and I breathe it in.

You must understand your tragedy, Mother once told me during one of her more lucid moments. *You must know the knife to understand how it wounded you.*

So I hold my tragedy's hands the way I'd hold a bird in spring freshly fallen from its nest. "I am real," I tell her. "I am flesh and blood. I am your daughter, and I am here."

"Stop taunting me," Mother whispers. Her eyes go wide and wild. She tugs on her hands, tries to pull them from my grasp. "Away! Away from me, thief of dreams! Away!"

She thrashes about, moaning long and low. Father, with starlight tears, moves to the vase on the table by the wall, and grabs sprigs of clary sage from within, bright purple blossoms filling the air with their subtle perfume.

Father refills this vase each day from Father Terra's Sacred Garden, back bent under the early morning light. He takes this task upon himself like it is his sacrament and will spend days paying his penance with guilt each time he must use them, as rare as that may be.

Without a word, he sets the flowers on my lap and bends to soothe Mother while I pull off my gloves. All it will take is a touch.

Mother rocks and moans. Her head hits the wall with a low *thunk.*

Father presses his cheek against her breast and closes his eyes.

Who, I wonder, do gods pray to when they are in pain?

Oh, this moment. So much layered, dark agony. So many wounds.

My vines grow long, wreathing my face in shadow. I lift the flowers.

"I'm sorry," I whisper, before finding a spot on Mother's arm and pressing them against her skin. It takes but a breath for the effect to take hold. Mother's eyes focus on me, then slide closed. Her body goes limp and she breathes slow and steady. When I am sure she is fully under and resting well, I pull the flowers away. They have grown into small bushes heavy with blossoms. The moment I release them, they shrivel, spent.

I do not like withered blooms. They remind me too much of my life.

Father lifts her in his arms and carries her to the bed they share. He will lay beside her tonight and watch over her while she sleeps, dying a little between each breath.

What must it be like to live only in gasps?

Once, many years ago, I said, "Even now, you love her." I had thrust those words at him with the intent to wound, yet I felt no pleasure when they struck their target true. For the beat of a heart, he let me see the depth of his pain and the wellspring of love that fed it.

"I do not love her *even now* or *despite*, Rosemary. I love her. It is as simple as that."

"But this hurts you so," I whispered. I knew well the agony of helplessness.

Father met my gaze and his eyes grew soft. "This pain is only the smallest part of it."

A moment later he breaks through my memories with a hand on my shoulder. "There will be better days than this," he whispers.

I feel the words more than hear them. Tears sting my eyes.

How soft hope can be, and still... it slices.

The vines of my hair had shrunk against my scalp in reaction to Mother's torment but now grow long and fragile petunias bloom, turning their faces to drink the sun's dying light.

I listen as Father picks up his phone and spins the rotary dial, calling Divine Dream. I know she will be here within moments with her notepad and pencil, drawing better things for my mother to see while she slumbers.

"I have not seen Mother so bad in a while," I finally say, for it is better to face the matter head-on than hide from it.

"It has been some time."

"If you'd told me—"

He smiles and the galaxies in his eyes dance. "I would not take you from your duties unless it is urgent. Today has been a bad day, that is all. Tomorrow, the sun will rise again. You know how these things go."

I do, but each time this happens, my heart breaks anew.

Father pulls me into his arms and I melt against him. Strange, how so long ago he terrified me. Now, my vines curl around his shoulders and the petunias open wider still, swaying in the breeze that always flows around him.

I lose myself in his arms, in the safety and familiarity that has become my sanctuary. I could spend an eternity being held by his embrace.

I pull myself together, step clear of his hold, and dab at my eyes. The room we stand in is large and familiar, with pale yellow walls and white trim. There, on the table by the phone, is a framed photograph of the three of us in Father Luna's Sacred Observatory. Three high arched windows look out at the garden beyond. Hanging in the second window is a small bit of stained-glass artwork I crafted years ago. I had gifted it to my father, the first present I ever truly offered him, and it has hung there since.

I am surrounded by memories.

Father gives me time to gather the shattered pieces of myself. He is silent with his love, showing rather than saying the words, and yet when he does speak, he always does so with such care and mercy.

The god of Creation is more lamb than lion.

"She loves you, Rosemary. Even when she doesn't know you, she loves you." He goes to the gramophone in the corner and turns on the piano music he so adores, then sinks into his wingback seat and I take the one opposite, feeling the leather fold around me like a hug. "But that is not why you are here."

I can hide nothing from him.

In the right light, my father's hair shines silver.

I lick my lips and suddenly find myself at a loss.

Words are such simple things, and yet when I need them most I lose them within the forest of my soul.

"Ah," my father says. "Are you ready to talk about it yet?"

Gentle. He is always so gentle. Somehow, it is the softness of his words that fracture me all the more. I break, then. A shatter so profound I am surprised he cannot hear it. Tears spill down my cheeks in rivers. My body trembles and a low wail flees past my lips like an escaped prisoner. Outside, the world seems somehow darker and more frightening.

I am a girl again, small and tender, and so very alone.

Hands rest on my shoulders.

"Not yet," I finally manage.

He lets me have my sorrow and does not begrudge my tears. When I look up and meet his eyes, I see they are full of solemn understanding.

How can he be so easy with this while it savages me thus?

My father's hair shines silver.

"Tomorrow, perhaps." But the way he says it tells me he knows that tomorrow I will not be ready either. I do not know if I will ever be ready for that conversation.

"Does it hurt?" I birth the words on a wave of agony.

Please, do not be in any pain.

My father considers me for a moment, head tilted to the side, almost birdlike. Moonlit clouds marshal along his twilight cheek-bones. The stars in his eyes spin slowly. "Sometimes, when the world is silent and still, I can feel each of my heartbeats."

My breath hitches. "Is it terrible?" I hardly dare breathe the words.

"It is the music of existence. Why would that be terrible?"

Because it is so fleeting, I want to say.

Because it means you are only temporary.

Because there is an end.

"I will love you, Rosemary, whether I am here to say the words or not."

My breath hitches. I picture this room, empty. My life, bereft. The world so large and frightening and I, alone to face it. No safe harbor. No port in the storm.

My father has always been eternal and now...

I can feel each of my heartbeats.

"I'm not ready to talk about this yet," I whisper, voice trembling, as brittle as I feel.

Silence, and then my father nods once and turns to the window where Luna pierces the dark and makes it bleed stars. "The moon," he finally says, "is beautiful, is it not?"

I do not reply, but I study that sliver of light. My blood rises like high tide.

"It does not stop shining, Rosemary. Even when it waxes." He hesitates. I feel his eyes on me. "Even when it wanes."

"Father—"

"We will not talk more about this, my heart. For now, sit with me and savor the night."

As if knowing I cannot bear another touch right now, he gives me space, settling back in his chair. Soft piano music surrounds us. Moonflowers bloom along the vines of my hair, petals catching the faint light. My father taps a rhythm along with the song, stars spinning from his fingers each time they beat against the leather armrest.

It is all so normal and yet...

I do not think I have ever felt so cold.

In the right light, my father's hair shines silver.

For a moment, I cannot breathe.

"Look at the moon, Rosemary," he whispers. "Just look at the moon."

THEN
ROSEMARY

Divine Dream was uncommonly kind, with a gentle touch and eyes that withheld any judgment. She drew a bath and then had my clothes taken away, likely to be burned. By the time she was done with me, I was wearing a finer gown than I'd ever touched, and my skin shone like polished marble in the bloom of twilight. Even my vines, once coiled against my scalp, had relaxed and on them were fat pink flowers, wide and searching for light.

I had taken off my gloves, and in my content state forgot to put them back on. My cane, when I touched it, bloomed, ivy running about its length, sprays of white flowers mixed into the chaos. It was Divine Dream's wide eyes as she beheld the foliage that made me realize my mistake. I had been so determined to keep my secrets, and now I let this one show.

She sat me on a plush blue sofa. Outside the window was a rose bush, flowers red as blood. Divine Dream set a spread of food on the small table before us: cheese, bread, honey so golden it looked like it had been harvested from the sun's own tears.

"Do you eat?" she asked.

"Who doesn't eat?"

I reached toward a crust of bread, slathered it with honey, and moaned when the flavors exploded in my mouth.

I was used to day-old bread and whatever fruit had been left to rot on the vine in our arbor's garden. I was not used to... this.

"Not all the Divine eat."

"I am not Divine." I spied a strawberry in a bowl and shoved it in my mouth, my eyes almost watering with its flavor.

Dream said nothing, just watched me, her eyebrows high and eyes wide. "Are you alone, child? Do you have anyone to care for you?"

I plucked another strawberry from the bowl and began toying with it. If I but touched her with this berry, I could make her feel flush with love or bestow unto her a choking sense of humility.

Suddenly, I realized the danger of my touch.

"I need my gloves," I whispered, setting the berry down.

Divine Dream stood and made her way to the chair, where she had set my gloves while I bathed. Every motion flowed, and I wondered what it would be like to have such grace. She watched as I carefully put them on. When I next touched my cane, the vines faded, as did the flowers, vanishing back to regular polished wood and when I looked outside, the world was not quite so bright.

"Do you have anyone to care for you, child?"

I looked at my hands, at the gloves that covered them. "I..." I had not thought to get this far, and so I had not planned a speech. "My mother has taken ill," I manage.

If possible, her eyes went even wider at that. I heard the door to the office open and felt Divine Muse enter, his presence comforting as a warm summer night. He filled the room with music, soft and in a minor key, and his face was pinched with worry.

"Is she your natural mother?" Dream asked, eyeing my vines. "Or were you, perhaps, found?"

Silence, and oh, the weight of that quiet. The layers of it. The texture.

"I need a job so I can move us into a better room, come winter," I finally said, making clear there was only so far she might push me for information.

More quiet.

"I am not here for handouts, nor am I here to be acknowledged. I want nothing but fair pay for a job well done."

I held my head high. I would earn what I got. I would help my mother by my own power.

Muse finally cleared his throat. He was looking at Divine Dream when he next spoke. "My brothers are returning, Rosemary, and they will need attendants. I think, perhaps, you would be well suited to them."

"Who?" Dream asked.

As an adult, I understand the subtext of this conversation, but as a child, all I saw was hope fulfilled. I saw a full belly and perhaps another room, this one with a fireplace so my mother could stay warm. And I would do this for her. I would earn it with my toil. It would be a symbol of my love for her.

"I think she would fit well with"—the pause fairly crackled with potential—"either Divine Aether or Divine Rain?"

Divine Dream studied me. "I should think she would fit best with Divine Aether. Is it not plain enough in the lines of her face?"

Muse smirked. "Yes, I think you are right." He looked at me. "Aether has never had a servant before. The god of Creation does not share his secrets. You will be a surprise to him, child. Dream will take you to his office, show you around. You will start tomorrow, but I will pay you three prayers today, in advance."

"I do not want handouts, sir."

"No, of course not." Muse grew serious, then reached into his pocket and pulled out three golden prayers, brilliant with their newness, with his face on each, and handed them to me one by one. "One is for the strain of your journey. Another is for telling us your story. The last is... consider it a security deposit. I am paying you to work for my brother, and to ensure you return for more, I am giving you but a taste of what I might bestow. I will personally pay you two prayers a day for work well done each day."

He dropped the prayers into my hand, each coin clinking as it struck my gloves.

I had never touched a new prayer. Prayers never made it down to the Narrows, and the ones that did were all tarnished, a breath away from disappearing, chipped and filed down, slivers of what they started out as. I would beg for what I could get, and when I got enough, I used my earnings to pay rent and buy food.

This...

He must have just bled his ichor to create these. They were still warm.

"Divine Muse, it is too much." I whispered the words, for in my hand I held the promise of a new life plus good food for my mother, perhaps a nice bone broth.

Maybe I could even afford medicine.

"You have given me the world," I murmured, staring at those coins. My eyes welled with hot tears.

"Oh, niece," he said and wrapped me in his arms. His body was warm and his embrace welcome. How long had it been since I had been held like this? How desperately I needed it. My life, I suddenly realized, had been churned by storms and here, for the first time, I was finding succor from the gale.

I came undone then, all of my carefully constructed walls crumbling.

There is a glory in the shatter, in allowing the cracks to surface and the ground to become unsettled.

We are, none of us, whole, riddled with wounds and trying to plaster them over as best we can. Yet here I had found someone who neither expected me to be strong, nor minded that I was crumbling.

Muse rubbed my back, hummed a song in my ear that filled me with calm. Finally, when I had collected the pieces of myself, he held me at arm's length and ran his eyes over me. "You are mine, Rosemary, and I am yours."

Simple words, but I felt the promise in them. With that utterance, Muse bound himself to me and I to him. We were a team.

I had never belonged before. Yes, I fit in the Narrows well enough, but I suddenly realized that fitting is different than belonging. My mother thought me a figment of her childhood as often as she recognized me as her daughter. It had been a long time since I had someone to go to when I was wounded or hurt or in need of a caring touch.

Divine Dream cleared her throat. "Rosemary, Divine Aether's office is not far."

For a moment, I was struck uncertain with how to proceed, for my leg was a low, painful throb and had not recovered from my long journey to this place. What is not far to Dream may very well be too far for me. But she... she was a goddess and how can I deny someone such as her?

So I closed my mouth and swallowed my pain, following her down the hall, around a corner, to a room sealed against the outside. The doors were thick wood and they opened with barely a touch. Inside, the room was dark. She moved to open the windows, two overlooking the same gardens as Muse's, though from a different vantage, and light streamed into the place.

This room was bigger than Divine Muse's, an office with a large mahogany desk, bookshelves full of leatherbound books lining one wall, and a fireplace along the other. There were tables scattered around and plush leather chairs. In the corner was a gramophone, and on the table sat an ancient wrought iron lamp. The room smelled like it hadn't been used in years, and dust was an inch thick, at least.

"How long has he been gone?" I asked.

Dream shrugged. "We do not think of time the same way as mortals, Rosemary. There is only long, and longer. Divine Aether has been gone long. I am afraid I did not realize how much work his office would require."

Yes, it would require work, but work was good. Work would keep me too busy to think. I could already feel my thoughts howling like many-fanged wolves, each one waiting to take a bite.

So much had happened this day.

"When does he return?"

Another shrug. "Anytime, really. He is traveling through Chaos, and who knows how long it will stretch these days? It is different for each soul who travels it. Sometimes it is short, sometimes long." She moved to the window, ran a finger along the pane and then grimaced at the dust. "My father, Divine Forge, felt the call to Create and went forth to bind himself to Chaos. Divine Aether was sent to help."

She spoke those words with such pride. I had no idea what she was talking about, but I nodded as though I did, and that seemed to please her well enough.

"Do you miss your father?"

"I do, but I am Divine enough to survive Chaos. I will see him eventually." She looked around. "Rosemary, if you return on the morrow, I will meet you here and help you clean. This is too much for one girl, and he will not wish to return to it like this. Aether is... particular."

If *you return on the morrow...*

With those words, she gave me the mercy of choice. These gods, I realized, were not how I had anticipated them to be.

"He sounds frightening."

"He likes his silence and his secrets. He is not scary, but he can be intimidating if you are not used to him. He was created in Father Luna's image. Aether is... the least diluted. He is the act of creation, while Father Luna is the purpose. One must have the other."

She spent the next hour showing me around, and then let me rest my leg for a time in Muse's office. Muse was gone, so I curled up on the sofa and fell asleep.

Strange, how comfortable I already was there.

When I woke, my vines had grown long, and bright blue primroses bloomed and closed along with my breaths. I watched them for a moment as I stirred and came back to myself.

The office was still empty and the sun was setting, and I noticed my dress had been given back to me, which was a kindness I had not expected. It was newly laundered, with the seam that had been splitting freshly mended. It was not a grand dress, not compared to anything I had yet seen in the Hall of the Gods, but it was mine. Before things got bad, Mother and I had threaded every needle, stitched every line with care, heads bent together in a spill of sunlight.

I put it back on and felt more myself. After this strange day, it was what I needed. Then, I left the Hall of the Gods the way I entered and disappeared.

Back to the Narrows.

NOW
BELLADONNA

The moment I show up at my mother's house for lunch, I know it is a mistake. There is a gleam in her eyes that I recognize. One that tells me she has been plotting.

Though there is something else about her as well. She is wearing too much makeup, her skin is paler than I am used to. Something here is not right.

"Your dress is lovely," she says, pushing the thoughts from my mind.

It is a beautiful dress, all straight lines and flashy beads, and far nicer than any I might have otherwise worn if I'd had to buy one at a shop today. "I borrowed it from one of Mother Sol's daughters. I'm afraid I do not have dresses anymore, Mother. I did not need them when I was ferrying, or in Dawnland for the years I lived there."

I hear the dulcet tones of a violin in the parlor, from Mother's gramophone, and I grow colder still, for she never plays music unless company is present.

"Years?" She steps aside and allows me entry. There is insult in the way she asks the question, as though the fact that I had tarried elsewhere without dashing right back to her is an offense.

It is strange, looking at her after so long away. It does not feel like I have been gone so long, but Chaos is ever-changing. Time flows differently there, and it is hard to judge. Years have gone by in what only felt like moments to me. Mother looks to be in her fifties now, while I am but a few years older than I was when I left. So much time lost, so much to catch up on.

How am I to reunite with this woman? Our relationship was never easy, but now I have spent nearly half my life away. We are strangers. I am not the pliable girl I once was.

The house stretches around me, and I take it in. I recognize every bit of this place. Mother has updated the furnishings and there is new wallpaper in the entryway, but I remember these walls. I remember those stairs and this door. So many memories of both happier and sadder times.

I think of Isra and the World Tree. Often she has spoken about feeling the echoes of previous generations engrained in that wood, as though their memories but wait for her touch. I press my hand against the wall and hesitate. Perhaps I will feel something, an echo of times past. But only silence answers my touch and Mother looks at me with a furrowed brow.

"Come into the parlor," she says, her voice pitched just so, words clipped and formal.

Dread clutches my spine with cold hands and I know we are not alone before I turn the corner. I can see the truth of it in every stiff line of my mother's body.

The parlor is a fine room, with maroon wallpaper. To the left are two large windows overlooking her prized roses. The bushes are large and so heavy with flowers the limbs droop. Fat honeybees, dusted with pollen, fly past the windows, busy about their tasks. Above the cold fireplace is an ancient photo of my father, from just before he left to ferry goods through Chaos.

My attention turns to the small writing desk in the corner. I know every whorl of wood, every chipped edge, every bump and divot by heart. I spent years there, practicing my perfect penmanship in a spill of yellow light, Mother lurking over my shoulder, examining each wrong swirl and swoop of my letters, marking them, and telling me how it will impact my marriage prospects if I cannot write a legible invitation to teas and brunch parties.

Something shifts, pulling my attention to the large, maroon velvet couch and there I see Basil and her son Oleander, two of the very people who caused me to run so long ago. Oleander's fingers toy with the metal inlay on the couch's arm. His eyes are troubled.

I fix a glare upon my mother, who is smiling as though she just won the moon. "My daughter, Belladonna," Mother says. She is simpering and it curdles my stomach. "Newly returned from Chaos."

She speaks these words as though my journey has won her something. She has ascended through me, and now I am the prize she holds against the world as proof of her insurmountable sacrifices.

"I remember you," Basil says. She stands and wraps me in her arms. I stiffen and panic rises in my throat, chokes me. The world crashes. The piano is too loud, the walls too hard, the very air screams. Basil holds on for far too long. Each heartbeat feels like forever. My breathing becomes labored.

Finally, she releases me, and it takes an effort of will to keep myself rooted.

Oleander smiles, and I notice his dimples. He is charming enough. I see the boy in him, hidden behind the man he has become. His gaze is assessing. I remember this sensation, the feeling of being touched... this other way. He is older now, showing signs of nearing middle age, while I am still ripe with youth.

Part of it is Chaos. Part of it is my blood. All of it makes me uncomfortable. Like I do not belong here.

Oleander says something, and I make the appropriate noise in response. We were friends as children and would have stayed that way until our parents started meddling. When we were old enough to understand their designs, we grew apart. The less time spent together, the better.

"Mother, what is this?" I ask, finally. Desperately.

Oleander and Basil watch, eyes wide and curious. Mother licks her lips. "They were visiting, Belladonna. That is all. I invited them to stay for tea."

Convenient.

Mother motions for me to sit, so I take a small chair near the cold fireplace. There is ash in that hearth, and I feel it in my soul. What a fool I was, to think my mother would have changed. That she would have wanted me here only to take an interest or get to know me again.

Basil is well-practiced at small talk and soon she and Mother are chattering like the best of friends. Oleander is silent, but I feel his eyes on me and I do not like it.

I should not have come. I left my daughter for this.

Still, Mother is looking at me, expectation etched across her features. I make myself act proper and smile at the right moments. My anger builds to an impotent inferno. Finally, Mother's lady, Daisy, arrives with a tray of cucumber sandwiches, a bowl of fresh fruit, tea, and lemon slices. Hunger directs my thoughts to the spread before me.

The afternoon is agonizing. By the time they leave, a headache is pulsing behind my eyes and I hunger for silence, to wrap myself in the quiet of Chaos. I long to be anywhere but here. To run headfirst into the wind and then keep going. The bars of this cage wrap around me, grow ever closer.

"He is a charming man," Mother says as soon as the door shuts. "He has grown into a very nice adult, Belladonna, and he is not married. Think of what such a union could do. Our two companies merged into one? Once the Divine face, we would control the trade out of Meadowsweet and he would control the trade within it. We would have an empire."

It takes me a moment to catch up.

Marriage? Empires?

"Mother—"

She waves a hand in the air, cutting me off. She is lost now, in her own world.

"He wants a strong woman beside him," Mother says and I follow her deeper into the house, into the kitchen. "Someone who will help him run a business. You'd have a nanny at home for the children. You could outsource the work. No more ferrying goods. No more Chaos and no more Divine."

"Mother—"

Into the kitchen we go, and she plucks a sprig of lavender from a vase and sniffs it. She is giddy with joy, her cheeks flushed and her eyes dancing. She is still pale, I notice, but less so now, as though possibility has infused her with new vitality.

"He is handsome, is he not?"

"He..." I hesitate. "He's fine."

"Fine? How could you say he is fine? His cheekbones alone—"

"He is fine, Mother. What would you have me say? He is very"—I wave my hands in the air—"blonde."

"Is that not pleasing?" Her eyes are daggers and soon I am pierced through.

"You have not asked me about my journey. You haven't asked what I did while I was away. You haven't even asked me how I am doing, Mother, and already you are trying to marry me off."

"He came to me, Belladonna. The moment you left yesterday, he showed up. You know what that means? You'll have men lined up for you. You'll be able to pick which one you want. Oleander would be best, but I'm sure there are other options. Oh, Belladonna, everything is changing now. When the Divine are no more, it will be families like ours who will run things if we make the right moves now."

She sniffs her lavender again and then sets the flowers on the polished countertop and stares at me. "You will have to move in here. It would not be proper for an unmarried woman to live alone."

"I am staying in the Hall of the Gods. I am far from alone."

"Even worse."

Silence stretches until I think I can hear it scream. Light slants through the far window and hits Mother just so. I see then, the cold calculation lurking in her hazel eyes. I understand why her quiet bristles.

The daughter she knew died when I left. She has already

mourned me. Now, I am a convenient stranger. I am a tool, and she will find a purpose for my use.

Disappointment is a bitter poison, and I drink all of it.

It is then that I notice a small sprig of rosemary not far from my arm. I pluck it from the counter and bruise the leaves. The scent of them slips into me like starlight into a temple. I remember better, easier times. Warm nights and soft moonlight.

"Belladonna—"

"I am leaving," I say, and it feels good to have that option now. To leave instead of stay. To have somewhere to go and a life to live that is mine and mine alone. "It was a mistake to come."

"Wait. I'm sorry. I'm old, Belladonna. I have already lived the better part of my life. Is it wrong for me to want to know that you are cared for? To want grandchildren?"

I flinch, my thoughts turning to Flora.

"I will not marry, Mother."

Rosemary. The scent soaks into my skin. Becomes part of me.

Mother's eyes go hard. "The business is in my name, Belladonna. Not yours. I let you run it, but it belongs to me."

"Are you threatening me?" Would she be so foolish? Mother Sol is my great grandmother. I have spent plenty of time in her Sacred Solarium. She knows my name and asks after me. She cares for me. My daughter has played at her feet. Surely my mother understands that no matter her threats, she cannot hope to stand against the full weight of my blood.

She seems to notice her error and her eyes fill with tears while her face goes soft. "Is it too much that I ask for some measure of security? Some knowledge that I will not be left destitute and alone? You could get an offer to ferry tomorrow and I will be here, in this house, growing older and older with nothing but shadows and silence to keep me company."

Her voice goes softer and quieter the longer she speaks, until the last words are a quivering whisper. I let the sound fade and I fill myself with the quiet that follows. It strengthens me in a way food never can.

I will be here, in this house, growing older and older with nothing but shadows and silence to keep me company.

She cannot hide her truth or pain from me and I see it now. She has spent years just like that: alone. In this hollow house, she has bided night after night staring at portraits of my father and cursing him for loving her and for leaving her.

She has spent birthdays and holidays alone. She has smothered herself in silence and bedecked herself in memory. Now that I am back, is it any wonder she chafes at the confines of this cage she has crafted for herself? In me, she sees a way out.

I understand all of this, and yet...

I am not the girl I once was, the girl who could not bear disappointing her mother, so she ran away instead.

"I will not marry," I say. I draw strength from the rosemary in my hands, the familiar scent of it, the soft press of leaves against my calloused skin. "Do what you will with the company, but I will not marry."

"Belladonna, you've been away a long time. I see now I am going too fast. Take time to rest and adjust. Think about this, is all I ask. I will keep the cards of whatever suitors come to our door but promise me you won't make any decisions now. Someday, you may find yourself lonely."

I want, so desperately, to tell her about Flora, but the words curdle on the tip of my tongue and I cannot do it. How fiercely would she use my child for her gain? Not only would she have a chance at a business empire through me, but through Flora she would have a direct connection to another Creation.

I have spent my life being manipulated by this woman. I will not allow it to happen to my daughter.

I make my way to my mother and press my lips against her cheek. It feels both cold and somehow hot. I keep myself from flinching, barely.

She was not always like this. Before my father left, I remember her as kind and gentle, caring for others and always smiling. However, like cream left in the sun too long, she soured. It happened slowly. Over time, I learned to never trust my mother, for she always wanted something from me and whatever I offered was never enough.

I was never enough.

But I see the woman I once knew in moments like this, when I press my lips against her cheek and, for a breath, hear her love carried on her sigh.

"I will visit you another time," I whisper.

I leave.

And she does not stop me.

NOW

ISRA

I rise with the sun.

The world is pink and soft. Mist clings to the earth and seems unwilling to let go. The first intrepid birds open their throats to welcome the day while Mother Sol sweeps her fingers across a brightening sky, healing the bruises left by night.

Dawn is a love letter to dreamers.

If I was in Dawnland, I would have already been harvesting blooms with my butterfly kindred. This is the quiet hour, when neither the denizens of night nor day reign. The forest would be thick with moisture and the gossamer sunlight peering through the canopy. Dew would collect on our wings, making them appear to be dripping with diamonds.

Instead, I am in Meadowsweet and I go where my antennae lead, tracking the sweetest smells deeper into Father Terra's Sacred Garden. Never before have I scented such heady blossoms. Each one is more potent than the last. I am drunk on this ripe morning, on the soft sunlight and the scents. I spread my wings and test the air.

Guilt suffuses me, like ice on a hot summer day, that I should be here enjoying this beauty while my brothers...

Manab.

Atheed.

I do not notice Father Terra until he speaks, shattering my thoughts. "It is an act of worship," he says, his words shattering the silence, "to glory in the morning."

Like a rose in summer, I bloom.

Father Terra sits before me. His presence fills me like water. The air is charged and the breeze turns to a caress. The earth cradles my feet. I breathe deeply and know that I am part of the world.

There is no mistaking who and what Father Terra is. His body is made from thousands of woven, moss-covered tree limbs. His hair is the green of grass in sunlight. Flowers grow from his scalp; small and white with yellow centers, they bloom and close, eternally seeking light. Acorn eyes fix on me and I shiver. Never have I felt so seen.

I bend my knee to my maker and spread my wings wide. The earth clutches my hands, holds them steady. The weight of this moment presses upon me.

"Father Terra, I humble mys—"

"Sit beside me, child." A loamy finger brushes the nape of my neck and I am transformed. Flowers grow from the notches of my spine and vines bind me to the soil. The earth wraps around me, and for a breath I am blooming and blooming and blooming. Oh, it is agony to become.

Then he takes his finger away and the sensation is gone with such speed it is almost jarring.

When I next look up, wisteria droops from Father Terra's shoulders and tiny rows of cabbage line the backs of his knuckles. His eyes are soft.

I wonder if I felt a fraction of what he feels.

I wonder if it hurts to be a god.

Slowly, I ease myself to my feet and then sit on the bench beside him. My heart beats so loud I swear he can hear it.

Birds and bees welcome us beneath a sky strewn with light.

Finally, Father Terra's voice rumbles through me. "It was not long after binding ourselves to Chaos that Sol, Luna, and I lost ourselves to Creating: Luna to the elements of dark, Sol to the light. I bent myself to the earth.

"It was Luna who found me after we had been about our tasks for..." Father Terra falters, as though trying to measure such a thing as time is beyond him. He waves a loamy hand in the air, his fingers covered in rows of weeping willows. Then, he begins again. "'Brother,' Luna said, 'pause a moment and behold what we have Created.' And so I did, for in all my time coaxing Creation from Chaos, I had forgotten to look up. I had not yet marveled at the sky."

He breathes deep, and I feel his eyes, heavy with sorrow, fix on me.

"The first night I witnessed stole my breath, and the day that followed returned it. It was a moment of such pure love, I used it to create my daughter, Falcon. Is it any wonder she had such an affinity for flight?" I open my mouth to speak, but he stills me with a touch. "I know my daughter sleeps, Isra. I have felt her fading. She is, after all, part of me. When she closed her eyes at the last, I stopped soaring."

Summer weaves its spell around us, and I am lost to it. So delicate is the light, so fine are the flower petals, so ripe is this wonderful earth... and yet this loss. It touches everything I see. To be severed of flight after a lifetime of it. To be so far from part of yourself. To suffer such loss alone.

We are not so different.

"Do not cry, child. It is the natural course of things. We have Created. Now it is time for us to give ourselves over and Sustain that which we have wrought." He pauses. "Nothing ever ends, it just changes shape. My daughter still lives in Dawnland and she always will."

Divine Falcon said much the same, at the last. It still does not make it easier. In her final days, as the bombs were falling all around and Dawnland seemed to tremble under the force of violence, even then my goddess smiled and said, "I am not ending, Isra. I am changing shape."

"She is not gone." Father Terra's voice trembles, and when I look at him a tear slides down his clover-freckled cheek. "That part of me... it is not gone." He shifts, and I notice now the slope of his shoulders, the bend of his spine. Sorrow has a weight and I see it press upon him. "Falcon wrote me a letter, many lifetimes ago, when the last ferriers went between Dawnland and Meadowsweet. She called you her 'children of the bright earth.' I look at you now and I think the title fits. No one could ever see you and not think of light."

Roses sprout from Father Terra's fingertips, the scent of them heady. He wipes them below my eyes to catch my tears.

I had thought I would need to soothe him. How is it that he is soothing me?

"Will you tell me of Dawnland?" he asks, and desperation colors his words. He is not a god now, but a father, eager for any word of his child, anything that might help manage the ragged edges that frame the space his daughter used to fill.

And so I weave for him the story of my home. I paint a picture of Dawnland as it was when it was ripe and full of life, peaceful. I take him through the university, where Manab spent his days, and through the library, where Atheed spent his. I introduce him to all of my siblings, even the ones who have not survived. I show him the Sacred Milkweed Grove, and take him through shopping centers and the arcades, restaurants, and parks I so loved.

I show him my life, all the things war took from me. All the things I've loved and lost: from the way the sunlight shines through the canopy after a rainstorm to my favorite nook in the World Tree, where I used to read.

I offer Father Terra as much of Dawnland as I can and he hangs on every word, smiling through it all like I am offering him the grandest gift. I give him this part of myself and watch as an endless cycle of seasons march across the terrain of his body.

Then, as my voice fades, I remember Flora and her need. "Father Terra..." I lick my lips. After all this, how can I bring myself to ask for more? "My niece has a certain need for milkweed."

Sunlight bursts from between his lily-covered lips and his eyes are almost lost within the folds created by his smile. "Of course. I should love to Create something that can be only hers, and for those who come after."

Those who come after. The words chill my marrow. I do not want to be here long enough for anyone to come after.

Milkweed sprouts from his arms and his cheeks and he smiles at me through the blooms. "I can picture what you have described, Isra, and I will spend tonight bending myself to the task. I think I have something left in me to offer Chaos. I think... I think I can manage this one last Creation."

His voice sounds so tired, and a wave of guilt crashes upon me for of course. Of course the wasting had not been relegated to Divine Falcon alone. She said as much, at the last. "This is but the start of it." I had just not understood the implication of her words at the time. Perhaps, more accurately, I did not let myself understand.

I do now, and it rocks me to my core. Will Meadowsweet be another Dawnland? I do not think I can stomach more war. And Father Terra. I do not know him well, but the world seems less bright at the thought of his kind mien not being in it.

"Nothing ends, Isra." Father Terra touches a mossy knuckle to my chin and his vine draws back from my wrist. He flicks fingers in the air, scattering flowers with every motion. When I next look at him, he is covered in honeybees. "Fly free, little butterfly. But do not forget to seek me out. You are a rare treat."

I do as he bids, and flee, my wings beating as though to hurry me along the path. Flowers reach for me in greeting and bees perch on my shoulders. The sun is warm and bright. I have never felt so alive. And yet I can swear I feel Father Terra's sorrow, the weight of his mourning tainting everything I see, turning it a bit darker, more bruised.

The Hall of the Gods looms before me, a palatial edifice made from polished white marble, the city of Meadowsweet arrayed around it like the skirts of a dress. Further out is the ocean, as far as the eye can see, a fathomless blue so brilliant it mirrors the sky.

It is not home, but I cannot help but marvel at the beauty of this place, as unique to me as I am to it. If I take a moment to see past my keening loss, I can appreciate the perfection of this Creation. I can glory in the Divine that made it.

"Isra?" The sniffle following that familiar voice sets my teeth on edge.

Belladonna is too bright to feel such sorrow.

I turn and see her. She has worked herself back into the shade of a willow tree, her knees drawn up to her chest. Marigolds sprinkle the ground around her like so many drops of captured sunlight. Her hair spills around her shoulders, a curtain of summer, and beneath that bright glow I can only make out the shape of the woman.

My antennae shift and I sense the fading light. It is later in the day than I thought. How much time had I spent with Father Terra? Most of the day, though it had seemed like only moments. I wonder if reality bends around the Divine. What must it be like, to exist both within and without time? Does it hurt to be torn so?

Belladonna sniffles again. I find a nearby rock and perch on it. I have been around her long enough to know that she will not desire touch, so I make sure I keep myself in my own space. When I face her, I look into her eyes and touch her there, where it matters most. "What happened?" I finally ask.

"I visited my mother," she whispers.

She has never spoken of her family, and I have learned not to ask after them. Now, I see why. There are some wounds that go so deep they never heal.

Belladonna shifts. I watch as she wipes away tears that shine like the sun. "I am an adult, Isra. I have lived on my own for seventeen years. How is it she can still hurt me like this?"

I think of my brothers, so far away, and how I ache for them.

I think of Father Terra and Divine Falcon.

"Love," I whisper, "is the knife that always cuts true."

"Isra." This is how glass sounds before it shatters. The light that makes her dims. "Do not leave me, I beg you. Do not let me weather this storm alone."

She breaks then, and I sit still, a lighthouse in the dark so she might always know where port is.

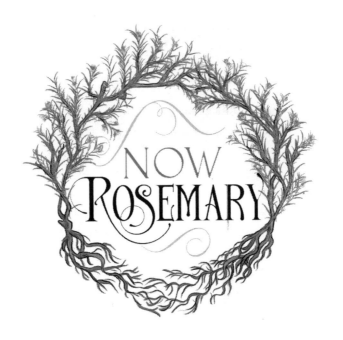

NOW
ROSEMARY

The next morning, I find myself in the main hall, where most of the other Divine have gathered. Across from me sit Father Luna, Mother Sol, and Father Terra. Even now, their Divinity presses against me. It requires effort to keep myself from bending low before them, and I wonder if anyone else feels the need to supplicate.

I look around. Ahead of me, one of Father Terra's sons stands, the leaves around his crown growing autumnal. My heart clenches.

I find Divine Dream along the side of the room, reserving a seat for me on an ornate stone bench. She has her notepad perched on her lap, her pencil already busy drawing whatever dreams she will grant people this day. Sun spills through the domed stained glass windows, painting her with rainbows of light.

I slip through the crowd and sit beside her, grateful to ease the ache in my hip. She flashes me a smile.

"What is going on?" I whisper.

"A ferrier came in several days ago," Dream replies, her voice a low murmur. "Brought a mortal from Dawnland, Divine Falcon's Creation."

That explains the crowd, I think as I look around. Everyone in the

Hall seems to be here, peering past shoulders and beyond elbows to catch a glimpse. While ferriers from other Creations did show up on occasion, the journey through Chaos was never easy, and so we rarely saw them.

"She is the strangest creature, Rosemary. Wait until you see her."

I can only imagine. Father Terra's line was nothing if not unpredictable, but the excitement in Dream's voice had me leaning forward, my cane bracing my weight. Still, I could not see over the heads of the Divine around me and my hip would not allow me to stand quite yet.

"How did she survive Chaos?" I ask. "She must have enough Divinity in her to allow it."

And yet, something about this is wrong. Ferriers are rare, but never before has one gathered such a crowd. I study the Divine and the emotions woven through them, tension in their stiff lines and worry in the cadence of their whispers. Beneath all of that is a certain dark foreboding.

This creature from Dawnland brings change with her. I know this the same way I know I have air in my lungs.

Dream smiles, but it is a sad thing. Pain, shared. Her pencil scratch-scratches along her pad of paper. A reptilian monster, this time, with kind eyes. "They brought news. Divine Falcon sleeps."

"She sleeps?" I whisper.

A vine grows around my trembling hands, holding them still.

Dream meets my eyes and nods once. "She sleeps, Rosemary."

The implication in those words, what they mean, fills me with frost.

For a moment, we go silent. The domed ceiling carries the susurration of voices well. Accented, lyrical, and lilting. Someone ahead of me shifts, and I think I see a flash of the brightest orange through a gap between elbows. There and gone in an instant.

Divine Falcon sleeps.

The words rattle until I cannot hear anything but them.

My eyes fill with tears; each one burns.

Dream's hand rests on my arm, squeezes, and when she speaks

again, her voice is softer and measured. "The woman from Dawnland looks to be part butterfly. She is truly splendid to behold."

She flips the page in her notebook and, a few scratches later, elbows me. "See?" She points at what she's drawn.

How Dream can capture so much emotion and nuance with a few lines, I will never understand. Still, the image before me makes me catch my breath. She is beautiful, this butterfly woman, with towering gossamer wings, but perhaps what captivates me the most is the sorrow Dream manages to convey in those dark eyes.

We all feel the heaviness that comes with realizing there will be an end. It is knowing that so bends the soul while seeing destroys it.

Still, I know she feels it, the weight of inevitability. It is in Dream's drawings, each one juxtaposed somehow. The ferocious monster with kind eyes. The butterfly woman steeped in sorrow. It is as though none of their souls quite fit the bodies they inhabit. Anguish as art.

I let her grieve quietly, in the only way she knows.

As though understanding the path of my thoughts, Dream squeezes my arm again. "Butterflies, Rosemary." She taps her paper, jarring me from my darker musings.

Ah yes, that. Butterflies.

"Let's go outside," she says.

Dream stands and shakes out her arms before running her hands down her pressed pantsuit and gesturing back the way I'd come. I follow, but slowly. My hip is agony and I lean all my weight on my cane, hating the way my right leg drags.

She does not lead me to Father Terra's garden, but rather to the front of the Hall of the Gods. The border of the yard where our sanctuary brushes against Meadowsweet proper is where Dream likes to spend time. She is a creature who thrives on the edges of things, and so that is where I often find her. On the edge of this world, and that. Drawing, ever drawing.

She takes her usual perch on a stone bench that sits beside a towering lavender bush, heady with bees. In an instant, she puts pencil to paper again. She furrows her brow against the sun and stares across the small margin of grass that separates us from the cobblestone street beyond. In the daylight, Dream is not quite so luminous, her mortality waxing just enough for her maturity to shine through.

"I feel like dancing tonight," she says. There is a mischievous glint to her moon-glowing eyes. "Come with me. We won't go far. I think we could both use it."

We could, I know it.

And yet, somehow, leaving these grounds feels like a betrayal.

Dream leans against my arm. "There is a small speakeasy, not far. We could drive if you prefer. There will not be so many people." She hesitates. "Rosemary, your father will not begrudge you these moments. He's aging, true, but not yet—"

I wave a hand, cutting her off.

"I'm sorry," Dream whispers. I feel her remorse in the way her fingertips tremble against my arm. "In truth, Rosemary, I need this. I feel like I cannot breathe when I am here. There is so much sorrow and fear. It presses upon me. It is not so bad to live, is it? To remind ourselves that we are alive? I yearn..."

But her words trail off, and before I can ask what she hungers for, she presses on.

"Please come with me."

"I will," I vow, for she is right. If I stay here, all I will do is count the moments. I will feel each of them slip through my fingers like sand.

I will think about my father's heartbeat and I will weep.

My mind turns back to the butterfly woman Dream drew. "What do you know of her?" I ask. "This butterfly woman."

Dream hesitates. She is careful with what she says, so she might best keep the privacy of those whose sleep she enters. She finally says, "She does not rest easy," and I know I will get no more from her than that.

"She brings change with her," I say, even though it pains me to form the words.

Dream nods. "The butterfly woman is as mortal as anyone in

Meadowsweet. She has no Divinity to feed Chaos and so she should not have survived her journey. Chaos should have devoured her."

Divine Falcon sleeps. That is the difference. She fed her Divinity to Chaos, satiating its hunger enough to let a mortal slip through.

The implications of this are vast. Creations are difficult to travel between and Chaos is hungry and unpredictable. Few Divine want to ferry. If the way becomes easier, so easy even mortals might manage it, then—

"It changes everything," Dream says. She picks up her pencil and draws.

A face reveals itself on her page. She has taken to drawing this figure more often of late. From the familiar features, so similar to my father's, I assume she is drawing her father, Divine Forge.

Songbirds fill the air. An automobile drives down the cobblestone street before us, black and gleaming. In the distance, a trolly chimes. Down the hill is an open-air market; voices carry to us on the salty ocean breeze.

"I need to forget, Rosemary. For one night, I need to forget."

What must this be like for her, with her father so far away, in a Creation of his own? At least I am close enough to comfort my own.

A hummingbird hovers nearby, sipping nectar. Strange, how life goes on despite our pain.

I turn my head and spy two women sauntering in our direction, already reaching into their purses for prayers.

"Let's go," Dream says, standing. "I cannot stand it when they offer prayers."

"Why?" Though I do not argue.

She hesitates as she studies the women. "I would rather be loved, Rosemary. Please, let's go inside."

She almost runs back into the Hall, leaving me to follow. I feel one of the women place my father's prayer on the ground where I just sat. My divinity pulses as the prayer disappears into the soil, strengthening my father's bond to Chaos, and, in turn, mine. For a heartbeat, I sense Creation all around, alive and thriving. I feel the frayed edges of Chaos lurking at the borders of Meadowsweet. I sense its hunger.

When I enter the Hall of the Gods, Dream is gone and the main hall is full of the Divine, so I decide to linger.

The crowd parts just enough, and for a moment, I see her.

The butterfly woman. Her black and orange wings arc above her crown with the tips nearly dragging along the floor. Her polished onyx skin is freckled with white. She is petite, with fine, sharp bones but it is her eyes that captivate me. Large and so luminous. The sorrow Dream drew was no lie.

I feel her gaze on me and shiver.

The crowd closes again, and the butterfly woman is lost.

THEN
ROSEMARY

Landlady waited for me on the front stoop when I arrived home that night. Old and wizened, her back bent like a question mark, she studied me. Her eyes were both cold and kind. "How'd it go today?" she asked.

I smiled. "Good," I said. "They offered me a job. It pays—"

Landlady's eyes went hard and sharp as glass. The transformation was so sudden, it struck terror in my soul. My bones groaned like pine trees after a blizzard.

She fixed her eyes on me and then took a drag on the cigarette clamped between her fingers. A row of children gathered behind me. Her boys, I knew. It was obvious who Landlady's boys were: they were always cleaner and better fed than everyone else.

My vines coiled against my scalp. A single spray of agrimony grew, yellow as sunlight, fed by my growing fear.

A lungful of smoke hit me like a slap. Sweet, that smoke. Now that I knew the gods who bled the ichor she laced her cigarettes with, it did not seem quite so harmless. I remembered the heat of his prayers as Divine Muse pressed them into my hands. Still fresh. He had offered up part of himself to make those prayers for me. Now, her callous use of them turned my stomach.

"My mother," I whispered, voice trembling. "Tell me she's okay."

"She's fine. You'll have her back soon as you pay me what's owed."

"But—"

The kids drew closer. Their faces pointed at me. They waited.

"It's for upkeep, girl," she said, thwapping me on the side of my head. My vision blurred and I saw stars. Tears stung my eyes. A boy behind me sniggered. Humiliation is its own kind of pain and I felt it then. The agony of being reduced.

"What do you want?" My voice was a whisper.

I doubt she heard me over the roar of the docks at our back and the speakeasy next door, doors flung open against the twilight. Music and the drunk and high staggered about the mud-churned street. A woman sang a bawdy song on the stoop across the way. Someone laughed.

It was all so normal.

Landlady did not need to hear me to understand. Surrender is its own language, spoken with slumped shoulders and a bowed head.

"Bet you have the good stuff, don't you? Now that you're up there, rubbing elbows with that what made you."

I saw then, with horrifying clarity, that I had been too trusting. Landlady had seen me coming, and all she'd had to do was wait. She'd known eventually I'd be desperate. She'd send me up the hill and I would be taken in by my own. And then...

Then she would get her ichor straight from the source instead of siphoning off whatever part-mortal wastrel ended up on the wrong side of the Narrows, or picking prayers from pockets. She'd keep my mother to ensure my return each day. With every coin I gave Landlady, her authority would grow, until she would run the ichor trade in the Narrows.

No one could supply pure like she could, because of me.

I'd think she hated me, hated the Divine, but I knew better.

Landlady didn't care a fig about Divinity, something she often proclaimed. Not many in the Narrows did, fading as it was. This was

the part of the city under no Divine jurisdiction. We were the forgotten. For Landlady, it wasn't about love or hate. It was about business,
and nothing got in the way of business. She would use me until the
Divine came down on her, or until I lost my usefulness.

The shavings from one freshly minted prayer, mixed with some
saw dust, could sustain the habits of an entire tenement for a week. If
I gave her one coin a day...

But that was half of what Divine Muse offered to pay me.

One would never be enough.

Her eyes gleamed as she watched me, dark and full of chilling
purpose. "One coin a day." She smiled. "It's only until you pay off
your mama's debt, you see. Costs a lot, watching her each day. And
you don't pay nearly enough for that room you're in. You're just giving
what's owed."

My mother's debt. Of course. I knew sitting her beside Landlady's
stove would cost me.

I had walked into my own prison.

The world closed in around me, pulsing like a heart.

"Don't worry," Landlady said, a fish-skin hand resting on my arm.
"I am not a cruel mistress. I take care of my own. You treat well with
me, and I will return the favor."

She did. I knew that much. Landlady's kids were a well-kept crew
and many longed to be a member. That did not mean I was among
them. I did not want to peddle ichor, and I had never enjoyed smoke.
I wanted nothing to do with her trade.

I thought of Divine Muse's kind, moon-bright eyes and knew that
beyond all of that, I could not harm him this way when all he had
done was help me.

I followed her up the three steps to the door, where she hesitated
on the threshold, her other hand clamped around the knob. Her nails
dug into my arm. Blood welled where they bit, swirls of gold and
ruby.

I had never questioned the color of my blood before.

"One prayer," she said. Then, gentler, "You'll be fine if you're
careful."

I wouldn't be, though, and we both knew it. Mother was sick. She needed a doctor and those cost money. I also had to make rent and buy food. I could afford this with Divine Muse's payment, but losing one prayer a day would cut well into any possibility of bettering our situation.

Or moving my mother into a better room come winter.

Slowly, carefully, I pulled a coin from the pouch I had secreted up my sleeve and handed it to Landlady. The coin, when held up to the light, was gold and gleaming, bright as the sun at noon. Divine Muse's profile faced me. I could not look into his eyes. He had been so kind to me, and to see his ichor used thus gave me great pain.

It was different now that he wasn't just an idea.

"Divine Muse," she said. "Are you his by-blow?"

I clamped my lips and held them firm. She would have my prayer, but she would not gain more.

"Doesn't matter," she grunted. "Your mother is already in your room. Was sleeping last I saw her."

"You left her there?" I shrieked, prayers forgotten. "Alone?"

"Are you daft? Of course not. Had her with me all day. Helped me roll cigarettes and give them to the boys to sell. She's got nimble hands." A pause. Her eyes go soft. "Put her in your room as the sun was setting, that's all." Kindly, that last bit, like she took pity on me. Perhaps some part of her felt guilty.

I pushed past her and limped down the hallway to the room I shared with Mother and then thrust the door open. She lay on the palette, sleeping peacefully. As soon as I spied her, all the tension left me. Relief felt like a storm breaking after a drought. My head felt light, and the room swam. My vines uncoiled and buds grew, eager to bloom.

"You have thirty minutes," Landlady said.

"Thirty minutes for what? I've already paid you."

"Thirty minutes to use the toilet and do whatever else it is you need to do. After that, your door will be locked. I'll open it in the morning." She jingled a ring of keys in her hand. "This is only until I trust you won't run away."

"You can't lock us in there! What if Mother needs something? What if—"

"You scream and I'll come running." She glared at me. "Thirty minutes."

Two of her kids stayed on either side of the hallway outside my door, while the others peeled off, some trailing after her, some turning around, likely to watch our window from the street. I was a prisoner in truth, it seemed, and my mother a hostage.

What had I done?

I do not know how to describe what I felt as the door shut that night. This was my home, never comfortable but a place I at least knew, a certain refuge against the world. Now it seemed as though I'd been thrust into a foreign land. The walls did not feel so familiar, the room full of shadows I could not pierce.

Mother slept peacefully enough while I tossed and turned, staring at the ceiling and listening as the woman next door, Lotte, worked her trade throughout the small hours, the wall vibrating with her moans.

It was late when my mother woke from a bout of coughing. Anxiety held me tight. I would scream for Landlady if I needed to, but the very thought of her repulsed me and I could not stomach the notion.

I held my breath and waited for the fit to end. I saw Mother's eyes open in the dark.

Would she know me?

"Do you need anything?" I helped her sit and wrapped an arm around her shoulders. How much these words cost me, to utter them so easily while worry drove my soul into frantic flight.

"Water," she said.

Relief then, for such a simple answer meant she was not drifting.

I stood and lurched to our small table, filling a cup for her, and then held it to her lips. It stilled the rattle in her lungs and her breathing eased and coughing quieted. Finally, Mother sighed and lay back, staring at the ceiling.

"I'm sorry," she whispered after the silence stretched long, and then longer still. Outside, a drunk shouted something at the fathomless sky.

"You have nothing to be sorry for."

She did not answer and I assumed she'd fallen asleep. Then, softly, "I am your mother, Rosemary. I should care for you." Before I could answer, she drew in a rattling breath and pushed on. "What do you have that she's after?"

I went still, for I did not want to upset my mother.

"Rosemary," Mother breathed. Her lungs bubbled, and tears filled my eyes. She was sick and we were trapped in this place. More so now than ever, and no closer to warmth for my efforts.

My heart clenched. What a fool I was.

"I got a job in the Hall of the Gods."

Mother's hissed breath turned into hacks. She rolled onto her side, coughed into a kerchief.

"You're sick," I whispered. "I can only beg so much. Winter is coming, Mother, and food is already scarce. The cold weather will make it so much worse and we have very little protection from it in this room. But up there... Up there they pay for simple work."

"You should be in school, Rosemary, not sweeping someone's floor."

"I'm going to clean an office." Keep it vague, I told myself, for my mother was brittle. One wrong move and she would crumble. I sensed that much in her, even then. She was always a breath away from breaking.

"Who took you in, my daughter?" These words, spoken low, held the world in them.

"Divine Muse, Mother. He was very kind."

"Ah." A breath left her, relief filling it.

Mother slept, and coughed, and slept, and I listened to her watery breaths. Felt each of them thrust daggers deep.

At last, she woke and I could see that something in her illness had turned overnight. Her lips were dotted with crimson.

Fear is a landscape all its own and I was lost to it then. Here was my mother, the only thing I had that was my own, and her lips were flecked with blood. "Rosemary," she whispered as the night bled pink. "Divine Muse is very kind."

How would Mother know if Divine Muse was kind?

It was the first time she let some of her mask slip and I peered beneath, suddenly realizing she had lived a whole life before me, and I knew very little about any of it. *Mother* was only one of her faces. *Willow* was a woman I had never truly met.

"Mother—"

But she was already asleep.

NOW
BELLADONNA

It is one of Father Terra's grandsons who finds me later that afternoon, after Isra met with the Most High. The leaves on the young man's oak branch antlers rattle as he hands over his missive. Fawn eyes dart about before he mutters, "Apologies, Divine Belladonna." With a nervous bow, he darts off in the direction from which he'd come. I watch as his furred legs disappear around a corner, a flash of a hoof and then, nothing.

The note trembles in my hands and foreboding settles on me like a shroud.

I want to stretch this quiet moment into forever, for once I hear the *snick* of the wax seal breaking, there will be no going back. As ever, it is silence that holds me and sound that shatters me.

I brace. Hold myself in perfect stillness, feed my Divinity with this throbbing, aching, overwhelming quiet. And then, I break the seal.

Divine Belladonna,

*   I am informing you that other arrangements must be made for your*

ferry, the Forget-Me-Not. *You have until the end of the cycle to collect your rig.*

Regretfully,

Sage

THE END OF THE CYCLE. That gives me two weeks to find another berth for my ferry or lose it to Sage's next auction.

It takes a moment for the full implication of his letter to sink in. If Sage will not berth my ferry, then I must find another place for it, and I must pay for that out of my own earnings. It isn't cheap.

But how could he toss me out like this, without warning?

Then, I understand.

I don't actually own my ferry. The ferry is in Mother's name, as is the business. I'm just a contractor. She allows me to run it, but she holds the authority over all aspects of the business while I'm in Meadowsweet. If she wants me turned out of one berth, wants to force my hand, this is how she will do it.

Apply pressure. Twist.

I do not know if it is rage or despair that overwhelms me first. For a breath I hover, torn between both before drowning in each of them.

I didn't expect it to hurt this much. Sometime, between first leaving Meadowsweet and returning, things changed. Before, my ferry had been nothing more than a certain kind of ship built from trees harvested by Father Terra's hands. It had been a conveyance that got me from one place to another and helped me thrive in Chaos.

My ferry is where I became an adult. It is where my daughter was born. It is so much more than a certain kind of ship. Part of my blood has soaked into that wood. My memories are etched there, as Isra would say.

These realizations hit me like weights, and I buckle under them. This is not just a conveyance, it is part of me.

My mother is threatening *me*.

Isra perches in the window seat, her wings flared wide to catch the fading light. The effect paints the room with ribbons of orange and yellow. Flora sits on the floor as Isra makes shapes dance across the walls. My daughter's giggle is sharp and bright.

Our eyes meet across the room. We have been together so long she knows all my signs and I know she can sense the rising tide of my ire.

"Go," the butterfly says. I am grateful she does not press me for details. "I will watch Flora while you are away."

And for all that I am glad she does not ask after my upset, her silence troubles me. Isra has been quieter since her meeting with the Most High, far more withdrawn, her silence almost... numb. Like she is disappearing within herself.

She has changed since being in Meadowsweet. The woman she is now is far different than the one I knew in Dawnland. In the act of saving her, did I actually do the opposite?

The note crinkles in my hand, reminding me what I am about. I'm wearing a suit. Mother won't like that, but perhaps that is the point.

"Thank you," I say to Isra, and then disappear down Mother Sol's golden hall, and out into Meadowsweet.

The day is bright and warm. A line of clouds marshals along the horizon, a portent of later storms. The air is thick with anticipation. Meadowsweet is a hive of activity, but I see none of it. I leave the Hall of the Gods, my mind buzzing, buzzing, buzzing.

I find myself at my mother's doorstep too soon. It is late, but I do not bother with knocking on her thick front door; rather I charge into the house, as though into hostile territory.

"Belladonna?" My mother appears from the kitchen, her eyes wide and her face is wan, pale as though she has a chill and I wonder, briefly, if she has taken ill.

We study each other. She had not expected me so soon, I realize. Before, when I was younger, I would have sulked first. I am no longer that untested child.

I dart a glance about, but her lady is nowhere to be seen. The house is quiet, and it feels empty. My presence, however, curdles that comfort.

I am a storm and I am breaking.

"My ferry," I say, the crumpled paper still in my hand.

"Ah." Mother nods and motions to the kitchen. "Have tea with me."

Have tea with me, she says, as though it is as simple as that. We will sip tea and I will see reason. I follow her because this must be dealt with.

I will not heap this legacy upon my daughter's shoulders.

The kitchen is lemon drops and sunshine. Daisy appears as though from nowhere and settles a tray of green tea and lemon slices on the table, and then disappears. Mother dedicates herself to the task of pouring, and then setting sugar cubes on the saucer beside our fine cups.

"My ferry," I say after she sips. I would rather drink poison than this tea. Sunlight spills through the open windows. This moment is soft. Why does it feel so hard?

"Really, Belladonna." Mother sets her cup on her saucer with a small chink. "You did not need to make such a scene. All you need to do is go make arrangements for your ferry."

"Sage's berth has been used by our family since our first ferrying run. Where do you expect me to go?"

"Oleander has availability in the berth his family runs."

So that is what this is about. I am not surprised. Mother's eyes gain a shrewd and calculating edge.

"You will allow him to court you."

"I will not—"

"You will," Mother hisses. She sets her napkin on the table and folds it just so. Somehow, her calculated movements feel like a slap. Like my outburst is not even worth acknowledging. Her nails are half-smiles and she taps them, each finger getting a beat against the polished oak.

This too shall pass is what she's saying.

I stand. The table rattles and tea and lemon slices spill everywhere. The sugar cube on my plate dissolves, saccharine and fading, like so much of my life.

Our eyes meet and our bodies are poised, the indrawn breath before frantic motion.

Why do poets never write about such moments? Perhaps this is not as grand as a soldier's life must be, but it is no less dangerous and intense for the smothering quiet. The knowing that hovers between us like an axe just waiting to fall. This quaint woman's war, where weapons are words, glances spear, and spilled tea and dissolving sugar cubes hold so much symbolism.

It has its own grace. It deserves a sonnet.

"I have a daughter," I whisper.

I do not think I could have hit her harder if I'd used two clenched fists and all my force. Mother goes pale, her hands shake and then she withdraws, disappears so deep inside herself I can sense neither her nor her silence.

"Her name is Flora."

"Flora," Mother breathes, then eyes me again. "A daughter."

This is agony. Agony to know I kept this from her. Agony to watch the revelation slowly unfold across her face. Silence surrounds us and I swear I am choking on it. Seasons change in the time it takes her to draw a breath.

"A daughter," she says again, harder this time. "Flora." And harder still.

There are so many different kinds of quiet, and the one she draws about her now is shaped like a sword. I have hurt her and she means to hurt back.

"Oleander is forgiving of mistakes, I am sure."

She bites each word like she hates it and her eyes are full of cold, cold steel.

Mistakes.

The word is thunder and it rolls through me.

"My daughter is not a mistake."

It costs me to say this. Each syllable carves a fresh wound. Here I stand, bleeding pieces of myself on my mother's polished kitchen floor.

Mother's eyes widen and she eases her tone, lowers the sword just enough. "Are you... married? Or... betrothed? In a... Are you in a situation, Belladonna? Is that why you are so averse to Oleander?"

The laugh I utter would wilt flowers if any were nearby. *A situation.* Always so polite, even when she thrusts the dagger. "It wasn't like that."

Mother stands, makes her way to me but, thankfully, does not offer her touch. I cannot handle that now. Not when I feel this fragile.

"What was it like?" Whispered are these words and she draws closer, almost too close, but I can handle this much contact. I can handle her brushing up against the edge of my silence as long as she does not shatter it.

I will give her something. An offering, perhaps, or a test. I cannot decide which.

"I heard stories of Dawnland's fabled fertility sciences and read about them in Father's books. It wasn't hard to find a merchant who needed goods ferried."

"Fertility..." Mother's eyes focus on something in the distance, and then fix on me. "Belladonna, are you well?" She reaches out to touch me, her fingers hovering in the air between us, but the touch is too much, too much. The kitchen draws tight, the walls pressing in. Colors swim in a dizzying kaleidoscope. Sweat beads my brow and my stomach roils. My silence screams and the animal in me roars. The light that makes me flares bright as lightning, blinding us both.

"DON'T TOUCH ME!"

Mother shrinks back, flings herself across the room and I gather myself, my cheeks flushing red. "I'm sorry," I say after I've given her a beat to recover. "Mother, I'm sorry. I..."

I watch as she distances herself from me and I become an island floating in a yellow sea.

Finally, I admit, "In Dawnland, with their science"—I blush—"the act did not require so much touch."

And I so desperately wanted a child.

"Is she... normal?"

Now it is my turn for my eyes to flare wide. "Normal," I hiss. "Of what use is normal?"

"Oleander won't—"

I am done. I am connected to my ferry, yes, but I don't need it if it means keeping this... weight... around my neck.

I have learned to never cling too long.

"Take my ferry," I say, making my way to the door. "And gift it to Oleander with a bow. Do with the company what you will."

"Belladonna, where are you going?" She shouts at my back as I am fleeing toward the door. Outside, the sky is smeared with amber. The tip of Father Luna rises in the east, a light in a field of perfectly ripe blueberries.

"I'm leaving," I say.

"Daughter, surely you understand—"

"You will not listen to me." Mother flinches and I know I struck a fatal blow.

"I'm listening now," she says, her hand hovering above my arm, as though aching to touch me.

Is she normal? The question will not let me go.

I shake my head.

And leave.

NOW
ISRA

The world is tilting toward sleep when I find myself considering my trunk. I have not unpacked it yet. I have not had the courage, as though opening it will make all of this real, I'm not ready for Meadowsweet to be real. But neither can I any longer live in this half-state, this dreaming daze where I think, at any moment, surely I will wake up in Dawnland.

Surely this is all a fantasy.

Yet, if I am honest with myself, this is not the only thing keeping me from unpacking.

I had not known I was leaving Dawnland and I have avoided my trunk since arriving. It is too hard to look at it, much less touch it, so I had Belladonna move it to the back of my closet where I would not need to see it so much.

Where I would not be so reminded of the betrayal that put me in this place.

I feel the jab of an injection.

I hear Manab's voice again, whispering through all that divides us, "I'm sorry, Isra."

How is it possible for my body to hold so many warring emotions? Love and hate, hope and hopelessness, war and peace. I am nothing more than contradictions bound by sorrow's thread.

Manab is my brother, and yet he took so much from me: my home, my family, my will. The wound he left is too painful to examine long. I had thought my brothers and I would always support each other and yet, when it mattered most, they only stood beside me long enough to push me away.

I miss them.

I hate them.

How long can I survive so divided?

Still, meeting the Most High had impressed upon me the reality of my situation. I am here now. There is no going back. Not for a while, at least.

It is time. Time to make Meadowsweet real.

This task feels monumental.

I kneel before my trunk. It is crafted from the World Tree itself and has survived generations of our family. Its handles are wrought iron and its lid is covered in an ornate carving of the World Tree encircled by twined roots. I trace my fingers along the lines and gasp as I feel the echoes, like tactile whispers, of those who came before.

For a moment, I am not so alone. If I close my eyes, I can sense them in this wood, feel the places each of them touched, understand the shape of who they were in that moment.

I wonder if someday someone will touch the World Tree, or this trunk, and know me. What a gift it is, that even my echo might help someone feel not so...

Isolated.

Connection is a powerful thing, and I feel it then. Suddenly, I am no longer alone. I press my hands against the lid of the trunk, close my eyes. My fingers move along the surface until I find a memory. I touch the edges of it, feel its shape.

My vision blurs and I am in Dawnland. It is the fresh morning after a storm. Howler monkeys call across the canopy, loud and familiar. Mist hangs in the air, turning sunlight into lace. A cluster of redcap mushrooms grow from the wall of the World Tree.

Before me is a woman. She is tall and slender, with one crumpled wing.

"I am not ready," she says. Her eyes are focused on the trunk before her and I can feel her sorrow as it wages war against anger.

"It doesn't matter if you are ready," a man replies. I cannot see him but his voice is harsh and cold.

"But my wing—"

"We don't need your wings. We only need your eggs."

The memory fades. Tears prick my eyes and my heart hammers. My family's history has not always been pleasant.

I move my hands around the lid, touching each memory, recognizing each monarch, understanding my relationship to them. I know each of them in turn and for a moment, I am not alone.

I save my brothers for last. Hesitating, I steel my heart before I touch their drops of blood.

It is Atheed I see first. He is crying as he pricks his finger with the pin. His voice is soft and his wings sag. "I love you, Isra. Forever."

Manab takes the pin and holds it to the pad of his index finger. Hesitates. Atheed rests a hand on his arm. "We don't have to do this," he says.

For a moment, it almost seems as though Manab might change his mind. He is poised, the pin pressing against the tip of his finger yet not cutting. His muscles are tense and his jaw clenches. "Yes, we do," he finally says, and then presses. A drop of blood falls onto the chest. "May you someday find peace, sweet sister," he whispers.

The memory fades.

It is touch that undoes me.

And memory that ignites me.

I do not belong here, in this strange world.

My lungs squeeze and squeeze. I press my face against the wood as though to push that much closer to them.

This is so much more than unpacking a trunk and settling into this new home of mine. This is a final goodbye. I cannot stomach another parting. I cannot face this world alone. Without my roost, I am nothing.

Cracks shiver through the bedrock of my soul.

I want to run away, to lose myself in Father Terra's garden, to do anything but face the things this trunk holds, but I cannot keep living with one foot in both worlds.

So I throw the lid open and breathe deeply, study what I find within. Perhaps I was expecting something significant, a gift or a trinket, some totem from my past that would help carry me into the future, but all I see are clothes. As many as my brothers could fit into this trunk, both formal and informal. I take them out and set them in neat piles on my bed.

None of these are appropriate in Meadowsweet, where modesty is a far greater concern than it is in Dawnland. In the heat of summer, it is not uncommon to wear a loincloth only, and some of the beast-kindred do not have bodies that lend themselves well to clothing at all. Here, in Meadowsweet, the clothes are so much... more.

I glance around my small closet. Mother Sol's daughters have been slowly filling it with dresses made for me by some of the finest tailors in Meadowsweet. Belladonna's paternal grandmother, Divine Dove, has taken it upon herself to fill my room with whatever comforts she can find. I have barely looked at any of it, only wearing a fine green chiffon gown once. The dress was far too constraining, with too many lines, too much fabric, and all those pearls...

It didn't fit.

No.

I didn't fit.

I grab a pile of clothes and stand. What I hold in my arms would take me through an entire season in Dawnland, and yet it is not nearly as much fabric as I see in the closet before me. All of those dresses, a few pant suits Belladonna had made for me, each of them pressed and stitched with care, made with consideration for my body.

But it is not the same. Here, the fabric is heavier than what I am used to and even when it is cut with my wings in mind, it still chafes.

Here, the air weighs on me differently. I feel as though I have to breathe more, harder, heavier, and the way the shirts are cut constricts my lungs.

I am thankful for Mother Sol's kindness, and her donation of clothes, and yet...

They don't fit. Not really. And the stack of clothes in my arms, all halter tops and cloth I would wrap around my waist and knot there, are not acceptable here.

I set my stack on an empty shelf and study what is arrayed before me.

So much fabric, so little of it mine.

My life had felt so large in Dawnland. Here, it seems so terribly, tragically small.

I grab the green chiffon dress and slip it on, as though wearing something from this place will somehow make me more part of it. There is a mirror hanging on the door to my closet and I steel myself and look into it.

I have not yet looked into a mirror since I left Dawnland, trusting Belladonna to help me prepare myself each day. I have not dared look into my own eyes. I am not brave enough to face what I will find there.

And yet, now I cannot stop myself. I trail my eyes up my body, starting at my feet, then up my legs and to my dress, olive green with gold trim. It is lined with small, gleaming pearls. I hesitate on that row of pearls. Hesitate, because there is still so much more of me to see. So much more to face.

Higher, then.

My wings are nearly as tall as I am, arching above my head and nearly brushing the ground, a brilliant mix of orange, yellow, black, and white. I recognize them. They are mine, whether I am in Dawnland or Meadowsweet. Despite all the uncertainty, there is still something that is mine.

My gaze slides across my slender shoulders, across the small green strap, up the slender column of my neck to...

Her skin looks like polished onyx, flecked with white. She is small and strange, chin too pointy, eyes too big and all-black. Her hair is a chaotic mix of black and white. Her antennae are slender and elegant.

She is a stranger to me, and yet... not.

I see Belladonna standing in my doorway. Our eyes meet in the mirror.

"You look beautiful, Isra," she says.

These words, spoken softly and with such kindness, are what break me. For so long, a storm has been surging in my soul, gathering its strength along the horizon, and I know I am moments away from it tearing itself open to drown entire cities.

You look beautiful, Isra, she said. The woman she finds beautiful is a stranger. I am not beautiful, but sharp and eager to slice.

"This dress doesn't fit," I say.

Belladonna scans me, her brow furrowed. "It looks like it fits."

"It doesn't fit, Belladonna." I cast my eyes to the window. Have these walls always been so stifling? We were not so separate from nature in Dawnland. Here, I feel as though I am being held apart from the world. The air is recycled, the walls do not breathe. The chairs have backs that are too wide for my wings, and none of the doorways are wide enough to accommodate my shape easily. Everything here is a struggle.

Suddenly this room feels more like a cage and I the strange thing trapped within. Can she not see how much this costs me? For me to stand still in this place and not bend under the pressure of everything terrifyingly new?

"This dress doesn't *fit*, Belladonna." I take a handful of the skirt and wave it around like I am proving a point with it.

"Then we can have it tailored to fit you better."

She is trying. I know she is trying. And her eyes are red-rimmed and swollen. I should go easier on her, but the hurricane has finally reached shore and there is no turning back now. I am incandescent. I am... fury. I am lightning and all I want to do is strike.

"I am small and strange, Belladonna."

"Isra—"

"I don't belong here! Not alone! I have never been alone. My brothers should be here. Why did you spirit me away and not them? Why am I worth saving but not Manab and Atheed?"

Belladonna gasps as though I'd struck her and I feel a fresh wound near my heart. She does not deserve this.

And yet.

And yet.

This dress. It chokes me. I feel like I am wearing someone else's skin. A great roar fills my throat and I dig my fingers into that soft green fabric. Pearls fly across the room, hitting the walls like raindrops in summer. The fabric tears, and oh, that sound is so satisfying. It feels good to finally shred something the way I have been shredded.

Belladonna doesn't stop me. Chiffon tears, green cascading through the air like bits of stolen summer. String and pearls hang akimbo off my body, and still it is not enough. This dress is a symbol of everything I cannot accept. I shed. I rend. I tear. I howl.

I rage against the injustices of the world, against the pain, my cloying, suffocating loss.

And when I am spent, I collapse on the floor, naked save a ribbon of green still clinging to my shoulder.

"Why?" I breathe.

"Manab told me you had agreed to go." Belladonna approaches me but does not touch, and her voice, when she speaks, is a small, rough thing. "That is the only reason I agreed to any of this. They said you knew you were leaving, you just didn't know when, and that I was to be ready when they called. That was all I knew, Isra, I swear it."

"You should have left me."

"If I can save even one soul, is it not my obligation to do so?"

"They are my brothers! What gives you the right to play with fate?" I sit, perch on my knees, and hold my wings aloft so I might face her fully.

"You are not the only one in pain!" Belladonna roars. I flinch, for in all the years I have known her, I have never once heard her shout.

Her eyes, when I meet them, are filled with tears, her cheeks wet. "You are not the only creature who has known hurt. Stop acting so small."

"Belladonna—"

"Manab put me in an awful situation, and he betrayed you in a way I cannot comprehend, Isra, but I... I left the father of my child behind," she hisses. "Do you have any idea what that was like? Do you know what that cost me? And then coming back to my mother..."

It is a churning, swirling vortex of hurt in her eyes that tells the story of her pain. She is already wounded. All I have done was work the knife deeper.

"I tried," Belladonna says, wiping at a tear, the gesture stiff. "I tried to make the right decision."

"Belladonna, I..." Part of me understands. Part of me doesn't want to understand.

All of me realizes, suddenly, that I have done wrong.

I will do better. I have to do better. I am an adult, not a child. Tantrums are beneath me. And yet I look around my room and see nothing but the mess I left, a shredded dress, pearls everywhere, a half-unpacked trunk and nothing more.

I am better than this.

I will be better than this.

Shame fills me until I burn with it.

Belladonna holds her hand in the air and turns her back on me. "I need silence." She presses her fingers against her temples. "This day is relentless."

A moment later, she is gone. I get to my feet and start cleaning.

NOW
ROSEMARY

"Rosemary."

Soft is that voice. So soft, I doubt I hear it.

"Rosemary, look at me."

Is she real? Do I hope? Do I dread?

I imprint this moment in my heart. The breath before I turn and see and *know*. The instant before the stab of pain as the wound reopens.

I turn in my wheelchair, a gorgeous contraption Father Terra made all those years ago, freedom when my body is ravaged by pain.

There she is, my soul croons.

How long has it been? It feels like forever, yet it has only been years, and not many at that. A breath, in truth. The beat of a heart. The blink of an eye.

Still, I see her and the world fades. Carved from a ray of light is Belladonna. Blinding and beautiful.

"You're back." They are the only words I can find.

She doesn't answer. Instead, she approaches me. Watching her move is like watching the sunrise. It is the dark parting to make way for the glory of the day.

"When did you return?" I ask.

She tilts her head. Belladonna is all angles: sharp chin, sharp cheekbones. She is the edge of the light's ray, the slice. Both harbor and hurricane.

"Days ago," her voice whispers along my spine.

Her answer breaks through my haze. She arrived days ago, and she did not call upon me. Years have slid between us and things have changed. This is a garden watered by pain. Suddenly, I feel very alone and the night is not so welcoming. Old wounds I'd thought long since healed open, suppurate.

Dark closes in. Belladonna's natural light diminishes. Her mortality rises just enough for me to see the woman beneath that glow.

Something is wrong. I can feel it the same way I feel the blood in my veins.

Not yet, I beg. *Please, not yet.*

I came here for peace. For a moment to breathe away from the Divine and all their aching. Suddenly, I want nothing more than to disappear to Father Terra's pine grove. I long to sleep cradled in the earth, twined by roots, and welcomed by the world.

For a moment, we stare at each other. I can smell the unspoken words adorning the edges of our conversation like so many forgotten flowers. The promise of summer long gone to rot.

"Divine Rosemary," she says, and I flinch.

Oh, the jagged beauty of the tongue.

"Is that all I am to you?"

Now it is her turn to flinch. She gestures toward a bench, perched between two bushes so heavy with flowers their limbs hang low. The ground around them bleeds pink. I maneuver my wheelchair beside her. The world is in the throes of transition. A spray of purple to the west as twilight gathers her army of stars and marches across a darkening sky.

As above, so below. I feel the moment quickening my soul.

"I had hoped to find you here," she says, voice soft and low. Her hands are in her lap, fingers twining together. "I had hoped... I had hoped you would still come."

"I wasn't the one who—"

"Rosemary—"

"I wanted to walk into the sea when you left, Belladonna." Each word breaks. I am speaking shards.

She meets my eyes. The tears on her lashes shimmer like tiny summer suns. Belladonna exists on the shivering edge that parts beauty from pain and I cannot look away.

I force my gaze to my hands, curled on the armrests of my chair. The woven branches are beginning to sprout despite my gloves.

"I have no right, Rosemary. I know. This is the last place I should be. I am..." Her shoulders heave. "I am coming here, despite."

I can hear the words she does not say. *I am coming here despite the pain.*

"I know I have done you wrong. I know." She leans forward and presses her hands over mine. Her touch is warm and welcome and I hate how much I crave her light. I turn toward her. I cannot help myself. I will always turn toward her.

The shimmer around her fades, and I see...

Broken vessel. Shattered vase.

She sniffles and I crumble. I have never been able to stand against her sorrow. "Belladonna, what happened?"

"Everything," comes her ragged reply.

Mulberry grows along my crown, small bushes thick with berries, their growth fed by Belladonna's sorrow.

"I have been afraid to find you," she finally says. Father Luna hangs low in a sky shot with dreams. Around us, night-blooming flowers open, filling the air with their heady aromas.

"Why?" For while there is plenty of history between us, she should know that even in my greatest pain, I could never bring her harm.

Belladonna sighs. "Your father told me, before I left, that leaving was hard but returning was often more difficult." She pauses. "I have found that to be true. And now that I am facing you, I do not know whether to beg your forgiveness or..." Her breath hitches.

She does not understand. She does not know that I have bound my Divinity to her. She is as much a part of me as my soul. My home is wherever she is.

"I have never stopped thinking of you," she whispers.

I open my mouth to speak but she stills me with an upraised hand.

"Even between seconds, Rosemary. Even then."

"Why did you leave?" The words are born on a wave of agony; years of it have been building inside. Was I too much? Was I not enough?

Years ago, after Belladonna left, I found myself in Father Luna's embrace, pouring out my soul to him. He held me through my breaking as planets and stars arced past the windows of his Sacred Observatory.

"She is gone," I whispered into his chest. "I drip or I pour, Grandfather, and I will ever wonder if it was the drought or the deluge that sent her running."

"I have a daughter, Rosemary." Belladonna's words are like snowmelt on my thoughts, and I come reeling back into the present, filled with winter's chill and longing for summer.

She curls in on herself, as though she expects me to lash out, to argue. Belladonna more kicked dog than goddess now and I wonder who hurt her so. Who dared make her think that she brought to the world anything but light? My hair springs a riot of flowers from woodbine to mulberry to nettle to lavender rose. I am a garden in the full thrust of the growing season. I am blooming, my emotions running riot in every flower.

I can hide nothing from her.

"A daughter," I breathe.

Something in my heart shifts, making room for another person.

I remember Belladonna spending nights poring over books in the library. I had asked her why Dawnland fascinated her so much. She had only smiled at me and said, "They have wonderful science there." I had warned her that the last ferry to Dawnland had been generations ago. Things change in that much time. But she had not been deterred.

I think of how reluctant she is to be touched.

And I understand.

"Are you angry with me?" Belladonna almost cowers and I cannot take this anymore. I cannot take this distance. The years between us are forgotten. The past does not matter. I slide out of my wheelchair and onto the bench beside her, though I am careful not to touch her. "Are you... disappointed?" she presses.

This takes me aback, and I study her, eyes wide. "Belladonna," I ask, "may I touch you?"

She hesitates a moment, closes her eyes, and prepares herself. Then, a nod. Only one, but it is enough. Permission granted. Still, I pluck a sprig of holly from my vines and offer it to her. She takes the gift slowly, timidly, and I watch as peace suffuses her. The lines of her body loosen and her sorrow, if not gone completely, is pushed to the side for a beat. Then I offer her a brilliant magnolia bloom. The very flower that Father Terra offered me as a child.

Of course I will love her daughter. She has already claimed part of my heart.

"I have forgotten the potency of your Divinity, Rosemary," she whispers as her fingers stroke the small red berries lost in the center of all that green, and she lifts the magnolia to her nose. Tears spill down her cheeks. "Thank you."

Only when I am certain she is at peace do I take her hand and entwine our fingers.

Her touch is a gift. Like skin over a wound, we are knitting together. Strangers to each other after all these years, yet the way her hand fits into mine will never change.

"Do you remember when we were children?" I ask. "We were in Father Terra's Sacred Garden. This very grove, if I am not mistaken." Of course it was this grove. There is a reason I come here each night. I rub my thumb across Belladonna's knuckles. She meets my eyes and I know we are sharing the same memory.

We'd been young, clumsy and awkward, full of emotions too large for our small lives. We lay on the ground, purple wisteria towering over us, honeybees buzzing about. Side by side and silent we were, until she reached over and grabbed my hand, wove her fingers through mine, the touch tentative and uncertain.

I was too young to understand how difficult it was for her to do such a thing. How many days she must have talked herself into that much contact. It was not until years later that I understood how much of herself she offered me that night.

"I remember," she whispers.

"I promised you that I would never leave you. I promised that no matter what turns life took, I would always be there."

"You have never gone back on that promise." Her lips curl just enough.

Overhead, the moon turns his gaze on us. I drink of Father Luna's light and feel it feed my Divinity.

"And I never will."

Belladonna shifts and sits so she can stare into my eyes, and I let her see the depths of my emotions. The pain. The sorrow.

The loneliness.

For a moment, neither of us speak. She opens the windows to her soul, and I peer inside. I do not need any Divine sight to see the pain lingering deep, her wounds a mirror of my own.

We are, both of us, bleeding light.

Finally, she sighs and wipes her eyes.

My thoughts turn back to her daughter. I want to meet her, but I do not want to push. I will let her chart the course and I will make myself happy with whatever she offers me.

I study her profile, her high cheekbones and full lips. The way she shimmers even when she doesn't mean to, like light cannot help but cling to her.

Belladonna's gaze touches my face, and then lingers on the riot of roses sprouting from my vines. "I would be the sun to you, Rosemary."

I remember, then, a poem I wrote her a lifetime ago, when I thought I was good at such things. We had not yet been so open with our affection, dancing around it rather than facing it head on. I had slipped the note into a bag she carried.

You are the sun
That shines on
The garden
Growing
Between my ribs

She never mentioned receiving the note, nor reading it. I thought perhaps she had spared me the embarrassment. And yet now, I know...

I glance at my watch and realize the time. I had promised Dream I would go dancing with her. It seems so far away from what is happening here and now, and yet I sense Dream desperately needs the activity, and I had promised her I would go.

I am talking myself into parting with Belladonna. This wasn't nearly enough. And in some ways, it was perhaps too much. I need time to think about how this makes me feel.

I need time.

"I must go, Belladonna," I say. "I will be here, whenever you should need me."

She nods, and I sense relief in the gesture, like being around me is overwhelming, and I cannot help the burr that abrades my soul in response.

I arrange myself in my wheelchair again.

"Rosemary—" I hesitate. "What if I should need a friend?"

I squeeze my eyes closed and a gust of air tears its way from my lungs. I will let her decide what we are to each other now. I have given her all of myself. I will take, happily, whatever she is willing to offer in return.

My ribs, like trees, cast shadows on my heart.

I turn toward her slowly as night turns toward day. "Of course, Belladonna. If friendship is what you want from me, I will offer it gladly."

But oh, it will cost me. My soul will be torn to ribbons. I will hemorrhage pieces of myself.

"Thank you," she whispers to my retreating back.

THEN
ROSEMARY

The morning came far too slowly. Each minute felt like a small eternity. Every breath was a span of forever.

I cannot tell you what it felt like, to wait thus.

Worry wrapped its hands around my throat. Squeezed.

I was ready for the day by the time the lock on the other side of the door rattled. I'd made Mother porridge, though she ate none of it and tried to hide her body-shattering coughs when she thought I was not paying attention. Landlady didn't look surprised to see me awake and well-attired.

She grabbed my arm as I dashed past her. "Mind yourself," she said. "This isn't forever. It's only for now. Not worth getting the high and mighty all worked up about something so... temporary." She released me and watched as I dashed past her, hardly seeing the two boys that trailed me. Mother's rattling hack echoed in the corridors of my mind.

I was trailed, as I'd expected, to where the fading edges of the Narrows gave way to the wide, stately rivers and swampland of Divine Rain's arbor, Landlady's boys left me, each of them glaring from beneath bushy brows and furrowed foreheads. I felt their malice like a touch.

Mother's coughing urged me on.

I hardly knew Divine Muse though I might know his countenance well enough. He was still Divine, as fathomless as the heavens. I could not guess what his reaction to me might be. Would he help? Would he think me a meddler? Did it matter?

I went on, for love is the fire that burns even in the rain. This was one way I might help the only person who mattered to me. Perhaps I had gone to the Hall of the Gods with the intent to work for what I earned, but desperation drove me to begging.

I would be okay.

I told myself this enough by the time I reached the Hall of the Gods, that I almost believed it.

The only true way ahead was to throw myself upon Divine Muse's mercy and hope his kindness would see me through to the other side.

There was a story I heard once, long ago, about Divine Muse uncreating someone who had raised his ire. The Divine were not often moved to wrath, but they did bend that way occasionally and the stories were fearsome indeed.

Still, my mother, it seemed, knew Divine Muse from her life before she had me. Straw flowers bloomed along my vines in a riot of colors. If they shared memories, that flower would make sure the ones Muse thought of were good.

Vulnerability shivered through me, etching my bones in frost.

So it was with trepidation that I entered the Hall of the Gods and made my way to Divine Muse's office door, shut tight against the morning.

I hesitated at his threshold and studied myself. I had not considered how I must look. I carried claw marks from Landlady on my left arm. My clothes were the same I wore the day before, not noticeable in the Narrows, but in a place so grand as this, it stood out. I had been up all night. There must have been dark rings around my eyes, and my vines were long and loose, the straw flowers on them wilted. Even my cane looked bedraggled and was dripping with mud.

I was unraveling in every way that mattered.

I drew breath, knocked on the door, and pushed it open.

"Rosemary, what—" Divine Muse's voice was a song.

"Divine Muse." I fell to my knees; my hip groaned and my spine screamed. My cane slipped and fell with a dull *thunk* on the plush carpet. "Something has happened, and though you owe me nothing, Divine One, I desperately throw myself at your feet. I pray to you for aid."

The song that always filled the air around Muse ground to a halt.

"What is it?" he asked.

No more friendly uncle now. Before me was a god in all his glory. His Divinity overwhelmed me. Driving me low and then lower still, until my face was pressed against the carpet, its soft weave abrading my skin. For all Divine Muse was kind, he was still crafted by Father Luna's hands. His glory far outshined what my young eyes could handle.

"My mother, Divine One. My mother. I beg you." Whispered were those words, timid. How would he look at me after I'd become so reduced?

"Your mother?" He asked, though not unkindly. His voice chimed like bells, and I moaned under the weight of that gaze. "Who is your mother, Rosemary?"

Tears streamed down my cheeks, blurred my vision. I heard him kneel before me, felt his hand rest gently amongst my vines—though he did not pluck a flower, I noted, merely touched them.

"Her name is Willow, Divine One. And she is very sick."

He hummed something low in his throat.

"And she is being kept. I cannot afford—"

"Kept?" Cold was that word. "What do you mean, kept?"

"Our landlady—"

"Landlady?" He shook his head. "Tell me plain, what has happened and why do you throw yourself at my feet?"

He drew back from me and gave me room to sit. My spine was fire and my leg locked, pain radiating from my hip, but despite that, I did not dare move. I kept my eyes focused on the carpet and remembered to make myself humble.

The story poured from me, and Divine Muse held himself still throughout it all, the moons in his eyes frozen, as if every part of him hung on the words I uttered.

Finally, after it was all told and my voice faded, Muse rested his hand on my shoulder. I went stiff in a way that betrayed how brittle I truly was.

My tears came unbidden and all at once. Gone were my plan, my carefully crafted speech, my arguments for aid. Here was a terrified child. My mother's coughing echoed in my heart.

Too much.

Too much rested on my small shoulders.

The world went dark, and darker still. My vision blurred and I trembled in a way that I had never yet experienced. I was being undone, picked apart piece by delicate piece.

"She is all I have in this world."

Muse rested his hand on my head, as though in benediction. My vines twined around his fingers, holding him to me.

Finally, "Come with me, Rosemary. I think there is someone you should meet."

I moved slowly, but my leg had locked from my time kneeling, and when I made to stand, it would not hold my weight, even with my cane bracing me. Muse grabbed my shoulder and helped me find my legs. His touch was cold, though welcome. His skin, when I looked at his outstretched arm, was dark as midnight. Night curled from him like smoke.

"Who are you, child?"

"Divine Muse, I am just a girl."

He studied me, eyes shrewd and knowing. "You," he said, "have never been just a girl."

"Divine One, my mother—"

"I swear, this meeting will only take a moment, Rosemary. I feel I cannot act before I consult my brother."

I froze, a rabbit in a trap.

"Most Sacred Divine Muse," I clasped my hands before me,

"please, I beg, let me go. I would rather you let me go than involve more of the Divine. I can make my own way. I can—"

As a child, my fear had seemed irrational. Muse had been kind to me, presumably his brothers would be as well. I had no reason not to believe that. And yet I was filled with such terror I felt carved of it. Now, looking back, I believe I knew what was going to come of this and I was not ready.

Some part of me, even then, recognized my father nearby.

"You will not," Divine Muse replied, his voice filled with conviction. There would be no arguing with him. He was Divine, after all. He could only be pushed so far.

I closed my eyes and let out a ragged breath. *Please*, I prayed, *let them be gentle.*

"It will be fine, Rosemary. We are family. I have bound myself to you. I would not let you come to harm." He wrapped an arm around my shoulders. "Keep your prayers, child. My brother, I am certain, will help you, but we must go to him."

Lightning arced through my body. I had done too much, and not rested nearly enough. When this was over, my pain would be steep, and steeper still.

Still, I could not focus on that.

Divine Muse led me, head bowed as if in supplication. I leaned heavily on my cane and followed through quiet halls and curious onlookers. My heart beat so loud I swore it echoed off the marble walls, a siren song: both signal and warning at once.

Here I was, walking toward my fate.

This wasn't about me, though, I reminded myself. This was about my mother. Getting her safe and keeping her that way. I did not matter so much, in the scheme of things. I could weather any storm. She, however, was coughing blood, and who knew what Landlady was doing to her while I was away.

Divine Muse did not speak as he led me, though he walked slowly and waited, watching carefully as I limped along, my right leg dragging, my cane groaning under my weight.

Thankfully, it was not far.

Still, he could have forced me into a wheelchair to hurry me along or carried me where we were going but he didn't. He let me walk and he paid careful attention to my pace, respecting what I wanted and what I was capable of, even then. He allowed me my ability and respected my limits, and gratitude washed over me at the respect he showed me by the small gesture.

I did not understand the way of the Hall then, how it shifted and moved depending on the need of those housed there. I did not understand how the space around me adjusted to my pain and made distances shorter for my comfort.

Finally, when I was near collapsing with exhaustion, a wall opened before us, and out from the gap spilled clouds of night, streams of stars, entire galaxies.

"Divine Muse," I breathed, "what is this place?"

He studied me, more god than man, glowing with the full power of what made him. I trembled before that gaze and the majesty filling it and was laid bare before him. There was no part of me he could not see.

It is no easy thing, to stand before the Divine.

"This," he said, his voice deep and grave, all baritone and minor key, "is Most High Father Luna's Sacred Observatory."

NOW
BELLADONNA

Grandmother Dove sits across from me, a ray of perfect light. Somewhere in her halo of summer hides my daughter. I can hear her giggles, and occasionally see fingertips and antennae poke through the glow as though through a curtain of lace.

Around us are all of Mother Sol's daughters who remain in Meadowsweet, for spending each morning together like this is a tradition, a time for family to gather and be together.

I am not the only grandchild or great grandchild here. There are many of us, sons and daughters, and their laughter fills the air with warmth.

I have ever loved Mother Sol's Sacred Solarium. It is the well from which I drink. After yesterday, I need this moment of Divinity more than I first realized, and I soak it in. Feel it become part of me. Still, when I am here, I cannot help but think of my father, which inevitably turns my attention back to the bruise of my mother.

I think about her manipulation, the cold way with which she uses me, and then purposefully turn my thoughts away. I will not let my mother ruin this moment as well.

The light dims and I can see Grandmother. Her smile is wide and her eyes are dancing. Throughout my life, I have loved being near Divine Dove. It is like being wrapped in summer.

Though she is different now. Her light is a bit dimmer and I can see laugh lines around her mouth. Grandmother turns the fullness of her attention on me. Conversations hum around us, offering some small measure of privacy. She adjusts Flora on her lap and leans forward.

"My son is alive, Belladonna," Grandmother says. Kindness oozes from her every word. "I would know if he was not."

She says this to me each time she sees me. I sense she needs to speak these words as much as I need to hear them, so I let her. It comforts me to know he is still alive, though I cannot help but feel like if he returned now, it would be to strangers.

I am lucky, I know, that my journey through Chaos only took seventeen years, rather than the lifetime it is taking my father. Still, I resent him. Even knowing the risk of how long his ferrying might take, he still went. He valued his contract over his family. Over me. In my life, he has always been a shadow.

Half a memory.

A fading face.

I shake myself back to the present. Despite my complex feelings toward Manab, I vow he will be a presence in Flora's life, and not a haunting one, but a warm one. She will know of the grand things her father has accomplished and someday, perhaps, she might even visit him.

"How is Isra?" Grandmother asks. It is uncanny how she can read me thus, as though she knows my thoughts before I speak them. I put it down to her long-lived years, but part of me wonders if her Divinity somehow guides her on knowing what to ask. *To understand kindness,* she once told me, *you must understand people.*

"She is depressed, Grandmother. I am afraid I did not do right by her."

Perhaps I have harmed her more than helped.

"Why did you bring her here, Belladonna? Why Isra?"

It is hard for me to answer this question. In the moment, it was not so much a decision I made as something that happened. I saw her laying on the floor, succumbing to Manab's medicine. Bombs were exploding all around. The World Tree would not stop shaking. Populist soldiers were closing in and I...

I could not leave her.

But I sense Grandmother is probing something deeper, something that lurks beneath the surface.

Why Isra?

The words rattle in my mind.

Grandmother smiles at me. She was crafted from the kindness that shelters Mother Sol's heart and bound to her form by sunlight itself. When Grandmother smiles, the world seems softer.

"Have you considered taking her to Divine Forest's arbor, Belladonna? Perhaps his connection to Divine Falcon would be some comfort to her."

Divine Forest. Of course. If there is anyone in Meadowsweet who will understand a fraction of Isra's loss, it will be him.

I stand with renewed purpose. "I don't know why I didn't think of that sooner."

"Be kind to yourself, Belladonna. It is not easy to come home."

It is then that light slants through the glass dome above, hitting her just right, and I see how she has changed. Even Grandmother Dove is fading, and my heart squeezes. She has crow's feet around her eyes, and some of her strands of golden hair have turned silver as moonlight. Signs of age.

My marrow freezes.

I think of Divine Falcon. I think of Dawnland.

"Go." Grandmother waves a hand. "My sisters and I will watch Flora today. I am certain Mother Sol might enjoy some time with her as well. Your daughter will be beloved."

She will be, I know, and yet I hate to part from her. From this piece of myself. Grandmother hands my daughter over and I hold her close.

I wonder if this is what it felt like for my father before he left, this slow rupture, this drifting away from part of himself.

Many years ago, Grandmother told me, "The truth is, I do not know how to miss my son. How can I yearn after my own heart? It's still beating, it's just... gone." That is how I feel when I am away from Flora. My heart is still beating, it's just somewhere else. I don't like it.

I lean down, brace myself, and kiss my grandmother's cheek. It is when I am straightening to leave that she stills me with a word and a touch on my arm. "Rosemary."

I freeze, rigid. Will there ever be a day when Rosemary does not undo me?

"Belladonna, so much has changed since you've been gone. It... it is not my place, but I ask that you go to the Narrows at some point. Go and see what Rosemary has done there."

Grandmother releases me. I hand Flora to her and leave Mother Sol's Solarium, out the side door to Father Terra's garden beyond. I have always loved this place, its perfectly chaotic organization, the sprawl of it, every flower imaginable open wide beneath a dazzling sapphire sky. Ahead, the milkweed grove looms, and I slow, collecting my thoughts.

I have gone about all of this wrong. I deserve all of Isra's ire and more.

I remember pearls hitting the walls like shrapnel.

Shrapnel piercing my heart.

So many wounds. All of this blood.

I push forward, pressing between two tall stalks of milkweed. Orange flowers float down, stick to my hair, become part of me.

Of course, this makes me think of...

Rosemary.

I cannot live like this, with so much regret. I must mend one wound before I can tend to others.

Isra is in the center of the small glade, on a grass-topped hill. Stalks of milkweed as tall as trees encircle her, all of them so laden with blooms they bend, forming a delicate orange roof. Isra is on her knees, her face pressed against a milkweed leaf that is as large as a dinner plate. Her eyes are closed, but I see wet streaks on her white freckles.

"Isra," I whisper. Her eyes snap open and she sniffles and sits up, releases the leaf. I feel like I am intruding on her Sacred ground. "I didn't mean to... I shouldn't be here."

She sniffles and I make to leave.

"Wait," Isra says. "Belladonna, wait, I—"

"I'm sorry," I spit the words at her before she can utter more. "I am so sorry, Isra. I have done all of this wrong. I thought I was doing the right thing, taking you here. I didn't know... I didn't know he had manipulated both of us. I didn't know until the last, and by then..." I picture her laying on the ground again, asleep as bombs detonate and the World Tree trembles, so vulnerable.

"Why me?" Isra asks. The words twist in her mouth until all I hear is the pain that forms them.

We study each other.

"I don't understand *why*," she whispers.

Grandmother had asked me the same question.

She deserves an answer. I search my mind, hunting for words. The silence around me thickens. My soul quivers, trembles. The sky feels so fathomless and blue. I feel like that sky, so wide and wild, undefinable.

Why, she asks, as though it is a simple question with a simple answer.

Why?

I saw her, laying prone on the ground with danger all around and...

Why?

"Isra, is it enough that I could not bear to let you go?"

She gasps and something in my heart flutters. I step closer to her so a breath is all that separates us. I can feel her, brushing against my quiet. I like the way she presses against me even though we are not touching, like her soul is reaching out to touch mine.

"I have done you an injustice and then heaped more mistakes upon that. Today, I would like to begin anew."

Her eyes light with familiar curiosity, an expression I have not seen since the calmer days in Dawnland. "What do you have planned, Belladonna?"

I hesitate. She has been afraid to leave the Hall of the Gods, I know. Perhaps going so far into the city will be too much for her. Too much change too soon, and yet as her breakdown last night attests, she is beating herself against the walls of this cage I have inadvertently put her in.

"It is said that Father Terra created Divine Falcon when he first beheld the majesty of the sky. He then turned and witnessed how the sunset transformed the earth he had spent so long Creating, and from the glory of that moment, he formed his son, Divine Forest." I pause and run a hand over a milkweed leaf, so green and soft. These plants feed my daughter and I honor them. "Divine Forest has not yet felt the call to go into Chaos and Create, Isra, so he has remained here, in Meadowsweet, Creating an arbor that... perhaps if it is not Dawnland, it is the closest we can come to it. I should like to take you there."

Her excitement is quick, and then dampens just as quickly.

"I am too strange, Belladonna. I... I cannot stomach the thought of gathering a crowd about me." Her wings tremble and I hate that I have done so little to mitigate her uncertainty or make her feel the least at home.

I smile. "I do not think you understand the strangeness of Meadowsweet, Isra. If anyone sees you, they'll know you for one of Father Terra's own. Come, please. Let me show you some of the wonders of Meadowsweet." I pause. "Will you trust me this far?"

Everything hangs on this question.

Isra hesitates, and the world waits for her answer with me.

"Of course," she finally says, and when she smiles, the sun shines a bit brighter.

NOW
ISRA

It is frightening, to leave the Hall of the Gods, and yet I cannot deny how much I long to be free of this place. It is grand, yes, and beautiful in every imaginable way, yet it feels like a cage. There is a city splayed around me and I have yet to see more than what I can glimpse through the window.

I could have explored the city alone, I suppose. Nothing stopped me save my fear. Belladonna is my safety blanket here. It is frightening to think of navigating this place without her beside me.

It is the language barrier that most worries me. Belladonna and I have been around each other for so long, we have created a hybrid language all our own, a smattering of hers, a dash of mine. I am not so good at understanding the speech here, unless those around me speak slow and enunciate well. The idea of getting lost and having to find my way, without words to help me, has kept me well rooted.

Now, with Belladonna, I am not so afraid.

There are three trolly lines that connect at the Hall of the Gods. Belladonna leads me to the line for Father Terra's quarter and fishes two of her grandmother's prayers out of her pocket, pressing one into my palm. She shines so bright it almost hurts to look upon her. There is no mistaking whose blood rides high in her veins. Soon, a green trolly pulls up before us, and a host of Divine get off, all of them as strange as I feel: a man with oak branches for antlers, another covered in leaves, a woman who looks to be part bird, and another whose laughter sounds like wind. The man who drives the trolly has ram's horns and hooves instead of feet.

"See?" Belladonna smiles at me and motions at my wings. "You are not so strange as you think, Isra."

I had been in Mother Sol's end of the Hall. I had not been too exposed to Father Terra's line, save for Father Terra himself. Mother Sol's daughters all look so... similar. Beautiful, yes, and otherworldly in their own way, but as strange to me as I am to them. Father Terra's line, though, I understand, for it is what made me. Perhaps these creatures I see look strange to others, but the seamless blend of nature with Divinity reminds me of home.

Soon, we are on the trolly, a conveyance with all manner of seats, some even carved for a body like mine, with narrow backs that allow me to sit comfortably and hold my wings in a more natural way. I cannot help but feel, at least a little, like I belong.

I close my eyes as the trolly starts moving and feel the air on my face. When I next open them a few seconds later, Belladonna sits before me, her sorrow so thick I can nearly taste it. Behind her, a sparkling sea stretches to kiss the horizon.

I realize, belatedly, that the city around me is different than I had yet seen it. Here, the trolly moves not down cobblestone streets, but through a vast, sprawling orchard. Between rows of trees were log cabins.

"Meadowsweet is broken into arbors," Belladonna explains. "Mother Sol, Father Luna, and Father Terra set their children the task of Creating. What ones feel called into Chaos go forth and Create there. The rest stay here in Meadowsweet and Create arbors. Think of it like a small world within a greater world. This is Divine Harvest's arbor. It is where much of the city's food is grown."

The next arbor we travel into looks to be nothing but stone. Rolling hills of granite, marble, amethyst, and onyx rise like ocean waves. There are houses carved out of these hills. I can see families outside of rocky dwellings, their skin polished like gemstones. "Divine Stone's arbor," Belladonna explains as I take it all in, eyes wide and full of wonder.

I had not realized how sprawling Meadowsweet truly is. From the Hall of the Gods, I realize, I see but a fraction of it, and the most mundane parts at that. Here, one arbor follows the next. After Divine Stone's arbor come ranches and a desert with houses, businesses, and entire factories built into the bases of towering cacti. After that, nothing but wildlife and grasslands with rivers running through it.

My heart lifts the more I see. This... this is not Dawnland, but the further I go into Father Terra's quarter of Meadowsweet, the more I understand this place. The nature that fills it, the way this part of Meadowsweet, at least, seems to speak a language I recognize. I am familiar with the way Father Terra's sons and daughters work with the world.

Finally, the trolly stops and Belladonna stands. She has not spoken in some time, and I see the pinched set to her eyes, the way her lips pucker. She is in pain. Being around others has never been easy for her, much less when they are strangers. She is sacrificing part of herself so she might take this journey with me. I will appreciate every moment of it.

Soon, we are standing on a platform. I breathe deeply and Belladonna watches me.

I feel it in my lungs first: home. It enters my blood and spills through me. My wings tremble and my antennae stand on end. I am filled with energy.

This is not Divine Falcon or Dawnland I sense, but it is near enough.

Tears fill my eyes. The heady loam of the forest suffuses my senses. Dappled light spills through a canopy of redwoods so tall I cannot see their tops. The trolly chimes and continues along its course, and soon we are alone.

I spin in a slow circle, taking in the forest and all its splendor.

I spy houses carved into the bases of these trees, and walkways of woven branches higher still. Stores and schools, even a moving picture theater can be spied through the branches. There is a small convenience stand across the station built from a large beetle carapace where a man with a black bear's ears reads a newspaper. Across the way, a boy darts across a path, his fox's tail bushy and red. A moment later, another child follows, this one with a rat's whiskered nose.

The feeling of being home, even though I'm not, is so powerful I nearly double over with it. I expect to see Manab and Atheed poking out from between the trees. This place is where Flora should grow up, surrounded by nature and by those who might understand what she may become.

"I'm sorry," Belladonna whispers, but the words crack and break into shards so sharp I bleed just hearing them. "I should have taken you here, Isra. If I had not been so focused on myself... If I had thought about your needs... It was an injustice to take you to the Hall when the Sacred Forest is right here. I... I'm sorry I have made this so hard."

She is tearing herself apart, shredding herself with guilt. Light flares from her in time with her sobs and I know I should not touch her. I know she will not welcome it without preparing herself first, and I know I should ask, but I cannot stomach her sorrow. I decide I am done with this distance and wrap my arms around her, holding her close.

Belladonna goes rigid against me. Even her sobs cut off on a sharp inhale. Then, a low moan of pain. I am about to let her go when her arms circle my waist and she presses her forehead against my shoulder.

"I have done everything wrong," she breathes.

I sense she is speaking about more than just me, so I don't reply. Instead, I offer her a place to rest her sorrows, a haven away from judgment. Once she has purged her soul, she steps away from me, wipes her eyes, and offers a shaking smile.

"I am not terribly familiar with this arbor, Isra."

"We should explore," I say.

Belladonna nods. "It's been a long time since we've explored. I've missed it."

Back when Belladonna first arrived in Dawnland, it was to the World Tree that she and her crew were taken. As we became friends, we would explore the rainforest together. I had thought myself familiar with every nook and cranny of Dawnland, but with Belladonna, I saw it with new and otherworldly eyes. Suddenly my home was unfamiliar, and glorious for it.

I have missed feeling wonder. I am anxious to immerse myself in a place that feels so much like home. I have needed the familiar, and Belladonna has given me all of it.

We spend the afternoon lost in Divine Forest's arbor, his small Creation. We sit in a cafe and eat lunch high in the canopy, then visit a petting zoo. Belladonna next finds a string of shops, each one peddling different exotic wares from Creations spread across Chaos. Then, we share a slice of chocolate cake from Grandmother Sycamore's Bakery, a lovely shop built into the base of a towering sycamore tree.

As the sun is setting, Belladonna pulls me into a speakeasy that had been built into an oak tree that had fallen generations ago. The door opens onto the beach. Within, yellow light spills on a room full of strangers enjoying the band on the stage, a group of five men with squirrel's tails playing various brass instruments.

Belladonna orders us food and we take it to the beach. A meat dish for herself, some lamb that had been marinated in an herb sauce along with rice, while I have a plate full of fruit, an assortment of flowers, some nuts, and a small cup of nectar with a mint leaf floating on its surface.

Such familiar food, a meal that I recognize. It is enough to make me weep.

The sea is not far off, and the ocean provides accompaniment to our quiet feast. The sun begins to set, painting the ocean with shades of amber. "What would happen to this arbor if Divine Forest felt the call to go into Chaos and Create?" I ask, thinking over all I have seen this day.

Belladonna sets her plate down and digs her toes into the sand. "Unless another Divine One binds themselves to that arbor shortly after they leave, it disappears back to Chaos. It has happened. It was happening to the Narrows when I left."

Her face suddenly goes pale and she clamps her lips tight.

I look to the sunset, watch the ocean waves, and munch on a berry. Flavor explodes across my tongue and peace fills my soul. I have needed this day, desperately.

I cannot bear the thought of any of this disappearing, going back to Chaos. Becoming undone. It is too magical to lose. Too much a part of me. Even now, I am not in Dawnland, but I know Dawnland is out there somewhere. It exists. And that... that is enough. I could not survive it if I knew it was no longer.

Belladonna looks over her shoulder at the arbor at our backs. I know the rhythms of this place. In the twilight hours, the day dwellers will be going home for the night, while the night risers will be coming out. Speakeasies dotting the beach fling open their doors. A large brass band sets up on a small stage on the beach. Someone drags out a few flat, square boards for dancing. Soon, the drums start up.

It is all so familiar, so much like Dawnland, I savor it. Beside me, Belladonna winces and then moans as the sound grows in pitch and intensity, overwhelming her.

It is too much. I watch as she fractures. Watch as she breaks. It begins with a tremor, and then a low wail.

"I am going to become sick from all this sound," she says. "Please. Take me away from here." She covers her ears with her hands. I know not to touch her, and yet I don't know where we are going, so I guide her in the direction of the trolly station as best I can.

Overhead, Father Luna's light pierces midnight and leaves a trail of silver in its wake.

"Where are we going?" I ask. A trolly appears with a sign on front that says, "Hall of the Gods."

"This one," Belladonna says. "We need this one." She gestures at the trolly with her elbow, for she still cannot release her ears. Her face is a mask of pain. Behind us, lights illuminate the trees, yellow and warm.

I must come back.

I help Belladonna onto the trolly. She is nearly sick, her face beaded with sweat, her pallor a deep grayish green. I have never seen her so undone.

"Belladonna, are you okay?" My hands hover about her like afterthoughts as I settle her on the wooden bench. She presses her forehead against the wall. The trolly is nearly empty, and what few others are on it move to the other side of the car, as though expecting Belladonna to heave on them. She might. She looks willing.

The trolly's bell chimes and she moans again. A moment later, we are off.

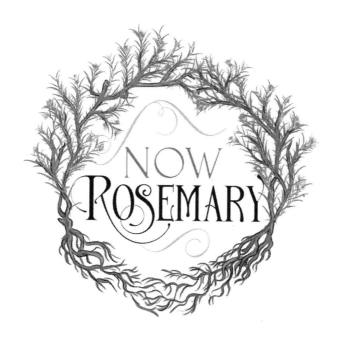

NOW
ROSEMARY

It is the morning glory climbing this trellis that I cannot look away from. For its one leaf, small and inconsequential as it is, should not be curled, nor should the edges of it be turning a faded yellow. Not here, in my Sacred Space.

I feel it in my soul, a blemish where once I had been whole. A spot of nothing where nothing should not be.

It is a wound, a small slice, but enough to start the bleed.

Around me, night embraces the world. The sea is not far off, and across the street is a row of towering apartment buildings that also double as planting pots, flowers growing out of each of them, tall enough to scrape the sky. Daisies sprout from the building across from me, and grapes large as dinner plates grow from the one next to it; the vines twining between windows are being used as clothes lines by enterprising residents. A door opens and music from a nearby speakeasy spills into the quiet, shattering my concentration. A trolly's bell chimes.

It is strange, when I think on it, that this is the place where I grew up. I had known that the Narrows was the way it was because the Divine One who had bound herself to that bit of Chaos felt the call to

Create and had gone forth to do just that. I had understood that the arbor of my childhood was degrading because it was being unmade. I had not understood what that truly meant, though, until I was much older.

After Belladonna left, I'd felt so rudderless and alone, I had longed to Create somewhere of my own. I had yearned for a place to belong.

And so I had bound myself to Chaos on the place where my old tenement rested. Now, the building has been leveled, and what resides in its place is a sprawling garden. The seat of my Divinity, the place to where I always return to know myself.

Yet, the morning glory. I cannot look away from the lush vine. It twines up the side of a square apartment building, the top of which serves as a garden plot for everyone in the tenement, green dripping down the sides of it like tears. My heart pounds and my vision blurs. I rub my hand over my sternum and feel an ache there, deep and burning.

"I have allowed you to Create," Chaos tells me through this leaf. "Now it is time to give over the last of your Divinity to sustain what you have wrought. It is time to give all of this to those whom you have made it for."

This is the natural order of things. This was always how it was going to end. And yet, it is different when the wasting stops being something that happens to other people and starts being something that happens to me.

That is how my father finds me: sitting on a bench in my garden, stroking a morning glory leaf and contemplating mortality with my cane propped against my leg.

His hand lands on my shoulder and I sink into his touch.

"My heart," is all he says, and in those two words resonates the fullness of his understanding. I lean into his touch. My vines grow long and wrap around his hands, as though holding him to me. He cups my cheek and I sob into his moon-glowing palm. Stars spin like fireflies around us before floating to the sky for Father Luna to do with them what he pleases.

Father's silence speaks for him. There are no platitudes for this moment. Nothing to ease this new ache. I will now, forever, be watching part of myself fade.

My breath saws out of me. Who am I if I am not Divine?

My arbor suddenly feels less welcoming. I can name each piece of myself I offered to Chaos to Create each of these buildings, to grow every flower, to pave every street. This is not simply a Creation or an arbor, but an extension of me.

This is my soul in this world, and I feel as though I am losing it.

"I sheltered you from it as long as I could," my father finally whispers.

...for as long as I could.

A wail climbs up my throat and dies there. When he touches me next, his hand is trembling and it no longer shines so bright. "You are still young," he whispers. "It will be easier for you."

He says this as though the words are meant to comfort me but they do not, for he is not so young. He is old as time itself and there will be no surviving this for him. He will become mortal, and he will fade, and all he creates will live on as a testament to what he once was.

I will live in this world he helped Create without him.

And it will be agony.

"It will be easier for you," he whispers as though trying to reassure himself. The tide of my emotion swells. Anger crests and sorrow crashes. My soul is storm-tossed and wind-worn, and I am no longer strong enough to contain its torment.

A low, shredded sob claws its way out of my mouth. "Can you not understand? Losing my Divinity will be hard but losing you will be so much harder."

"Rosemary—"

"This ache"—I clutch a fist over my chest—"has its own heartbeat."

My father settles on the bench beside me. I feel his attention but I cannot face him. Not right now. I am not strong enough. So, I stare straight ahead and watch as the moon uses the ocean as a mirror to admire itself. Stars spin as though drunk with the wonder of the dark.

"How am I to live in this world without you?"

"The same way you always have, my heart. One day at a time." He draws near to me. I smell the ozone that clings to him. Then comes the whisper, "There will be better days than this."

I sob then. Come apart in his arms. I shred myself until I am nothing but tattered bits of soul. When I am empty, he helps me knit myself back together.

"It is better this way," my father whispers as though to himself. Night sinks its teeth into my heart and I bleed stars. "I am not strong enough to let you go at once, my daughter, so I must give you up slowly, in pieces."

That does not make it hurt any less.

"Rosemary," he breathes against my crown, "I finally understand what a moment is."

The wonder in his voice sends silent tears spilling down my cheeks. There should not be so much glory in this long end.

"Does it hurt?" I finally ask.

There are any number of things he might say in answer, but he considers my question and I love him for it. "Do you remember when we went to the beach when you were a child, and you filled that doll with sand?"

I remember that afternoon well. The beach is not somewhere I go often, for sand is hard for me to navigate with my leg and often leads to added pain. That day, however, I had been feeling well and my father had been anxious to explore Meadowsweet with me. We had gone to a moving picture show, and then to eat ice cream at the beach. I had found a burlap sack, and my father had begged some string from a nearby merchant. I spent the afternoon filling my sack with sand and making a doll of it.

"Yes," I answer.

"Remember how the doll kept leaking sand?" I nod. "That's what it feels like. My Divinity is leaking out like sand. It doesn't hurt, Rosemary, it's just different."

The night holds us close, comfortable and quiet. Moonflowers bloom, followed by jasmine, and what small creatures who call the kingdom of night home wake and go about their business: mice in the tall grasses, owls in the trees. A gentle breeze off the ocean cools my heated soul.

"There is something I would say to you, my heart," my father says, resting a hand over mine, pulling my attention to him. "We are both still alive. Let us act like it."

His words are not unkind, and when his eyes meet mine, the galaxies in them spiral somberly, as if in minor key.

"Each day my Divinity wanes a bit more, and each day, Rosemary, I feel a little more alive in a way I never have before. Is that not worth celebrating? I understand moments now, my heart, and I cherish them. Will you not cherish them with me?"

"Father, you cannot ask me not to be sad."

He shakes his head. "I am only asking you to try to be happy as well." He hesitates and I see an old man before me, bent spine and wispy gray hair, age spots along his bald pate and all those wrinkles. Then, I blink, and he's back to the man I know, only with gray touching the hair at his temples.

"Father?"

"I'm facing the unknown, Rosemary." His breath shudders out of him. "And part of me is very afraid."

Who do the gods pray to when they are afraid?

"I do not know who I will be when this is all over," I whisper.

There is a truth in those words that chills me to the bones.

We're going forward now.

There is no going back.

THEN
ROSEMARY

"Quietly," Muse said. The dark spilling from the gap in the wall wrapped around him, wreathing him in a cloud of deepest night. The moons in his eyes glowed, twin beams of silver cutting the black just enough. "We may enter, but softly, child. Sacredly."

He did not need to tell me this, for I felt the moment press upon me like so many hands. Divinity was heady indeed, and with each step I took, it grew stronger, until I could swear my bones were glowing with it. My blood ran like a river cresting with rapids. Night closed around me. Rather than being terrifying, it was comforting, a presence I somehow both knew and understood.

The darkness cleared, and I found myself standing in a grand observatory fashioned of the finest glass, with a ceiling so high ten men standing on each other's shoulders could not reach it. Beyond was the universe, galaxies spiraling and dancing in chaotic streaks of light. I gasped, for this was not the sky I studied through my window each night. No, this was...

"Oh," I breathed.

Never had I witnessed such glory. Here I stood, beholding creation.

"Do you see?" Divine Muse whispered. "Certain sacred things only happen in darkness."

"This is—"

"Father Luna's Sacred Observatory."

Softly, he had told me to enter this place. *Sacredly*.

Oh, the weight of that moment. How it did not break my spine, I will never know. I could feel Most High Father Luna all around, less man and more sensation. It swallowed me. Creation itself flexed and flowed all around and I was driftwood lost to its current.

I fought to keep myself upright when every part of me wanted to bend.

I was not strong enough.

Divine Muse's gleaming hand landed on my shoulder and offered a sympathetic squeeze. I drew strength from that touch and smiled at him, shocked to see that in this place, the lines of him blurred making him seem ephemeral. He glowed like the full moon on a bright summer night. There were no storms massing along the planes of his night-woven body.

My gaze drifted across a polished stone floor, touching on some topiaries before focusing on two people in the distance, silhouettes standing near one of the glass walls and staring at the cosmos beyond. A moon whirled past, scattering stardust in its wake.

In the air were fireflies, their soft yellow bellies glowing in the darkness.

The two figures turned and I felt their attention settle on us. "Sit here," Muse said, pressing me gently onto a stone bench. I sat, grateful for the reprieve, and dug a knuckle into my hip. He waited until I was settled, and then nodded once and continued down the path.

A moment later, I heard Muse speak, tone soft and impossible to understand. Then, came an answer, voice so low I felt it rattle my bones.

I kept my eyes focused on the scene ahead, on the stars, the spiraling dance of the cosmos beyond these windows. Divinity filled me, and even my weary leg seemed to take succor from the sensation, strength given by proximity to the Most High.

It is impossible to explain Father Luna.

Formless and fathomless, he came to me suddenly and curled around me like smoke. I did not know the night held so many hues and textures until I was wrapped in all of them, from shades of polished onyx to the violet-kissed edge of twilight and everything between. There, I spied the birth of solar systems. In another breath, the gaping maw of Chaos.

Night spun about me and in the depths of it I saw the mists of Creation and the three Most High waking to find themselves the only creatures in all of Chaos, newly formed and swollen with divinity, throbbing with the will to Create. I watched as they learned themselves. Then as Father Luna grew lonely. Finally, eaten through by a need to have something of his own, he scooped a handful of Creation and some of his own soul, and from it, formed his eldest son and the first of the gods, Divine Aether.

A hand crafted of stardust touched my arm, jarring me from my vision. My bones emanated a soft, silver light and my blood surged in response. Midnight strengthened my muscles and dreams softened my skin. Moonflowers bloomed wide on the vines of my hair.

Father Luna was not what I expected. Or perhaps, I did not know what to expect and so he was exactly that. He was what I could not fathom.

It took him time to pull his darkness in and craft himself something that looked like a body. Man-shaped, he was the chaos of night and the passion of dreams given substance. His skin flowed with ever-changing shades of dark, and his eyes were full of cosmos. Instead of hair, stars spun about his crown, and his ear was stabbed through with a ray of purest moonlight. He smiled at me and I heard the song planets hum as they spun their way through eternity.

Was I to bow? Prostrate myself before him? Pray? How is one supposed to greet one of the Most High? No one had prepared me for this moment.

Yet, I did not fear him. Not truly. It was more the idea of him that frightened me rather than the man himself. He was hard to look at for long, for even while forming himself a body, bits of him were eternally spinning off, changing, rearranging. It was like watching smoke in a storm. Part of me wondered if perhaps he was so chaotic on purpose. Perhaps he did not want to be seen.

But he was beautiful as well. I never knew the dark could be so glorious.

"Father Luna," I said, bending as low as I could while sitting. My hip twinged, angry at this new angle.

He made a gesture like shooing away a fly, and a wisp of night spun from his hand to dissipate in the air like smoke. "I am an old man, nothing more."

"Sir, you are—"

"Please turn away from me," he said, voice trembling. The galaxies beyond the glass slowed their dance and grew dim. "So much of me is missing. I do not want you to see all that I lack."

Shifting, I stared out the windows, color flushing my cheeks. I related to his words, too much.

"My son tells me you have requested aid."

My blood hummed. I rubbed my arms, warding them against the sensation.

"Most High Father Luna," I licked my lips. My voice trembled. "My worry is beneath you."

Divine Muse had told me he'd take me to his brother, not the Most High. I was not prepared for this.

"Nothing is beneath me, Rosemary." He rested a hand on mine. It was warm and covered in moonlit clouds. "Tell me what happened."

So I spun my story for the second time that day, aware of Muse and his brother slowly approaching as I spoke. Most High Father Luna did not interrupt me. He folded his hands in his lap and studied the cosmos, nodding as I spoke. The longer I talked, the easier it became to forget who this was beside me and speak freely.

I daresay, I found Most High Father Luna's quiet companionship... comfortable.

I had not looked at the third man before this point. He stood beside Muse, quiet and wrapped in a darkness I could not pierce, but

I saw his eyes well enough. Wide, they were, and full of wonder. In a mirror to the chaos I saw outside the observatory, they also showed the endless dance of the cosmos.

Our gazes met and something in me shifted.

What had Mother said all those years ago? I had taken it as a fantasy of hers, yet the words had stuck to my ribs despite all this time. It was the sorrow in her voice that held my attention. The way each word trembled. The tears she thought I could not see.

Your father is creation itself and he loves you so very much.

Blood tells its own story and I knew then I was casting eyes upon my father for the first time. I gripped my cane, my gloves slippery with cold sweat.

He could not love me. Not someone so august as that. He would likely be glad when I took my limp and my vines and left his sight, never to be seen again.

"I only need help. My mother is ill. I need to pay off Landlady and I need to move Mother away from that place. If you can help me that far, then I will indenture myself to your service. I will work until I can pay off what is owed."

I would repay.

For my mother, anything.

Silence answered and my soul was brittle.

I took my cane and stood. "I'm sorry. I... I shouldn't have come. Forgive me."

"I will help you," Divine Aether finally said. His voice was a low, husky rumble. The moonflowers in my hair bent their slender stems toward him. "Will you take me to her?"

I studied him then, my father. His eyes were soft. Too soft for someone that Divine. It frightened me.

As a child, my mother had been full of stories. One had been the tale of a woman, the eldest daughter of a merchant family with just enough of Father Terra's blood to matter. The woman had fallen in love with a god, but the god had been called away and the woman... she had been cast out by her family and was now alone.

I had thought it a tragic fairytale.

"Will you take me to her?" he asked again.

His desire burned brighter than the sun. It hurt to look at him.

He loved her.

He loved *her*.

I sat before him, his daughter, and he did not move toward me. He did not introduce himself, nor so much as acknowledge me beyond what he must.

I knew then that I would take him to my mother and he would gain her back and then I would truly be alone. Everything with the Divine requires payment, I'd learned as much in the Narrows. This is why I did not want to ask their help in the first place. I did not have enough to weather losing what little was mine. Yet Divine Aether would keep my mother healthy and safe. That was truly what I needed, wasn't it? I vowed to protect her, at whatever cost. It did not so much matter if he loved me. Perhaps he would let me stay on as a servant so I could at least be close to her.

Perhaps he would be kind, in time.

I'd offered my indenture.

Pain. I had never before felt its like. My eyes burned with tears. The world went blurry. A spear of moonlight wrapped around me like arms. Like a noose. Like fate.

"You will care for her?" I whispered. "You must bind yourself to that oath, Divine Aether, or I will not take you to her. All of this is for her."

"I so swear," the god before me rumbled and I felt his Divinity pulse, an oath he could not break.

"I will take you to her," I said.

Divine Aether fixed his eyes on me and I could not imagine what he was thinking. I am not ashamed to admit, I trembled.

He would hate me by the time this was over. As much as he loved her, he would hate me, for my mother was different now than however he remembered her and our survival had fallen upon my shoulders. When he saw how far his beloved had fallen...

I had done my best. Surely he must see that.

It took every ounce of bravery I could muster to whisper, "Come with me, Divine Aether."

NOW

BELLADONNA

I wake the morning after visiting Divine Forest's arbor feeling bruised and aching with it. My head throbs, and my soul has been wounded. I pushed myself too hard yesterday. It will take days for me to repair the quiet that surrounds me. Days for me to heal from sound.

Still, I cannot stay in bed forever, no matter how much I wish for nothing more than silence. Isra is in the apartment beyond, her soft footsteps slide over softer carpet. Birds chirp, and a breeze drifts through open windows.

My room is bright, white walls with white furnishings and white decorations. Mother Sol had this room decorated for me as a child, when she understood the nature of my Divinity. White, she said, is the quietest color.

I slide my legs over the side of the bed and wince as the movement causes pain to pierce my eyes and my stomach roils. Even the sound of my robe sliding over my skin is too much, like sandpaper against the soul.

Weak. I am so weak and I despise myself for it.

I cast my eyes out the window and seek out the border of Meadowsweet. Not too far, and I would be lost in Chaos, in the silence provided by the absence of Creation. Strange how the one place that seems to drive so many mad is the one place I long to return to. And yet, I cannot. I cannot raise my daughter in Chaos. I cannot live so isolated and alone. I cannot let sound chase me into impenetrable silence.

I cannot be this weak.

I make my way to my wardrobe and pull out the pantsuit that Grandmother Dove had made for me. The jacket is violet and double-breasted with white pinstripes. A matching white vest is worn beneath, with nice, tailored trousers.

"You look beautiful," Isra says, her voice a whisper. I spin around and the world spins with me. For a moment, bile rises and I press a hand against the wall to steady myself. "I'm sorry to startle you." She creeps into my room, her wings folded tight behind her. Guilt hangs heavy in the air between us.

I should address it. I should comfort her. Remind her that I undertook the journey yesterday of my own volition and I regret not a moment of it, no matter how I feel today. Instead, I smile.

"My mother never let me wear trousers," I explain, gesturing at myself. "I always was forced into dresses. *You are not a man, Belladonna, so you will not dress like one.*" I mimic. Still, I can hear her voice. Still, it pains me. "Grandmother Dove had this made for me as soon as I returned."

It is so much more than just a suit. She accepts all of me.

"I never saw you in a dress in Dawnland," Isra said.

"It was easier, when I was away, to live how I wanted." I think of the dress I had to borrow to visit my mother and how uncomfortable I felt in it, like I was putting on another person's skin. I think of Isra. *I don't fit.*

Isra opens her mouth to speak, but a knock sounds on the apartment door. I feel it rattle within my skull. So much sound. A whole world of it. How am I to live like this? Always sick, or on the cusp of it? Always either wounded or healing?

Rosemary, years ago. "There are gradations of pain, Belladonna," she had whispered. "I am familiar with all of them."

Isra hesitates, unsure if she should stay with me or answer the door. "Please telephone Divine Aether, Isra. Ask for Divine Rosemary. Tell her... tell her I need her assistance, should she have a moment."

Rosemary. She is the answer to each of my riddles.

Another knock, insistent this time, and Isra disappears down the hall to our phone nook while I open the door. I am not surprised to see Oleander on the other side, though I was not expecting him. Still, there he stands, cap clutched in his hands. He looks wrong here, in Mother Sol's brightest wing of the Hall of the Gods. Dressed in thick wool and dour black, he is a wound in an otherwise brilliant hall.

Yet, he does not look angry or even particularly determined, but rather ashamed. His silence is bruised, too, but perhaps in a different way than mine.

"Come in," I say, peering into the hall to make sure his mother isn't also present.

"I'm sorry I came so early," he says, putting his hat on a peg by the door. "I heard Mother Sol's daughters rise with the day."

"I am but a great granddaughter," I say, motioning him toward the foyer. "But I tend to keep early hours."

Isra appears a moment later and I make introductions. Her wings flutter, betraying her anxiety as he studies her.

"Tea," Isra squeaks when she can take it no more, and scurries from the room.

"Fascinating creature," Oleander breathes, staring at the space Isra had just vacated. Finally, he rouses himself. "We should sit, Belladonna. There are things we must discuss."

Marriage, I am guessing. He will expect me to walk to the altar willingly and be grateful for the opportunity. A thousand curses colored with my mother's name fill my mind as I follow him to the sitting area. He takes the couch and I take the chair across from it. A moment later, another knock sounds and the door opens. I know instantly who will be there and part of me unclenches, as though by proximity alone Rosemary makes me better.

"Belladonna," she says. Her voice is husky and low and her eyes are red-rimmed and swollen. She's been crying. Guilt holds my heart in cupped hands. Whatever she is dealing with is more important than my woe and still, I called her here to tend me as though she's a servant, as though I deserve it.

I am weak.

Rosemary's vines grow long around her heart-shaped face; belladonna blooms along their length, and she plucks a flower and offers it to me. Our fingers brush as I take the bloom. In the beat of a heart, Rosemary's Divinity suffuses my soul. Belladonna, my name-sake flower, fills me with silence. I bask in the still, calm waters of peace.

The world grows brighter and sound less abrasive. My stomach eases and the pressure behind my eyes relents.

Finally, I can breathe again.

"Cousin," Oleander is standing again, and it takes me a moment to realize he is speaking to Rosemary. They are cousins? How much do I not know about her? "I had not thought to see you here."

"In the Hall of the Gods, Cousin Oleander? You had not thought to see me where I live?"

Oleander winces. "No, I..." He runs a hand through his hair. "Belladonna left, Rosemary. I hadn't thought to see you *here*."

Rosemary's starlight freckles shine bright against cheeks suddenly suffused by cloud cover. Her forehead turns the black of a starless void, and slowly that color spills, like tears, onto her cheeks, wiping away the clouds and covering her starlight. Her vines shrink and she leans heavily on her cane.

"Ah," is all she says.

One small sound, and she forms a dagger of it and stabs true. I feel the knife go in, twist, and then I am bleeding.

I have done so many things wrong.

There is a mighty crash in the kitchen and a small yelp. Rosemary follows the sound. Oleander reaches forward and stops just shy of touching me when I make to stand and follow. "Please, Belladonna, let me say my piece."

"Speak," I say.

I spin the sprig of Belladonna in my fingers. The moment I release this bloom, my headache will come rushing back, but for now, it is kept a distance away and I can finally think clearly.

"Belladonna, our mothers have been scheming."

"I know that." I snort and bring the blossom to my nose. I can hear nothing from the kitchen and I cannot help but wonder what Isra and Rosemary are doing together in there. If they are getting along. This meeting, I realize, is important to me, and the fact I am not there to witness it is like having a briar in my sock.

"Your mother was going to let Sage sell your ferry. There was a line of eager merchants waiting to buy it."

Something in me goes cold and hard.

It is so much more than just a ship.

"Why?" I whisper.

Is that my voice? That brittle thing? That shatter?

Not even I know what I am asking with that question, but Oleander answers anyway. "Word has spread that a mortal has survived Chaos. Now, she has been seen in Divine Forest's arbor, so the rumors are true. Merchants are superstitious at the best of times. Yours was the ship that brought her, so they are all looking to buy it and start ferrying their own goods. Cut out the middle man, as it were. Perhaps Chaos is weakening enough, with the Divine fading, that now even mortals can ferry goods."

This is what my mother wants to reign over.

"I bought your ferry, Belladonna. I paid a ridiculous sum for it, and I have it in my berth."

Those words fall on me like bombs and shrapnel pierces my soul. Do I dare hope? Is there someone in this world who might help me? Dare I believe it is Oleander?

"I will not marry you," I say. "Not even for that ferry." But oh, it will hurt. It will hurt to let go of something that has become part of me.

Still, if it gives me freedom from my mother's machinations...

"I am not here to persuade you to marry me, Belladonna."

Oleander stands and starts pacing. "Our parents are scheming, yes, but can we not come to a similar agreement without all of... that? If we are to enter a new, mortal age, perhaps we should go about it differently than our parents would have. I am far too mortal to survive Chaos, Belladonna, but you aren't, and you have connections to other Creations. I have connections in Meadowsweet. I can help you move your goods and offer you a place to store your ferry. All I want is a percent of the profit. In return, I'll fund your journeys."

I cannot speak. Cannot think through the roaring in my ears. Did he truly say what I just think he said?

"I bought your ferry as a gesture of goodwill."

"That's a big gesture," I say.

"I figured I'd have no shot if I let your mother sell it to prove a point." He licks his lips. "Belladonna, your ferry was owned by your mother—"

"Now it's owned by you."

"But I don't want anything from you but a trade agreement, don't you see? We can come to an arrangement between us. Hire lawyers and make contracts. It would be smart business sense, especially in this coming age. Our mothers are not wrong about that. But we do not need to marry to come to such an arrangement. And if none of that sounds pleasing to you, I'm amenable to a payment arrangement for your ferry. I want nothing more than for you to hear me out."

It takes me time to find the words. "How am I to believe you won't hold this against me, use it to pressure me into a bad deal?"

"You'll have to trust me until we get contracts signed." Oleander meets my eyes. Behind him, Isra and Rosemary stand in the kitchen door, side by side and watching. Rosemary's hair has bloomed a riot of flowers and her cheeks are flushed with moonlight.

Have I misunderstood him so greatly?

"I have to think about this. I gave my crew time off. I won't discuss anything further with you unless we all agree."

"Understood." He looks relieved even with this much.

Rosemary shifts and her cane taps against the floor, drawing attention.

"I should go," Oleander says.

It is striking, that none of us argue.

He makes his way to the door and hesitates. "Come to my berth should you want to discuss this further." He takes his cap from the peg and a moment later, disappears out the door.

NOW

ISRA

The door closes behind the man with a soft snick and Belladonna lets out a breath, yet neither Rosemary nor I move to go to her. It seems we are both uncertain about what to do now. Does she need comfort? And will it comfort her more to be with people or without? It's impossible to tell. She sits in her silence, not so much as moving, and we leave her to it.

The sprig of the jade plant Rosemary had given me, an offering of friendship, is clutched in my fingers and my wings flutter, stirring the air just enough to carry the scent of fresh flowers to me.

Rosemary is intoxicating. It is the nectar in her eternally blooming flowers that so enchants me. I scent so many different flavors of it, and I hunger. I cannot stop looking at her, at the flowers blooming about her, or the way her vines move, like snakes seeking something to cling to. Her skin changes like a chameleon's, ever rolling waves of night, twilight, and dawn. The freckles along her cheekbones glow like stars, and her eyes are wide and full of nebulas.

Who is this creature?

She leans on her cane and motions to the patio door, open to a wide deck overlooking Meadowsweet beyond. I cast my eyes to where

I know Divine Forest's grove is, and I cannot deny how desperately I long to be there. Wind sweeps past us.

"She needs silence," Rosemary says, glancing at Belladonna, and I see something in her gaze, a certain quiet longing.

I expect her to leave me here, watching over Belladonna. It is the least I deserve after putting her through so much pain, but still...

"Spend the day with me?" Rosemary asks, eyes bright and hopeful.

I do not second guess myself. I have tasted freedom once, and I am desperate for it again. More, the scent that clings to Rosemary makes me feel alive in a way I have not in a while, and I do not want to rid myself of it yet.

Beyond that, though, like rain in a thunderstorm, lurks the knowledge that I will help Belladonna most if I am not present right now. She needs quiet, and outside of Chaos, she can only get that when she is alone.

"Yes," I say.

Rosemary smiles and I feel as though I have never seen so beautiful a sight. Her crown is wreathed by a halo of jasmine and snowdrop flowers, open wide and flush with summer. The moon on her cheeks is high and shines bright as the nebulas in her eyes dance.

Belladonna has shifted to lie on the sofa, and I pause to cover her with a thin blanket.

"Rosemary," Belladonna murmurs. And oh, how she cradles that name, as though she'd carved each letter from the bedrock of her soul.

"I'm taking Isra," Rosemary says. Her forehead is pinched and eyes narrowed. A sprig of meadowsweet grows near her temple, and she plucks it and offers it to Belladonna.

Belladonna hesitates before accepting the flower, and it is as though a bomb goes off in Rosemary's soul. The woman I saw who had been so friendly and open before, so easy with me despite my strangeness, is gone. She has transformed into this trembling, wounded creature that stands before me now.

"It will give you peace, Belladonna, that is all."

What history rests between these two? I am seeing a new side to Belladonna now, a side I have never seen before. Tender and vulnerable.

And Rosemary...

Her flowers droop, her vines curl against her scalp. It hurts to see her wither.

Belladonna takes the flower and her body eases, muscles uncoiling, the furrows on her brow smoothing. "I was going to take Isra to meet Divine Forest today. Instead, I find I must rest. Can you take her in my stead, Rosemary?"

"Of course."

Belladonna's breath hitches. "And then... come back?"

Rosemary hesitates and her eyes dart about as though she is cornered. She curls her hands over the head of her cane and I hear the sound her gloves make as she clenches them tight. "If that is what you wish from me, Belladonna."

Belladonna smiles, her eyes sliding closed. It is as though she does not hear the surrender in Rosemary's voice, nor does she see the weeping willow branches weaving through her vines. I do not need to be familiar with her Divinity to know Rosemary is in mourning. I understand the quiet way of pain. The smothering silence of grief.

I rest a hand on Belladonna's shoulder and she starts.

It strikes me then, how comfortable we have grown together. We have always been friends, true, but now something more lingers between us. I recognize Belladonna's rhythms and I understand how she works. I know how to live in a space with someone who needs quiet to survive, and it does not bother me.

And she...

She is easy enough with me to allow herself to relax into slumber. That was not always the case. She had been timid and afraid when I first met her. It took time to coax her from her shell.

I wonder what drove her there.

Was it Rosemary? Surely not. The goddess does not seem like one capable of bending others with cruelty.

Still, there are mysteries that surround Belladonna and I am eager to learn more, perhaps from another vantage.

I follow Rosemary out. The hallway beyond is bright as sunlight and Rosemary is silent for some time. I walk beside her, allowing her to set the pace. Her limp is pronounced and she grunts low under her breath each time she moves her right leg.

Finally, when we are alone, Rosemary stops, a hand on my arm. Suddenly, I am uncomfortable. I don't know what rested between Belladonna and Rosemary, but I am a creature of the air. I understand currents, and I know the one traveling between them is powerful indeed. Have I encroached somehow? Have I offended? Have I done wrong?

Uncertainty feels like a noose around my neck, cutting off my air.

Rosemary is steeped in Divinity, so much so, it aches to be around her. The power of her presence is overwhelming. Her touch on my arm burns. Who knows what could happen if she was so stirred to anger. There will be no withstanding her terror.

"Do not be afraid of me, Isra," she says, slowly, enunciating each word with care and precision, then pausing to make sure I understand. It is a kindness I appreciate more than she knows. "I seek only to thank you."

Her words drip with sincerity and I wonder how difficult it must be to be so soft and survive in such a hard world.

"Thank me?" I ask. "For what?"

"You have loved her when I could not. It eases me to know that she has not been alone all this time."

"I— You're welcome."

She smiles and then turns before I can say more. I follow her down the hallway, to the main entrance to the Hall of the Gods, and then down another hallway, this one immediately familiar as Father Terra's. Its walls are crafted from branches woven so tight, it is impossible to see through them. Instead of carpet, grass cushions my feet, and each of the doorways we pass is wreathed by a profusion of flowers.

In the same way I understood the Sacred Forest the day before, I understand this place.

Soft flower-laced grass softens my footfalls and my wings flap, stirring a concoction of scents from fertile loam to nectar-rich flowers. Rosemary, when I look at her, is blooming. Her vines hang long, wrapping around her arms and even her cane; her crown is covered in a riot of color. The scent of her slips into me, makes me...

Want.

A door opens down the hallway and a man I know instantly to be Divine Forest appears. He is tall and angular. His skin looks to be bark and instead of hair, he sprouts leaves. His eyes are green as sunlit moss. "Divine Rosemary," he says, pressing his lips against her cheek. "And Isra of Dawnland. I was hoping to meet you. I felt you in my arbor yesterday."

He ushers us inside.

His room is not truly a room, for it is impossible to tell where the Hall of the Gods ends, and where Divine Forest's forest begins. Trees surround us; so thick they are, I can hardly see through them. Aspen and oak, yew and pine, all mingle. The ground is pebble-strewn, and a small stream rushes past to my right. If there is a ceiling or stars, I will never know, for it is obscured by a canopy of leaves so green it aches to look upon them.

"Sit," the god says, and three trees move, shaping chairs of themselves for us.

For a moment, I don't know what to do, and so I sit and I fret. If Belladonna was here, she'd ease me into a conversation. Rosemary, however, is silent. Her eyes scan the room before she licks her lips and finally says, "Autumn is kissing your leaves, Divine Forest."

There is something in those words, something that makes my heart hurt, and I turn my attention to the aspen leaves above me, see then the green edged in yellow and notice the carpet of brown beneath my feet.

Forest's smile wanes. "We are all approaching autumn, Rosemary," he finally says. "It is a glorious season."

It is impossible not to see the panic flash through Rosemary's eyes.

"My father says it does not hurt, only that it is different."

Is she looking for reassurance?

"Divine Aether is wise."

Divine Aether. The name rattles through me. No wonder Rosemary's Divinity is so potent. No wonder there are nebulas in her eyes.

Divine Forest turns his attention back to me. "Isra," he says, his voice deep and sonorous. "I have heard stories of Dawnland and still, it would do my soul well to hear of my sister's Creation."

I think of Dawnland.

I hear bombs.

Guilt, then, for his eyes are full of such sincerity, such hope, and I know I am about to snuff that light.

"Tell me of my sister," Forest says. Never have I heard such heartbreaking kindness, such soul-crushing desire. "Tell me what befell her Creation. I want to hear it from you."

I don't want to do this. I don't want to face yet another god and tell them the one he loves sleeps and her Creation has torn itself apart in her absence. I don't want to stand here, alone, and face his sorrow.

I am not strong enough for this.

I want Manab. I want Atheed.

Belladonna would know what to say.

Anyone. Anyone but me.

Rosemary reaches out and grabs my hand, squeezes. The lace of her gloves is soft. "It is okay, Isra," she says. "Speak your truth. It will be welcomed here, no matter how painful."

It is those last words that undo me.

Speak your truth, she says, as though this will be easy for me. Yet she does not—cannot—understand. I am a mortal. I am a butterfly away from her roost. I am strange and inferior. I am nothing, and Divine Forest—

He has spent an eternity with Divine Falcon. They were Created together and lived together, side by side, for a time I cannot fathom.

I am to look in his eyes and say...

Here is your fate, God. Here is your future. I carry it with me on gossamer wings.

"Isra, trust."

Rosemary's words drip with kindness. A breeze blows through the forest. Water trickles over rocks.

Perhaps it is the silence that does it, or the flowers, or Rosemary's newfound friendship, or the way Divine Forest's eyes cloud as though overcome by a winter storm.

Perhaps it is the fact that I have never felt so alone and lost.

I have never felt so small.

Whatever it is, my tears come unbidden, and the sobs that tear through me are raw and real. A war is being fought in my soul and I can no longer contain the damage. Sorrow tears its way out of me, a violence all its own.

There are so many ways to bleed.

"Divine Falcon sleeps, God, and her Creation has torn itself apart. I come here as a refugee. My brothers... they conspired a way for me to survive."

Whatever story they had heard, I doubt it was that plainly spoken, for they look at me as though stunned.

"Tell me, please." Oh, these fragile words.

I don't know if I can. Each night I roll a different part of what happened over in my mind. Piece by piece, I deal with what happened, but still, I have not managed to see the whole thing, much less speak it. It feels too big.

"There are things I cannot say," I whisper. "Pieces of this story I'm not yet ready to face."

Divine Forest nods. "I will take whatever you are willing to offer."

NOW

ROSEMARY

Morning light spills through the windows. Mother sits on her favorite window seat looking at the garden beyond. She is calm today. Soft music plays from our gramophone and I perch in a nearby chair and read stories from one of her favorite books. She hums along to the tune. I would think she is not even aware of my presence, save for her pause each time I stop speaking, her body poised as though waiting... waiting to see if I will continue.

We do this each morning we are both able. This is all she will allow. All I can afford to give. A story. Words strung together by the thread spun from my heart. Something soft for her to hold on to while she drifts.

She is my mother and yet to her, I am a stranger.

It aches, this love.

Like an ocean wave, I crest. I break.

Still, we do this. Our ritual. I have learned over the years to stop hoping she will recognize me, and yet still I find myself aching for her to turn her eyes on me. I long to hear her call me by name.

To know me.

To love me. Not the dream she thinks I am, but *me*.

It is calm this morning. Nothing but the two of us and this music. Almost, I can forget. Almost, I can pretend.

Almost.

My life has become a cage crafted of almosts.

Suddenly, Mother sits tall, her muscles coiling tight. "It is morning," she says. "We must prepare ourselves, Rosemary."

She stands and holds a hand out to me. There's a twinkle in her eyes and I know she's not here, not now, but then. When I was a child.

"Where are we going, Mother?" I ask, setting the book aside. I speak my question carefully, cautiously. It is impossible to tell if whatever memory she's reliving is good or bad, light or dark. So I brace, unsure of what is to come.

Father, I notice, has restocked his supply of clary sage. If I need to make her sleep, I can, though I will not use it unless I must. Unless there is no other option.

I face my mother, see the nervous anticipation in her eyes. We are alone. It's just her and me, and her memory haunting the space between us like a specter.

"Where are we going?" I ask her again, leveraging myself to my feet and then gripping my cane while my hip cracks and groans. My body settles like an old house. Every day, it gets a little worse as I age and my Divinity wanes.

"It's time," she says, eyes wide and wild. Her hair is all gray now, a hint of color spun through there, if I look hard enough. Her face is lined with wrinkles.

"Time?" I ask.

She nods, breathes deep and throws her shoulders back. "It is time to face my parents. To show them who I have become. To introduce them to their granddaughter." She weaves a hand through my vines. Pale pink evening primrose blossom along my crown, their petals opening and closing along with my breaths. "They will not be able to help but love you."

I remember when she said this to me, years ago. I was but a girl at the time, we still had food and a nice place to stay. We still had hope.

These were the words that changed everything.

Her voice is soft and it seems she is looking at me and seeing me, but what she sees is a girl, not the adult I have become. Here we stand, so close our toes nearly touch, and yet we are bisected by time.

"They cannot help but love you."

It is the hope in her words that breaks me, for I know well the day she is remembering. She left part of herself in her parents' house that afternoon and has never been the same since. I can see the scene play out in her eyes and I relive it with her.

"What is this, Willow?" her father, Aster, roared, face ribboned with rage. So terrified was I, I hid behind my mother's legs and trembled.

"She," my mother replied, fire in her voice, "is my daughter."

No. Not this. Not now. I am not strong enough to face that day again.

"Mother," I say, keeping my voice gentle. I never know what to do in these moments. Am I to remind her of the present, or live with her in the past? Do I distract her? Do I focus her? There is no map for this, and so I feel my way forward. "I would love to meet my grandparents, but perhaps another day. Today I should like to read with you."

Mother's eyes go wide and she focuses on me. On *me*. Our gazes lock and we see each other, finally, as we are.

I capture this moment and wrap it in amber, keep it tucked safely within the forest of my soul.

"Rosemary," she breathes, and even her voice is sharper, focused.

"Mother," I whisper, pouring all of my heart into that one word. Tears sting my eyes and something buried deep both shatters and heals. There are so many things I want to say to her, so many things I want her to hear. *I love you* hovers on the tip of my tongue. *Always. Forever.*

She opens her mouth to speak and I wait breathlessly to find out what she will say.

Then she blinks, her eyes go soft and the moment is broken.

"Please sit." I keep my voice soft, but there is a scream etched into the walls of my throat.

Thankfully, Mother sits.

A knock rattles the door and I hear it open and then shut. Dream, probably, and I am glad for it. I need a moment to myself. I need to go to my Garden. I need to breathe.

Suddenly, Mother stands again. "We must prepare ourselves, Rosemary."

Dread coils in my stomach.

"What is this, Willow?" her father roared, face ribboned with rage. So terrified was I, I hid behind my mother's legs and trembled.

"She," my mother replied, fire in her voice, "is my daughter."

Aster reached around my mother, grabbed my arm, and yanked me out. The motion twisted my leg and I let out a yowl and fell. He half-dragged me to his feet and dropped me there, between them. "This is what you destroyed us for? This is why you ran off? For this... thing?"

I pulled my legs to my chin and tried to make myself small.

"Rosemary is a girl, Father. Not a thing." Her voice was pitiful and broken. She reached to grab me and Aster rested his hand heavy on my head, keeping me well rooted.

Panic surges and rings clear in my voice when I cry, "Dream, please!"

A moment later, she is there, her pad of paper in hand. I wrap my arms around her waist and bury my face against her. "Give her something else to see, Dream."

Dream begins to sketch.

Mother: "We must prepare ourselves, Rosemary."

A moment later, "Oh, that's lovely."

Dream's hand lands between my shoulders, rubs away the pressure there. "I gave her visions of butterfly-laced fields of lavender, Rosemary."

She lets me cling to her for as long as I need. Finally, I lean back and wipe my eyes. Mother is sitting, her face pointed toward the sunlight, a smile curling her lips. She looks so peaceful.

"Do you mind if I go outside for a moment. I need... I need..."

Dream nods, her eyes soft and full of concern. "Of course. Take whatever time you require."

I feel her watching me as I leave. I am so lost within myself, so worked up and torn down I do not see where I am going. My feet guide me through the Hall of the Gods and into Father Terra's sunlit garden until they can carry me no more. I collapse on a bench beside a lilac bush overcome with blossoms.

The memory falls on me like water and suddenly, I am drowning.

"What is this, Willow?" her father roared, face ribboned with rage. So terrified was I, I hid behind my mother's legs and trembled.

"She," my mother replied, fire in her voice, "is my daughter."

Aster reached around my mother, grabbed my arm, and yanked me out. The motion twisted my leg and I let out a yowl and fell. He half-dragged me to his feet and dropped me there, between them. "This is what you destroyed us for? This is why you ran off? For this... thing?"

I pulled my legs to my chin and tried to make myself small.

"Rosemary is a girl, Father. Not a thing." Her voice was pitiful and broken. She reached to grab me and Aster rested his hand heavy on my head, keeping me well rooted.

He snorted. I felt his gaze on me, burning. His voice, when he spoke, was softer. "The god who sired her has cast you out, hasn't he? And now you come here begging for scraps."

"He didn't cast me out."

Aster laughed winter. "Then he forgot about you."

My mother flinched. The motion was subtle, but it was enough.

"Ah," her father said. "I see the way of it now. You had a child with a god. He promised he would be back to love you until the end of time. Now he is gone, doing whatever it is they do, and you are left with his bastard child. Did he at least tell his temple staff to fill your needs?"

She hesitated. "He did, but—"

"If you didn't want to be judged as a god's castoff and temple-dependent, you should have been more careful."

"Father, I need a job and no one will hire me."

"You're a castoff, Willow!" he shouted, then glanced at me. "If you got rid of the girl, perhaps dumped her in the Narrows, we could... revive some of your reputation. Someone will marry you. Rowan's son is desperate. He's got a head for business. You'd never want for anything."

"No."

His eyes went hard and flat. The air thickened, grew cold.

"Even now," he hissed.

"Even now." She was so small when standing against her father, and yet her bravery made her seem a giant to me.

"Get out."

"Father, please. I miss you. I love you."

"Get out, Willow."

"Please." She was sobbing now. "The temple supplements our income and food, but it isn't enough. Now that he's gone, there are less prayers in circulation, less donations, less tithing. All I need is a job. One lowly job. Just put in a good word for me. You don't have to acknowledge me as your daughter. Please. I am good at sewing. Tell a tailor I will help."

"Get out!"

"We are starving, Father!" She fell to her knees, pressed her hands together in supplication. "No one will hire me!"

"That isn't my problem."

"You told them not to!" my mother wailed. "And now all of Mead- owsweet knows that I am both a castoff and a cast out."

Aster turned his face away. "It isn't my fault you abandoned your own kind."

"You are digging our graves. She is innocent. A girl. If you hate me so much, at least spare her."

"You made your choice."

Mother moaned.

"At least let me see—"

"Your brother will have nothing to do with you."

"Father—"

"Look at the results of everything you accomplished when you dallied with the Divine. You are destitute, your child is broken, her father has abandoned you, and your family is ruined. It is only through the barest shred of good will that Larch didn't sue us for all we were worth after you walked out on your marriage. It's through that family's grace that we have a business at all anymore. That we aren't Narrows-bound as well." His toe prodded me and I shifted. "This creature limps. She grows plants from her

scalp. Have you seen her eyes? Her skin? I cannot have you here, and I will not. I don't know you. Leave."

"Father."

It was not a plea or a question, just a word, and she savored it like she knew that would be the last time she would speak it in this context.

He released my scalp and I rushed to my mother. Her fingers trembled when they touched my shoulder.

Aster breathed deep and closed his eyes. For the beat of a heart, he looked to be in pain. "I have no daughter."

A touch on my knee brings me back to reality, gasping.

There, before me, is a child. Small she is, but certain. Our eyes meet and she smiles.

"Flora!"

I know that voice. I study the child with renewed interest. Her nubby antennae, her dimpled cheeks, the light in her eyes.

"Flora! How can you be so small and so fast? Come out, come out wherever you—"

Belladonna flies around the corner, her light painfully bright. I cover my face with my hands and flinch. A moment later, the world dims and I blink away the assault as my eyes adjust.

"Rosemary," she says.

A smile curls my lips. "Your daughter seems to have found me."

Belladonna's answering smile is as uncertain as mine feels.

"She is beautiful, Belladonna."

Flora toddles across the path and laughs when a butterfly lands on her nose. Belladonna sits on the bench beside me, not touching but so close I can feel her press against the air that surrounds me.

It is enough.

"Thank you," she says.

We sit in comfortable silence, watching Flora play in the morning light. My mother seems so far away now, as do her memories, though it will take a while for this bruise to heal.

"You ache, Rosemary." Belladonna hesitates, then rests her hand on mine. How I wish I could feel her touch through the lace of my gloves.

"I always ache."

"Your heart, not your leg."

"It does," I admit. A tear slides down my cheek. It feels like a betrayal. Thistle sprouts from my crown and my vines pull tight, coiling around my scalp.

"Tell me what hurts."

I shake my head. There is no word for what I am feeling. But she has never needed words to speak, to understand, to hear or be heard.

Another hesitation before Belladonna leans her head against my shoulder.

It is the connection that undoes me. The contact. I have been lost in a desert, and here is water to quench my thirst. For the first time in years, my soul is at peace.

"Rosemary," she whispers. "I did not leave because I stopped loving you."

My breath hitches and I close my eyes.

So many things are ending, and yet I feel hope sprouting in the ruins left by yesterday.

Flora giggles as she chases a grasshopper down the path.

THEN
ROSEMARY

God Aether was silent and careful with me, allowing me to set the pace. He was kind enough to study my limp and cane from the corner of his eye rather than openly staring. Still, he had a fathomless, overwhelming presence. Wherever he walked, people bowed low in reverence and respect, their admiration plain on their faces. Never had I seen someone so beloved.

"Where are we going?" he finally asked after the silence had dragged on long, and then longer still.

I missed Muse. For all he was Divine, he did not frighten me nearly so much as Divine Aether.

"Surely not far," the man beside me mused.

He had no idea. He had no notion of the situation we were entering. He would see where we lived, the room we rented that I barely kept us in by begging and with odd jobs, and he would hate me.

"The temple, I suspect. She knew that was a refuge," he said when I did not answer. He sounded almost chipper, like this could not truly be so bad.

I remembered a temple, many years ago. It had been a grand place, with blue tiled walls and pictures of wind. When we stood within that space, our voices echoed. I thought the sound I could create there to be terribly impressive. However, one day we had gone for our weekly allotment and the priest had met us at the door. "I'm sorry, Willow. He's been gone for so long, we didn't even get a tithe this week."

No, I could not think of that now.

The weight of what was to come nearly broke me. I would give him my mother, and then perhaps I would disappear. I knew how to hide. I knew how to not be seen. I would stray from his wrath, and when the storm calmed, I would leave. Walk into Chaos. See what it had to offer. There would be no standing against an angry god, and I was not fool enough to try.

Perhaps, if I was truly blessed, he would take up my offer of indenture and I could stay close to Mother while working off my debt.

This winter would be the end of her in that clapboard tenement.

I would do anything to help her. Even if it meant losing her. For I knew he loved her, it was writ plainly enough across his features. I, however...

"Divine Aether..." My voice trembled and he stopped and faced me. I blinked away the tears gathering. Sunlight streamed just beyond the portico where we stood, so peaceful despite my torment. Divine Aether's eyes landed on me, and my cheeks flushed and burned. I could not bring myself to look at him. My cane felt like a brand, something pointing out how flawed I truly was. "It is a bit further than that."

"Ah," said he, pointing toward the driveway. "Well then. My man is already waiting with the automobile."

Still, he did not understand. His automobile, fine as it may be, could not traverse the roads where we were going.

This was a mistake, I wanted to shout. *It's all a horrible joke. Forget this. Forget me. Please, just forget. Let me go. Do not make me feel even more shame.*

Minutes later we were standing before a fine black automobile. A young man got out and opened the door wide. I hesitated before entering. I had only seen these contraptions from a distance. I had never been so close. The idea of sitting within one was both frightening and intoxicating. What freedom this vehicle offered, to go anywhere and not ache while doing so...

"Surely you have ridden in such a conveyance before?" God Aether asked, sensing my hesitation. I shook my head and his brow furrowed. "It is safe enough, child."

He helped me inside, his touch gentle, his regard quiet. I thought, if I were not so broken, he might love me, and winced as the knife twisted.

I sat upon a plush leather seat. Divine Aether traded words with the driver and took the seat across from me. After rapping a hand on the window, the engine roared to life, making me jump, my hands gripping the seat.

"It's just the motor," he said. "Loud, yes, but nothing more. Where are we going?"

"Toward the lower city," I said. "Through Divine Rain's arbor."

Again, his brow furrowed, but he only nodded. He rolled down the window between him and the driver and gave him instructions.

The car started making its way down the hill, toward the ocean. Soon, we turned a corner and were well within Divine Rain's arbor where we waited beneath a towering kapok tree, its leaves blotting out the sun. Finally, a barge was brought to ferry our automobile across the wide river.

"What is your name?" he asked after some moments of quiet. The engine had cut and the journey on the barge was peaceful. I sat beside Aether on a wooden bench, watching the arbor slide past.

"Rosemary," I replied, voice a murmur. The river was wide, twisting, as sensuous as a snake through a tropical wonderland.

"Rosemary," he said. That, and only that.

Finally, our barge docked on the other shore and the automobile's engine roared to life again, past shops and cafes, restaurants, and schools. I would have loved to enjoy it, for my only time in Divine Rain's arbor was traveling through it. With my mounting dread as we drew ever nearer our destination, I saw none of what we passed.

Soon, the line of half-present buildings that marked the Narrows loomed before us, ephemeral and foreboding. A wrongness that I felt in my soul. The road became pockmarked, then potholed, and then stopped altogether. Our driver cut the engine.

The quiet was expansive. Not even birds chirped in the canopy, and the trees looked bedraggled and sick, shrouded in the mist of unmaking. Before us, the demarcation of the Narrows looked insubstantial and haunting, an eternal cloudy day, with buildings that were but echoes of their former glory, fading more each time I passed them.

Once, I had heard, the Narrows had been a palatial district, castles and manicured gardens as far as the eye could see. It had hosted the casinos, the gaming and gambling of Meadowsweet, carefully controlled by a denizen of vice if the stories told true.

I could not imagine such a thing.

Even being this close to the border where Chaos fed made me feel as though I was being unmade, too. Affected by proximity alone. Weaker, somehow, as though just being here depleted some of my energy.

Faint wisps of sunlight pierced the canopy. It was still morning, I realized, somewhat shocked that I hadn't lost hours with this drama.

"Here?" God Aether said. Very few people lived this far on the outskirts of Divine Rain's arbor, but I knew he was likely hoping I was one of them.

I turned to finally study this man.

I had done my best not to look at him overmuch while we traveled. His presence was enough to battle on its own, beholding his glory made it that much more difficult. Now, when I rested my eyes upon him, I saw that he had changed in the time since we had left the Hall. He was older, his hair gray, back bent, voice quivering. This far from both his temple and the Hall of the Gods, he aged before my eyes. Now, he looked more old man than god, and his hands trembled where they clasped his knees.

It was shocking, to see him thus. I did not know a god could look so mortal.

The Divine do not travel so far down the hill very often. I had always thought it was because they had abandoned Narrows dwellers, but looking upon Divine Aether, I realized there might be other reasons behind their avoidance.

I shook my head. "Divine Aether, I live in the Narrows."

The driver appeared, opened the door. "I can't drive the rest of the way. The road isn't good enough." Even our driver looked older now, though not by much. He had aged, from a man in his prime to one of middle age, gray at his temples.

Aether glared at the insubstantial edge of the Narrows, the tumbling buildings, the few lonely drunkards staggering around. "Surely you jest."

"This is not a joke, sir. This is my life." He frightened me, yes, but even he could only push me so far.

We got out of the car. I stretched and then strode past him, past the Narrows' insubstantial border and onto the muddy sprawl of streets with Divine Aether a silent presence at my back. I felt surprisingly bad for how this journey would ruin his fine shoes, his pressed pants.

Guilt is a wolf that bites when least expected. For all I had to feel then, what I felt most sharply was guilt about my decision to do this, to bring the gods into my life and meddle in my affairs. Perhaps I could have gone about this another, more subtle way. Perhaps there was a different course for me to take to achieve safety for Mother without bringing all of heaven down upon us.

How can anyone know, in the moment, that they are doing what is best? Perhaps I had just made this worse.

Yet my mother was ill and she needed care. I knew that much.

So Divine Aether followed me into the Narrows, without a thought for his fine shoes or his suit pants.

With each step, we attracted a crowd of beggars and drunkards and wastrels, until I felt as though the entire Narrows was pressed around me, all of them whispering behind their hands. My vines coiled against my scalp and refused to bloom. My leg ached. My soul was raw.

I could not come back here after today. I was too known. I would have to find other quarters of the city to hide if God Aether turned me out. Perhaps Divine Clematis's arbor, which housed many of Meadowsweet's factories and often welcomed those without homes.

Further down the hill we went, and further still, to the last ratty row of tenements that butted up against the docks. The worst part of the Narrows. The part I called home.

Usually loud, full of constantly shouting voices and the chaos of life, the surrounding area was silent as a tomb now. Everyone had stopped, gathered to watch what was transpiring. God Aether, even wearing his wizened mortality, attracted attention. There was no denying what he was.

"I cannot stay here long," he said. He looked uncomfortable, older by the second. "I have no sway in this place. It is untethered to Creation."

"Then we should hurry," I said. I was anxious to be out of there, away from those curious gazes. Ahead of us was my tenement. I swallowed. Stopped.

"Here," he said when I reached the stoop where Landlady met me the day before, the word more curse than question.

I can only imagine how our tenement must have appeared to him. My father, descending from on high to the worst of the Narrows, the poverty-stricken streets where society's boils come to fester. The air was laced with the smell of ichor and smoke and I wondered if it offended him, to know that Divine blood was being used for these ill ends.

I climbed the three steps, opened the door, and made my way down the long hallway. Landlady stood at the end, smoking her ichor-laced cigarette. Her eyes widened when they fell on me, and I heard God Aether growl something low in his throat before pushing past me to face her.

"I can unmake you as easily as you were made, woman." His voice was a low, terrible rasp, his face a breath from hers. "Show me where she is and let me have her, else I will find a way to drag you out of here and I swear on all that I am, I will uncreate you and ensure you feel every agonizing moment of it. You might hold sway in this court, but you and I play different games and you are out of your depth."

For all Landlady had never had a place for the Divine in her life, she looked truly frightened then. Though Divine Aether was nearly mortal and weak with it, he had the power to find a way to get her out of the Narrows, to a place she could be dealt with, and that prospect likely chilled her to her marrow. She had not thought this through.

She trembled and pointed a shaking finger toward my door.

The hall filled with people, watching, waiting. The world hovered on the edge of a knife, eager to bleed.

I opened our cracked door and winced as the hinges screamed in the silence. Aether hissed out a breath, and for the first time, I truly saw our threadbare room, our pallet covered in flea-ridden sheets, and our rickety table.

Wind whistled through the broken window.

Shame is such a tame word for what I felt then, as the reality of my paltry existence crashed upon me. I knew I did not live in a palace, but now, with this imposing man filling the space...

Winter filled my veins and clouds massed along my horizons, churned by a sharp north wind that sliced like a knife.

I fixed my eyes upon our one chair and...

I was all brittle soul and the sound of shatter.

"Divine Aether, please look upon us with kindness." It was perhaps the most desperate prayer I had ever uttered.

His eyes fell on her and...

"Willow." He breathed her name, filled each letter with every raw, wounded, suppurating part of himself. He bled her. He ached her. With a low moan, his mask slipped, and I glimpsed the constellations of his grief.

I know the sound a god makes when he breaks.

It happened with a gasp.

NOW
BELLADONNA

I find myself at my mother's doorstep when dawn's light has barely crested the horizon. The streets are silent and still and the shops are closed, their windows dark. The Blue and Rose Tea Shop on the corner smells of baking bread, but even that door is shut tight against the early hours.

I couldn't sleep, is the truth of it. Too much unfinished business, too many thoughts.

Still, I know my mother's rhythms. I understand her patterns. She is awake in her house now, probably readying herself for the market.

I knock and the door opens wide. Mother stands before me clutching a basket, with Daisy beside her. She has her market dress on, I note. I recognize it from my childhood, though that was years ago and this one looks new. Mother's eyes widen when she sees me and she hands the basket and a list to Daisy. "Go to the market in my stead, please," she says, her voice soft. Timid, almost.

Daisy looks between us, uncertain, and I muster a smile I hope to be reassuring. Finally, she scampers off, leaving us alone.

"Belladonna," Mother says. "I hadn't expected you."

Our eyes meet and hesitation stands between us, all unavoidable, pointy elbows.

"Please," she finally says, stepping aside, "come in."

There is a thin black line of weatherstripping that sits under the front door, dividing inside from outside. A battlefield all its own.

I cross it, invade Mother's territory.

Her house is dark, silent, and still. The door shuts behind me with a snick. Mother leads me into the kitchen and then stands at the counter, tapping it with her nails, her eyes looking anywhere but at me.

Finally, "Oleander."

It is all she says, but it is enough. Fire fills my blood again and old rage comes roiling to the surface. "He showed up at my apartment." I glare at her. "He wanted to talk business."

Mother sighs. "I hope you were kind to him, Belladonna. He is being more than generous to still entertain you, considering..."

She doesn't need to finish the sentence. I can hear her plain enough.

Considering your daughter.

I cut my tongue on the words I long to say. It is no use arguing with her and yet I can feel an argument simmering. Like a spider in a web, Mother will draw me in.

"He has asked me to go into business with him," I say. "I have set up a meeting with my crew to examine the offer."

Mother nods, taps her nails on the counter, and looks out the window.

"He will not require marriage." I sharpen each of those words and aim them at her.

Her lips tighten, pucker almost. "You are young, Belladonna. You will get lonely."

"I do not need to marry Oleander to stem the tide of loneliness."

Her answering chortle is sandpaper against my soul. "Someday, when you are older, you will realize—"

"Mother—"

"I am not telling you to marry him, Belladonna. I am saying

someday you will want a family of your own and you should be open to entertain such notions."

I glare at her. I should not have come. I don't understand why I am surprised when I keep returning to this place and find that nothing has changed.

And still, the knife twists.

Mother does not look at me, but rather over my shoulder. Silence gathers between us and it is then that I truly take it in. The way it stretches and strains, the way it puckers, as though wounded.

My eyes trail across the walls. Over my father's portrait. Over the table.

And stop.

In a pool of sunlight is a small blue stoppered glass bottle. There is liquid inside and a spoon on the saucer next to it. I cross the room and reach to grab it.

"Belladonna—"

"What?" I snap. "Is this something you don't want me to see?"

I lift the vial and study the label, then set it down again. Hemp oil, prescribed from Doctor Rose.

Medicine.

I think back over the times I've visited Mother, how during each of them, I noticed her sallow coloring.

"I have cancer, Belladonna." She chips each of those words off her granite soul and offers them to me, hard and sharp and gleaming.

My breath stills. My heart stops. My mind races.

Suddenly I am fourteen again, realizing my mother had faked an illness to get me into a special, mortals-only private school.

How much of this, I wonder, is real?

And then I shake myself, for not even my mother would lie about something as dire as cancer.

There was a time, in Dawnland, when I became so used to the sounds of bombs falling that I stopped truly noticing them. They became something I learned to exist alongside, a regular part of my life. Panic was my new normal. Worry and waiting defined my days. Would this bomb strike me? End me?

I learned to stop running. There was nowhere to hide.

And then, one day there was silence, and I realized that silence is a certain kind of war bringing a terror all its own. Not all bombs whistle as they fall. Not all grenades explode. Sometimes the rending is quiet.

I close my eyes and grasp the counter, swaying on my feet as the news blows through me.

I think of the glass bombs in Dawnland.

That is how I feel now. Like a bomb, I explode.

I clench the countertop with a white-knuckled grip and keep my voice even, somehow.

"How bad is it?" I finally manage.

Mother shrugs. Still, she will not look at me. "Bad enough. The treatments seem to be doing what they should. My doctors have high hopes."

I drag in a shuddering breath. I need to get away. I need to be alone. I need my own kind of silence.

"Do you understand now, why I wish to see you with someone like Oleander? A man who will elevate this family and stand strong beside you while we usher in this new age? I will not be able to take care of you forever, Belladonna."

She looks at me then, and her eyes are full of tears. They tremble on her lashes.

How much of this is real?

"I only wish to see you cared for, with a family of your own."

I do not know whether to scream or cry.

"I have a family of my own." My words are sharp enough to draw blood.

Finally, she spears me with her gaze. Her eyes are bloodshot. "Sure," she dabs at her nose with a kerchief. "I suppose that is a kind of family."

"Mother—"

She shakes her head. "Don't pity me, Belladonna."

Strange, that she should land there first. Out of all the things I feel, pity is the least of them.

"—Rosemary asked me to marry her, before."

"You left," Mother finally says, "so you must have declined her." She sounds both horrified and relieved. "You've been gone so long, most have likely forgotten about your... proclivities."

I would have thought, after so many years, I would not be so hurt by her callous disregard, but I am.

I am.

"I never answered," I say. "I left before I could."

A pause. "Why?"

"I was being pulled in two different directions, and I love both of you. How was I to choose? To say yes to one would be to hurt the other, and I did not have that kind of strength. So I ran." I level my eyes at her. "I saw an opportunity to perhaps get something *I* wanted, Mother. I knew I would not get the chance to do this again, and so I took it. It was impulsive, but that is what I did."

"And Rosemary?"

I remember Rosemary the other day, distraught in the garden. "I did not leave because I stopped loving her, Mother."

"Oh," Mother sighs. There is so much emotion in that sound. So many layers and textures, I cannot parse it all. If Rosemary was here, she'd understand, but I... I only hear pain. "Oh."

"I will not apologize for who I love." Stiff shoulders, straight spine. Our eyes meet, and it's Mother's gaze that slides away first.

Surrender. Retreat.

For now.

Finally, she sighs and all the tension leaves her. "I love your father," she finally says, her eyes flicking to his portrait. "Even now. Even after a lifetime apart, I still love him." She walks to the wall and stands a few feet before his picture. Studies it. Her eyes lose their focus, and I know she is back, years ago, before it all went wrong. "The sun rose and set in his eyes and I was there for all of it. But I did not understand, Belladonna. I did not understand that it is different, to marry a god. They have no understanding of time, no concept of mortality. They do not know what it is to be temporary, and it is so easy for them to forget. If I can help you avoid that, I will."

I wonder which is worse: to be abandoned or forgotten.

Mother takes a seat at the table. She looks exhausted, and her face goes pale. I eye her medicine bottle. "It helps ease the nausea," she explains.

"Do you need more?"

Another sigh. "Perhaps. Mornings are always hard."

I think of Rosemary. She has certain skills, abilities that could help. "Mother," I say, probing the topic with a delicate touch, "if I could find you help by Divine means—"

"No."

"For your nausea, that is all."

She hesitates, and it's that hesitation that slices, for she would not hesitate if it was not truly awful.

"Are you safe here, alone?"

"My lady cares for me." Her answer feels like a door slamming in my face. "This is my home, Belladonna. If your father returns, this is where he will come. I sit each night at this table, pour myself some wine in the very glass I drank from on our wedding day, and talk to him." She shakes her head. "I'm fine here. I have Daisy."

I have Daisy.

Ah, there's the knife, twisting just so.

She has Daisy.

She does not have me.

How is it possible to both love and loathe someone this profoundly? When it comes to Mother, I am eternally at war.

I brace myself, steady my soul, and reach across the table in invitation. My mother stares at my hand as though she's never seen it before. Then, slowly, she takes it in her own. Silence shatters and the world comes rushing in. I grab her fingers, crushing them in my grip. Her little mew of pain brings me back to the present and I unclench my grasp and smile in apology.

"I would like you to think you have me too, Mother."

"Do I, Belladonna?"

I hesitate. Does she? Do I want her to have me?

The front door of the house opens, saving me from answering. I glance at the clock on the wall. There are things I must do this day. And now, I desperately need solitude.

"Go." Mother stands and Daisy appears, basket laden with fresh food from the market. I see the leafy tops of carrots, a loaf of bread, some berries, a jar of honey. Mother and I make our way to the door and hesitate there, uncertain of how to proceed. Finally, she musters her familiar distain and says, "That color would really look so much better on a dress."

I remember a time, many years ago. Rosemary had been carrying a glass of water when her hip gave out and she tumbled. The glass broke, shards spraying everywhere.

I found her not long after, sitting on the floor of her kitchen, an island lost in a sea of shatter.

"I am tired, Belladonna," Rosemary had said through her tears, the words jagged and raw. "Tired of watching you walk carefully around the wreckage so you do not cut yourself on pieces of me."

I feel like that glass now, scattered across the floor.

"I will be back, Mother." I would bring myself back to visit her... sometime, when I was a little less raw. A little less wounded.

There are things I want from this place. Things I left in my room that mean something to me. Books from my father, letters I'd written to Rosemary and left there, and trinkets from my childhood I want to give to Flora.

I study my mother's gray hair, her wrinkles, her sick pallor.

Time grows ever shorter.

NOW

ISRA

"Tell me, Isra," Divine Forest says, "is my Creation not beautiful?"

We sit in dappled light, high in the canopy of his arbor. Forest watches me sip my coffee with warm amber eyes. The leaves on his crown are almost entirely yellow now, with brown at the tips, and the lines on his face are deeper. I look away and shift my wings to ease the strain on my back. He reminds me too much of Divine Falcon as she neared her end.

We have cafés such as this in Dawnland, though the drink they serve is called ka'kau rather than coffee and is brewed either sweet or spicy. Manab always enjoyed his spicy, while Atheed liked his sweet, and Zahia had preferred hers half and half. My tastes varied, depending on my mood.

Before the war became so bad, Divine Falcon would often sit with us at Ssavathi's Shop in the Imperial District, a favorite haunt of ours. Ssavathi's was near the World Tree, and so was often filled with the wasps and wandering spiders that guarded us coming on or off shift. It was a safe place, a home away from home. Divine Falcon would make herself comfortable and, with eyes half-closed, listen to us talk or argue or debate for hours. She always so loved a lively discourse.

I miss her.

I miss Dawnland.

I miss all of them.

No. I will not think of that now.

Still, Divine Forest is studying me, waiting for me to say something. What had he asked? *Is my Creation not beautiful?*

"It is lovely," I admit with a smile.

It feels like home. Almost.

The wide forest pathway where we sip our drinks is elevated above the mud-churned ground. Bridges and staircases connect the trees, allowing easy commerce and travel to the businesses housed in the upper levels of the forest. On the corner, I see a lift set well within the trunk of a maple. The walkway is full of people scurrying to and fro, merchants shouting prices, food cooking on carts. We sit across from a small arcade where I can see children playing a game involving balls and pins.

A boy with a young hawk's spotted wings careens past, bumping our table. He grins and giggles in apology but is gone in a blink. A moment later, his mother appears, frazzled, her feathers sticking out at odd angles around her flushed neck and face. "Forgive my son, Divine One," she says, pressing a shining, newly minted prayer onto the table. Then, she is gone and the prayer disappears. Goes wherever prayers go. Becomes god food.

Divine Forest hesitates, then reaches forward and touches the spot where his prayer used to be. His eyes lose their light as his smile fades. Wind rustles the golden leaves that line his crown.

I blink and see Divine Falcon again, sitting in the World Tree, at a table much like this one. She presses her hands against the surface and studies them. Her knuckles are swollen and knobby, her skin liver-spotted.

Her voice echoes through the corridors of my mind. "Already, I am diminished."

I know what he is facing. I hear the words he is not saying as he studies the whorls in our table's wood.

I watch as two women, each with rounded mouse ears, approach the café's counter and place their orders. There's a flash of gold as Divine Forest's prayers change hands. I wonder what he feels when his ichor is being used.

In Dawnland, we did not have prayers like those in Meadowsweet to help strength the Divine bond with Chaos. Falcon, instead, created beads, golden and gleaming, with her ichor. She would spend months fashioning them into necklaces and then gift them to each monarch when they hatched. It began as a symbol of the pact between us: she would Create and we would watch over that which she Created. Over time, however, our necklaces became a symbol of our imperial lineage.

Toward the end, I had taken mine off and hung it on some ivy clinging to my bedroom wall. It did nothing more than remind me of all I had lost. The imperial family had been destroyed, and Divine Falcon was edging toward her rest. There seemed no reason to carry it anymore.

I left it there, with three beads still on the chain. I wish I had it now. I would gift it to Divine Forest so he might have at least part of his sister with him.

"I miss her," I whisper.

His eyes find mine, warm and soft, and he reaches across the table and clasps my hand. "I do too," he says, then straightens. "Come with me, Isra. I have requested your presence today because there is some-thing I wish to show you."

The space around us stills as Divine Forest makes to leave. A few bow, a few tip their hats, some just smile. Everyone, however, acknowledges him. It is easy to tell from their warm regard that Forest is well loved in his arbor. It should have been thus for Divine Falcon.

Instead, there were no bows or tipped hats. No smiles and little regard.

I will always carry the weight of that in my soul.

I follow him as he moves through his arbor, along the walkways, his feet ringing on the boards, and down to the hard-packed forest floor. We tread on pathways that wind through towering, mist-shrouded redwood trees. The crowd parts around us like water around a stone. Forest moves at a quick pace, determined, his jaw clenched, his shoulders stiff, as though whatever he is about to show me requires a certain amount of will to face.

I realize I only saw the barest bit of his Creation when I visited with Belladonna. He leads me deeper into his arbor and I watch as life unfolds before me: schools carved out of the trunks of trees, playgrounds with brightly painted equipment, grocery stores, theaters, libraries, an open-air market set next to a lake flush with recreational boats and picnicking families. Entire trees are carved into towering apartment buildings with clothes lines strung between windows. We pass a bakery set within an oak tree, the scent of fresh bread wafts through its open door. Overhead, all around, the walkways are full of residents. So much life. This is a world all its own.

Dawnland was like this once.

Now, it is a ruin.

Manab. Atheed. I rub a fist over my heart.

Finally, Forest stops at the edge of a wide, sun-dappled glade filled with knee-high grass and poppies sprinkled throughout like rubies. A narrow, winding path bisects this place, lined with purple lace flowers and clumps of yarrow. My eyes follow it, past a few large boulders, and down to the center where...

I gasp.

For there, before me, in a pool of lemon-yellow light is a towering cedar tree, with branches so wide they nearly blot out the sun. Green tufts of pine shiver in the breeze, casting shadows across the glade as the wind toys with them. The warm, brown trunk is large and craggy. It would take hours to circle it. Vines climb up a trunk covered with red-capped mushrooms and a profusion of flowers, sprays of purple, bursts of red. In the center of it all is a brilliant emerald door with wrought iron adornments along the edges.

I know this place.

I know it like I know my own heart.

And yet, I am acutely aware that while this is similar to the World Tree I call home, it is not, in fact, my home. The tree in Dawnland takes days to span, not hours, and it climbs so tall, no one has ever reached its top. Atheed used to tell a story about how the stars truly rest in the World Tree's highest branches.

Our doors were painted monarch orange, not emerald.

But the shape is similar, the form is right. It is so close to what I know. I look at that tree, and I see home. I feel... *home*.

And yet, I am not home.

Therein lies the knife.

Divine Forest smiles at me, a sad, knowing thing, and then strides toward a boulder beside the path not far ahead and perches himself upon it. He does not face me, and I sense he is offering me privacy, a moment to accept what I am seeing before we discuss it.

I take my time beholding the wonder that is before me and when I am ready, I lift my wings high and make my way to Divine Forest. The air is redolent with the scent of nearby wildflowers and hunger churns in me. I have not allowed myself much nectar recently, and I feel that now, the loss of my nourishment and the need for more.

"This," Forest says when I reach him, "is where I bound myself to Chaos."

It is as though cold water has been dumped on me. I blink and the past is merging with the present. I am with Divine Falcon again. I am with Divine Forest now. I am home. I am not. My knees go weak and my wings flap as I ease myself to the stone beside Divine Forest. His loamy hand lands firm on my shoulder.

"Falcon and I spent many eternities here learning the ways of Creation. She set about Creating birds and butterflies and bees and I focused on forests and meadows and..." he waves a hand in the air as though it is nothing. Then, "She always had a fascination with this tree."

"Why?"

"She said it bridged the gulf between the land and the sky."

I remember a time, not long before Divine Falcon found her rest. A storm had just cleared and the air was full of sun-speared mist. "You are a child of the land and the sky," she had said as she studied departing clouds, "and forever you shall be torn between the two."

I suppose we were not so very different from the tree we called home.

"It was not long after Divine Falcon went forth to Create that I decided to bind myself to Chaos. It was this place, where I felt closest to my sister, that drew me."

He goes silent and I wonder what pieces of himself he sacrificed to Chaos to allow him to Create all of this.

"I have bartered pieces of my soul for everything you see. There is not much left of me, Isra. I am fading. It is happening faster now, with Falcon gone." A bird calls from a branch of Forest's tree. A swallowtail butterfly spirals past me, bright as summer.

This day is too beautiful to be so filled with such pain.

"I have no children, no spouse. I grow ever more tired, ever more depleted." He studies his tree. "With you here, I feel closer to Falcon, more prepared to face this transition."

Dread coils in my gut. I hear Divine Falcon, when she first told us of her fading. "You will be my caretakers, at the last." We had no notion of just how much it would hurt.

Nothing ever ends, it only changes shape.

"Will you sit beside me at the last, Isra?" Forest asks. There is desperation in his voice, as though everything that happens next will hinge on my answer. "Will you help ease me through this transition, now that I go to Sustain all I have Created?"

Though I know those words are coming, they still wrap around my soul and squeeze. Watching Divine Falcon fade was an agony I wish to never relive. She had been our protector, our safety, the only family we had left. I remember days with Manab watching out the window for enemy soldiers while Atheed and I tended to Divine Falcon.

My soul is riddled by shrapnel and bullet holes.

War fills my dreams.

Forest is not just asking me to keep him company, he's asking me to add another wound to my tally when the ones I already have are not yet healed.

For a moment, the forest fades and I am back in Dawnland. A bomb whistles and terror strikes me, both familiar and horrifying.

Sweat beads my brow and my heart races. I look up, expecting to see something falling, expecting to wonder where it will land, but the sky is clear and there are no bombs. I am not in Dawnland, but Meadowsweet. Here, there is no war, save that which lives within each of us.

I can't go back there. I can't relive that. I am not strong enough.

I turn to face him, to tell him... something... but stop when I meet his sad eyes.

I have no children, no spouse.

No one deserves to be alone at the last.

Not for the first time, I wish my brothers were here. I think they would appreciate this moment, the ability to do this all over again. But the right way this time, in a Creation that is at peace rather than war.

And that, I suppose, is the thought that makes up my mind. Perhaps, by honoring Divine Forest, I will also be honoring Divine Falcon.

"Will you... will you do this, Isra?"

Will you do this?

With a sigh, I straighten my spine, throw back my shoulders, and set myself upon the path.

"Divine Forest," I say, reaching over to clasp his hand in mine, "I would be honored to love you into the last, and beyond."

A breath pushes out of his lungs, so profound is it, the grasses around us sway from the force of it. "Thank you."

NOW
ROSEMARY

I am in Father Terra's garden when she finds me. It is night, the moon is full and I am drunk on its shine.

"You glory in the dark," Belladonna says, emerging from around the corner. A smile curls the edges of her lips, just the hint of one but I feel it all the same. Like summer on my soul.

Her glow is faint and I realize that whether she knows it yet or not, her Divinity is changing as well. I see mortality shivering about the edges of her, the woman hidden beneath Mother Sol's light.

No, I will not think about this tonight.

I have come here to run away from all the dark, heavy things waiting for me in the Hall of the Gods, from my father's advancing age and Dream's ever-increasing disquiet.

From myself.

And Belladonna, I know, is running as well.

Strange how we find each other when we most need sanctuary.

"I must be away from here tonight. I need to forget, Rosemary. For one night, I need to be young and carefree and..." She clears her throat. "Come to the beach with me?"

The night is thick and the stars spin in their midnight abode, yet she is all I can see, her smile, the way her eyes gleam even in the darkness.

I nod, and Belladonna's laugh sounds like the answer to a question I didn't know I've been asking. She tucks her hands in her pockets and leads me to the large, circular driveway, where there are usually automobiles with drivers waiting at all hours, anxious to carry us to where we need to go, for an extra prayer or two.

"To your arb—" one driver, a man with mushrooms growing from his crown, starts to ask.

I cut him off with a wave of my hand. I do not want Belladonna to find out I am bound to Chaos from a driver she does not know. It should be me who tells her and that... that is a conversation I am not sure I am ready for yet.

Every day I am a little less Divine. Every day I hurt a bit more, I am a bit older, my heartbeat feels ever more important. I do not want Belladonna to worry about me. Not when she is trying so hard to smile.

"To the beach, please." I press two prayers into his hand. Then I think, because which beach? I would like to be close to my arbor, and yet I am not sure I am ready to show Belladonna that part of myself yet. "Silent Sand," I finally say. It is well within Father Luna's district and shares a border with my arbor. As well as being small and intimate, it is easier for me to navigate. The sand is harder there, the boardwalks are longer.

The man opens the door for us and we pile in. Soon the motor is roaring to life, and we are on our way.

Our driver heads toward the beach through Divine Muse's arbor, where no two streets are the same. We turn a corner and drive down a narrow lane of glass blowers living in their cunningly wrought glass houses, each different than the next. Then, a street of musicians and crowds dancing on the sidewalks outside of speakeasies, doors flung open to welcome the dark, and another of play houses with their lights on and lines of people waiting outside in their finest evening wear. Finally, we drive past a square of fiber artists with their weavings adorning every wall. Divine Muse's arbor is a place of art halls, galleries, exhibits, plays, moving pictures, and whatever kind of creative outlet one can imagine, where art is celebrated and done out in the open. It is all colors, sound, and chaos, a place I love for how alive and vibrant it is.

Belladonna, however, stiffens as we travel through it, as though being here pains her. It is a true assault on the senses and I realize my error. I never would have made the mistake of bringing her here years ago. My mood darkens as I lose some of my humor.

"Don't," Belladonna says. She reaches for me and then stops herself. Her hand falls to the pleat on her trousers and she toys with it. "Don't think about what was. Only think about what is. Live in this moment with me, Rosemary. Please. For tonight, let us just be *us*."

Us.

How sweet that word is. It sings through me.

"Okay," I whisper, then run my fingers along my arm, a gesture from our youth. It began when I realized how touch-averse Belladonna truly is, and yet how much she longs for contact. Never wanting to harm her, I came up with this sign. It is subtle and unobtrusive and each time I make it, she knows that in my soul, I am holding her close.

Belladonna sees the gesture and her eyes go wide. "You remember!"

"Of course I remember." How could I forget? Her every breath is imprinted on my soul.

Finally, we pull up to the shore. Our man opens the door. "Need me to wait?"

"No," I say. "Thank you." There are public telephones all around. We are in Muse's district still, though a quieter part of it. The buildings that line the beach are squat and square, nothing special. They are filled studios rented by those who prefer quiet when they create. It is no wonder that Belladonna has always loved this part of the city.

Our driver nods, his mushrooms bouncing. Then he gets in the automobile and drives away.

Belladonna smiles and then turns toward the ocean. Her footsteps on the boardwalk ring hollow. She walks slow, close enough if I should need help, but far enough to leave me with my thoughts. The sea breeze tosses her sun-spun hair and toys with her sports jacket. She shoves her hands in her trouser pockets and glances back at me before descending the three stairs to the beach. "Are you coming, Rosemary?"

I would follow her anywhere.

There is a ramp beside the stairs and Belladonna waits for me at the bottom. My hip grinds with each step sending lightning through my body. I clench my molars around a moan. Ramps have never bothered me before, but now each step I take makes me gasp. Belladonna's eyes cloud and I hate my body for ruining this moment.

This is mortality, a voice whispers in the back of my mind. *It is grinding bones. It is pain.*

"I'm sorry," I whisper when I reach her side. I grasp my cane and lean against the ramp's railing to catch my breath. My eyes fill with hot tears. Suddenly this night has claws.

"Whatever are you sorry for, Rosemary?" Belladonna's voice is soft, nearly lost by the roar of the surf at her back.

For my pain, I want to say.

For being a burden.

For ruining this moment.

"Beloved"—her smile is soft—"you do not need to ache alone."

Simple are her words, and yet they spear my soul. Our eyes meet, and...

I am falling in love all over again.

Even now.

Especially now.

"We can turn around, call a car if you would like." She puts a foot on the ramp, and I still her, my hand hovering an inch above her arm, so close to touching.

"I want to be here, Belladonna."

Her eyes ask me if I am certain and I nod.

The ocean is not so far. I kick off my sandals and Belladonna leans down and loops them around her fingers, then she takes off her white wingtip shoes and loops them over the fingers of her other hand. The sand is soft between my toes and painted silver with Father Luna's touch. It grows harder the closer we get to the ocean, which is easier for me to manage, barely.

Soon, we are at the shore. Water washes over my feet and I am bathed in sea spray. Laughing, I spread my arms wide while Belladonna shouts, one long, low, wordless roar.

Then,

Quiet.

A pause.

This breathless silence.

The sea throbbing, the moon shining, the stars... Oh, those glorious stars.

I am drunk on this night. Lost in this moment.

A golden thread of sweet agony stitches through me. It hurts to love this profoundly.

"Rosemary." She breathes my name as though it is a prayer.

"Belladonna," I answer, and the ocean rises like the beat of my heart.

Her smile slips and she draws nearer, close enough I can feel the heat of her body, even if we are not touching. She is wearing a tie and I grab onto the end of it, feel the silk slip through my fingers.

Belladonna studies me and then licks her lips. Her mood changes, becomes serious. "My mother had arranged for me to marry. It was to merge businesses with—"

"Oleander." My cousin from my mother's side. Of course. He ran the Meadowsweet side of this ferrying business, putting up ships when they were in port, and acting as a fence between ferriers and merchants. Why did I not see it sooner?

"It was all but done, Rosemary. Mother had signed the papers, the whole thing had been arranged. She'd even ordered stationery. It was so far planned, she had bought a dress for me to wear. All she was lacking was the bride."

And I... I had...

"And then you asked me to marry you, and I was torn. Pulled in two different directions: my mother on the one and you on the other. Suddenly I could not breathe. All I could think was how desperately I wanted a child."

"And you did not think you could come to me with this?" The cracks in my soul can be heard in my voice.

"It wasn't... it wasn't like that, Rosemary." She turns away from me, crosses her arms, closes herself off. "Living with my mother was not easy. I learned, when I was very young, to never speak of the things I truly wanted for she ever followed the scent of my desire and twisted all she touched."

Belladonna is holding herself now, staring across the sea. I have never seen her look so vulnerable, as though she is seconds away from rupture.

"My father had collected books as he ferried. A few of those were on Dawnland. I read of their fertility sciences, far more advanced than anything in Meadowsweet. Suddenly I found myself at a crossroads. I knew if I stayed, I would have to deal with my mother, who would never understand—"

"And I?"

This story wounds. How many ways can a soul bruise? It seems I am determined to count them all. Here is a new one, fresh-pressed, turning my sky into a stormscape.

Belladonna sighs and turns to face me. "I knew you would never leave Meadowsweet, Rosemary. I thought that I was sparing you from having to make the same kind of decision I was suffering through. I wrote you so many letters, trying to explain."

"I have spent my life feeling unworthy of love. Being with you was the first time I truly felt—" My breath hitches. A sob claws its way up my throat. "And then you left."

It destroyed me, to realize how easily I could be forgotten.

"I'm sorry," she sobs. "I did this all wrong. I acted without think-ing. I brought you so much pain."

There was a time, not long after Belladonna left, when I had found succor in Father Terra's arms. Moss had grown across his chest to pillow my cheek, and briar roses bloomed along the notches of his spine.

"What troubles you so?" he had asked.

"Father Terra, I love too—"

"You love, Rosemary," he whispered low in my ear. His voice rolled through me like boulders down a mountainside. "You love. That does not make you weak."

"I abandoned you," Belladonna says, her voice pitched to carry against the waves. "And I will never stop apologizing for that."

Everyone leaves, a voice whispers in my mind. *She already left once. She will leave again.*

But what if she doesn't? another responds.

"I will spend my life trying to make this right, Rosemary. I hurt you in so many different ways and I will never forgive myself for that." Belladonna hesitates and uncertainty fills her eyes. "But I will never apologize for Flora."

"I would never expect you to." Nor would I want such a thing. Flora is a gift.

Belladonna's voice fades, and I stare out at the sea, at the reflec-tion of the moon on the tempestuous water.

"Is there anything left of us, Rosemary?"

It would be so easy for me to say yes, to open my arms to her and find myself home again. So easy to pick up where we left off.

But we are not the people we used to be.

This beach borders my arbor. If I want there to be any future to us, I must show her that part of me. And yet, the very notion sends fear through my bones. What if she sees what I have Created and finds it lacking? I picture her looking across my arbor, disappoint-ment etched on her features, or polite acceptance.

I cannot decide which will be worse.

Still, it is time.

On this heady, heavy night.

"Beloved," I say, my voice filled with regret. With dread. She will never know the effort it takes to be this vulnerable and remain standing. "There is something I must show you."

She studies me. Her hesitation draws long, and longer still.

"You think I will not love you after I see whatever this is."

I sigh and shrug. There is no use hiding from her. She has always seen me.

"I love you on purpose, Rosemary."

That is all she says, and yet I understand her well enough. Love is a choice as well as an emotion, and she made hers.

THEN

ROSEMARY

Mother roused when Divine Aether held her in his arms. She opened her eyes and focused on him, knew him in a way she only rarely knew me anymore. When she reached out and cradled his face, he closed his eyes and cried stars.

And I...

I unraveled.

How long had it been since she had last touched my face like that?

"Beloved," she whispered, her voice so sweet, the way I remembered her speaking to me when I was younger. "You've returned."

"Of course I did," God Aether replied, burying his face in her hair. Inhaling her. "I swore I would."

"I thought you had forgotten me."

"You are like the moon, Willow. I see you even when I am not looking."

The world gathered outside our open door, watching this private reunion. I witnessed Divine Aether spilling starlight tears across our tiny tenement, illuminating it like the night sky. He pressed his forehead against Mother's and whispered something. Mother clutched his shirt and pulled him close, and then closer.

Their lips met, a sweet, sacred touch.

I thought I knew what it was to feel deeply. That by the time I had reached the ripe age of twelve, there was not so much in the world that could surprise me.

I was wrong.

I watched them kiss, and I was overcome. Mother knew him. Divine Aether knew her. The world looked on and I... I was...

Forgotten.

Beloved, she called him, so easily when my name often came to her tongue only after a struggle with memory. They formed a world, the two of them, bodies pressed together, breaths mingling. There was no room in there for three.

I was a child. All I saw was absence.

Pain is not a word that encompasses the fullness of that moment. To be riven, sundered, split, the agony of my soul came pouring out, hot as lava, and I not a strong enough vessel for it.

I watched that reunion for as long as my heart could handle. Watched, as each moment they drew ever closer and I further away. Until finally, I could no longer breathe through my pain, or see through my tears. With one last look at the couple, their soft smiles, I turned my back on them.

I could be there no longer. There is only so much a child can handle.

So I ran. I wove through the crowd, disappearing out the back door and into the Narrows. It would be easier to be alone, to let them have each other. To hide myself in one of the arbors of Meadowsweet and lick my wounds.

They did not need me.

No one—not even Landlady's boys hired to trail me—noticed me leave, and perhaps that was the saddest part of the whole affair.

I took to the streets, not noticing where I was going as tears spilled down my cheeks. My leg was an ache, a low throb that ended somewhere near my heart.

I begged for a paltry meal at lunch, and then made my way toward Divine Clematis's arbor. It was not too far, part of Father Terra's quarter. Once I was away from Landlady's turf, I breathed easier. My stomach growled, but I was used to that. Later, toward night, I realized my vines were attracting too much attention here, and so I stole a bit of cloth from someone's line and wrapped it around my hair, hiding what I could.

Night came with its damp and chill. I huddled in an alleyway and tried to keep from being seen. The moon cut a path of silver through the dark and I reached a hand out, as though I might grasp it.

I did not know then what I know now. The moon sees all its light touches.

It was Divine Muse who found me, looking just as ancient and wizened as Divine Aether had earlier. I had not slept and was aware of each sound, but still I did not hear him. He crept to me with a whisper of motion, more cat than man.

"Sweet child," he whispered in his quivering old man's voice. He pulled me into his lap and wrapped his arms around me, and I clung on tight.

One simple touch was all it took for all of my brittle to break. I sobbed against him, curling myself small as a child, wet his shirt with my tears.

He did not speak, just held me through my storm, tugged the kerchief off my head, and ran his hands through my vines. I was covered in mud and dirty from top to bottom, exhausted, my soul in turmoil. Still, he was there, giving me succor from the gale.

When I calmed enough to speak, he said, "I was worried."

Perhaps it was the gentle tone of those words that shook me. Regardless, I fell apart again. He stroked my back through the worst of it.

"Does it surprise you to know there are people in this world who care, Rosemary? That when you disappeared, Divine Aether was frantic, and it was Father Luna who talked him down from unmaking the Narrows piece by piece in an effort to seek you out? Father Luna so desired to find you, to ease your aches, but he cannot survive leaving his Sacred Space, so I said I would go forth into the night and discover where you had hidden yourself for the thought of you out here, alone, turns my stomach. Divine Dream has been pacing the halls, chewing her nails to the quick. Your mother has been—"

"Divine Aether will care for her."

How well I had taken to my sorrow.

"Why did you run, niece?"

I sat up, sniffled. Mud squelched as I moved.

"What need have they of me when they have each other?"

I had no more tears to give. My body had wrung itself dry. Now, my soul was on fire, a low, agonizing burn.

"What will you do?" Muse's voice was soft, his rheumy eyes focused on me.

I shrugged. "Disappear, I suppose. To live. To survive. I will make my way."

"Hmm," he said. "Like you have so far? You, with your few years, have put a roof over your heads, fed both of you, kept yourselves safe enough. I'm sure you could survive out here and do well in this jungle if you desired, but Rosemary, you could have so much more."

Something shifted low in my soul, a certain truth aching to be breathed into being.

"I want love." The words came blazing out from between my lips like a forest fire. Not even the stars burned so bright in their firmament. "I want to be loved and... and I want to be seen. To have someone speak my name, and not by accident."

I did not know this would hurt so much. I did not even know my father and still, his lack of regard wounded.

Muse studied me in the low light. The moons in his eyes ceased their spinning and hung still, suspended. His hair was gray and his face lined, but he wore his mortality well.

"Rosemary," he whispered, "I will never speak your name on accident and I love you with my whole heart."

I thought I was done crying, but my sob was so loud, someone down the way leant out the window and shouted, "Would you shut up! People here are trying to sleep!" My sob turned into a strangled, barking laugh and even Muse chuckled, then went still.

"You have spent your life looking for succor from the storm. I understand that much, Rosemary. And I know a lot has changed for you recently." A pause. "I offer you my temple, my hallowed halls as a place for you to rest your weary soul, a refuge to pause and let these changes settle within you. Will you accept that? Will you wait before you make any decisions?"

I did not answer.

He sucked in a breath. "Truthfully, I cannot abide the idea of you out here, in the mud and filth. I had hoped... I asked Goddess Dream to meet us there, with a bath and a meal."

"And Divine Aether? My mother?"

"Your mother is being attended to by a doctor even as we speak. Divine Aether will grant you time. But Rosemary, your mother misses you and she worries. Aether... I have never seen him in such a state."

I let his words sink through my skin, to my bone, to my marrow, and heard the truth in them, as well as the need.

I mattered. To someone, suddenly, I mattered.

"I will do this," I said. My stomach growled its agreement.

Muse stood and held a hand out to me. With a grin, he led me up the hill to where an automobile waited, then bid me wait while he stretched a blanket out on the seat so I would not get the leather muddy. A few minutes later, we were driving through Divine Muse's arbor to the Grand Meadowsweet Theater, which doubled as his high temple, the place where he bound himself to Chaos.

The Theater was open to all in Meadowsweet, regardless of their station or the arbor they called home. Divine Muse organized plays and performances there, as well as art shows, and admission cost but a prayer, for those who could afford it, though no one was ever turned away. There were stairs to the front door, yet he'd also thoughtfully built a ramp to the side of them, and I walked it slowly, my body a keening of agony with each step. My cane groaned under my weight.

Divine Dream waited for us at the front door, relief evident as she spied me. "Rosemary," she said. "I was so worried." There was a luster about her I learned to recognize over the years, owing to the night and the dreams filling it. Divine Muse appeared beside me, smiling with his divinity riding high. No more old bent man. Now the god had risen beneath his skin.

"Will you see her bathed and fed, Dream? I must go to the Hall and tell Father Luna and God Aether what happened." He turned his attention on me, and even in my morose state, I could not hide from his intoxicating smile. Like the sun, it brought me to life. Jasmine bloomed in my mud-covered vines, fed from the wellspring of my burgeoning hope. Perhaps, with God Muse beside me, all would be well.

Perhaps his love would be enough.

"Of course," she said. "I had your caretaker draw a bath already, and a meal is also waiting. I don't know why you are so cross with her, Muse. Lavender is a perfectly lovely woman."

"She loves everyone but me." But there was a glint in his eyes that told me he was joking. He winked at me. "Lavender loves control, Rosemary, and does not like when I am around to wrest it from her."

"Oh hush," Dream replied. "This child doesn't need to know about your personal drama. Come inside, Rosemary."

Muse kissed my cheek and then disappeared into the dark while Dream led me inside.

The Theater was a grand place; a huge crystal chandelier hung from the ceiling and the floor was polished marble, with a curving, red-carpeted staircase to either side of the foyer leading to the upper levels. Signs here and there pointed to various art exhibits or theater seating. Bathrooms were well marked, and everything was so clean it fairly glowed.

A woman bustled to us, more mortal than divine. She had a round, comely shape and gray hair. Her eyes, when they found me, were filled with concern. Lavender, I assumed. She did not look frightening.

"Come along, child. I've got a nice bath drawn and some food made up. I'm afraid there's no saving that dress or those shoes, but we'll get you right in no time." She wrapped her arms around me and tugged me toward a back room full of steam and the scent of soap.

She gracefully pretended to not notice my tears.

NOW

BELLADONNA

Rosemary leads me away from Silent Sand Beach to the road that lines the boardwalk. It is empty this night, and quiet. The night would be peaceful if it was not for the foreboding that hovers between us. Rosemary is clenched, nervous.

Whatever we are walking toward frightens her, and so it frightens me.

I want to stop this. Turn around. Go back to where we were an hour ago, laughing and carefree. No past, no pain, only now.

I want to dash forward. *Show me your secrets, Beloved. Let me see the darkest recesses of your soul.*

I am, as ever, torn.

She leads me forward, silent as the grave, her limp pronounced, her spine stiff. Every line of her is pain, and if I could but ease her ache. The vines of her hair have curled tight around her scalp, no flowers blooming. The woman I had been with is gone. Before me is someone else entirely.

It happens slowly, and then all at once.

I notice, first, the buildings surrounding us. Different now. Rounder, somehow. Leafier? Are there flowers growing from those planter-shaped tenements? Flowers tall as trees, with petals so wide, they could serve as umbrellas in a rainstorm, or shade on a hot day?

"Rosemary," I say. "What is this?"

And that is when I see her, and I know. For Rosemary...

Rosemary is blooming. Her skin is moon-bright and glowing, and the nebulas in her eyes cast a pink glow wherever she looks. It is her hair that captures my attention, though, for her vines are long and a profusion of flowers so numerous they look heavy enough to break her back are arrayed along their lengths. Yet Rosemary wears them as though they weigh nothing. As though they are the lightest part of her.

She has on her ever-present gloves, but here, in this place, nothing can keep her from her nature and whatever her hands touch becomes covered in flowers. Her cane blooms a riot and ivy wraps from it, around her hand and up her arm to keep her steady. My breath catches. She is beautiful. Every piece of her. Beautiful in a way I had not known beauty could exist. Divinity pours from her, pulses in a steady heartbeat, a lullaby for dreamers.

"Rosemary," I say again, my words a whisper.

She leads me forward. Still limping, I notice. Still aching.

She does not answer me, so I follow and take in the buildings as we progress.

Each one is a planting pot, the outside walls are filled with apartments, and within, instead of a courtyard, are the flowers, or grapes, or berries, or fruit trees, or... So tall, these plants grow, they look to scrape the sky. We pass an apartment building crafted from a purple planting pot, from its center grows a resplendent bush. Blueberries as large as my hand grow in clumps along willowy branches.

None of the buildings have stairs, I notice. Ramps, everywhere.

Oh, Rosemary. She has created for herself a world, and she can access all of it.

A row of flowers lines each street, and on the corner of every block is a garden, full of ripe and ready produce, cut and come again.

This is paradise. This makes the rest of Meadowsweet look like a desert. This... this living garden. This bountiful harvest. This goddess of giving.

We arrive at a small, rectangular plot, inconspicuous and understated, save for the Divinity I feel wrapping around me in welcome and I know that this is where Rosemary's purest self resides. Here, finally, I am seeing *her*.

There is a small picket fence and she opens the gate and bids me enter her temple.

It is then that I notice the outline of a foundation marking this garden, large enough to fit a tenement.

"Rosemary, what is this place?"

"This, Belladonna," she says, easing herself onto a small stone bench with a grunt. It is set well within an arched trellis covered with long red pole beans and cucumbers. "This is where I lived before I met my father. After... after my mother became unwell. This is where it all began."

"What happened? How... how did it get to be yours?"

What else can I say? It is rare for second generation Divine to bind themselves to Chaos, and Rosemary is younger than most who would dare attempt such a thing. Still, she had done it. Something drove her to do this.

I study my hands.

She is a goddess in truth now, with a world to rule over that is all her own. I look up, expecting to see her differently, but when our eyes meet, she is still my Rosemary. Still as familiar to me as my own heart.

She shifts, uncomfortable. How had I not known she had all of this inside her?

"After you left, I was... alone. Bereft. Lost. You took my soul with you, Belladonna. Part of it, at least, and I... I was rudderless and I needed, desperately, somewhere to call my own. Somewhere I would belong, no matter what. I wanted to matter, Belladonna, to somebody."

"You always mattered to me, Rosemary."

"But not enough for you to stay." She sighs and plucks a flower from her hair. Overhead, the moon hangs like a pearl in that jewel box of a sky. "I was desperate and wounded and not thinking. I formed this bond because I was devoured by loneliness. I came here, to the tenement where I was raised, found my old room—thankfully with no one in it—and fell to the floor. I called to Creation and—"

And then, the thought strikes me. Creation requires bargaining with Chaos. She offered up pieces of herself for everything I see, sacrificed bits of soul. Like the night sky, she is shot through with starlight.

Oh, Rosemary.

"I offered Chaos my heart, Belladonna, at first. I thought, if I could gift it my heart, then perhaps I would no longer drown in this sea of emotion. But Chaos did not want my heart."

"Then I tried specific emotions. Will you take from me my love? My pain? My anger? My..."

Her voice trails off. She runs her hand along a pale pink rose growing from the shaft of her cane.

"My father once told me that Divinity is just Chaos given purpose. If we listen hard enough, Chaos will tell us what it wants. So I listened. Chaos did not want my heart, for I would need that to Create and Create well. It did not want those emotions. So, I offered up pieces of myself and Chaos rejected one after the next. I thought, perhaps, I was not worthy."

"What did you end up offering, Rosemary, to establish this bond?"

Rosemary's breath shudders out of her. "Chaos wanted to experience an emotion. Something powerful." She hesitates and how I long to bridge the gulf between us, to wrap my arms around her and hold her so she hears the beat of my heart and might know she is not alone, will never be alone again.

Suddenly, Rosemary crumbles. Starburst tears spill down her cheeks and her shoulders shake. She covers her face with her hands and moans. I rub the space between her shoulders and give her what time she needs to compose herself.

"You left and I was... I was alone and ruined. I thought perhaps I could ease this ache and give Chaos something it wanted at the same time." Her words are muffled behind her palms, but I hear them well enough. "I let Chaos experience any hope I had of you returning."

I squeeze my eyes closed. I do not know what I am feeling, but it hurts.

"And now you are here and I... I broke when you left, Belladonna, and I did not heal right. This—you—do not yet feel real."

I take in the majesty of the world around me, this Creation sprung from the flotsam and jetsam of Rosemary's soul.

Beauty from pain. Creation from agony.

The fact that I had driven her to this point.

Forgive me, Rosemary. Forgive me.

I steady myself and reach toward her, lace our fingers together.

"You come here and you see a garden, beautiful and blooming, but what this is, Belladonna, is a Creation watered by pain. I have unmade the Narrows piece by piece, and I rebuilt it using the stuff of my soul. Part of me already resides in Chaos to Sustain everything you see. Now, I come to this place so I can feel what it is to be whole."

I remember a time, long ago, sitting in Father Terra's garden beside a rosebush, heavy with blooms. "How is it anything fragile survives?" I had asked.

"Even porcelain gains a cutting edge," Rosemary had replied, "if shattered."

She is soft, my beloved, and yet there are edges to her now, a certain sharpness that did not exist before.

"I am fading, Belladonna." She whispers the words. "It started not long ago, but it is happening. Every day, I am a little less Divine. Every day, this place takes a bit more of me, and I feel less of it. My mortality is waxing, and my pain—" She clamps her lips shut and shakes her head. Her eyes fill with unshed tears.

Finally, she whispers again, "There is so much pain."

I stiffen and go cold. I remember Divine Falcon—her gray hair, her wrinkles—and cannot help the sob that steals past my lips. The world cannot be this unjust. I cannot get Rosemary back only to lose her so soon.

"My father thinks I will survive it. I am middle-aged by mortal standards and my arbor is still young. I have not offered so much of myself to Chaos yet. I will... I will live the remainder of my days as a mortal and I will ache."

A low wail flees past her lips, such a shredded, painful sound. "I am watching them fade, Belladonna, by increments. All of them. My father, my uncles, my grandparents. One day my father will lay down, exhausted, and he will not get up again. Each breath I take brings that moment closer.

"He tells me this is for the best. This was always how it was meant to be. 'We did not Create this reality for us.' He asks me to live, to experience, to do, to be, but how can I? How can I... breathe... when I have no air? My Divinity is fading, true, but they are ending. They will wink out like lights, one by one, and I will feel it all. I will *feel*. And I will have no garden to go to. No flowers watered by pain, no sanctuary to call my own because I will be mortal, and this will no longer be mine, but everyone's. And those pieces of my soul I offered to Create all of this... those will be everyone's as well."

What can I possibly say to that?

"Rosemary." I wipe away a tear. "I'm here."

She sighs, and her muscles unclench, her fingers uncoil around mine. I had not noticed she had gripped my hand so tight.

"I gave you my soul years ago," she says. The night grows thick, and thicker still. "Belladonna?"

"Yes, my darling?"

"Will you love me... after? When I am mortal? Will you love me, even then?"

Does she not see?

Does she not understand?

"I love you, Rosemary. Then, now, and always."

Rosemary trembles and then shatters. Her sobs are hoarse and harsh, each one knife-sharp and bloody. She covers her face with her hands and her cane clatters to the ground. Elbows propped on knees, she curls in on herself and unravels.

I ease my arms around her and pull her close, so her tears soak through the linen of my dress shirt, then my skin, all the way down to my bone, my marrow. Rosemary's anguish becomes part of me.

"It's okay," I whisper against her crown, rocking her as I rock Flora when she is upset, "to be the ocean, trying to make sense of the wreckage."

I hold her close, this wilted flower. This broken-winged bird. Earthquakes stir her marrow and hurricanes mass along her horizons.

She is shaking, shaking, shaking...

Shaking loose anything that is not soul.

NOW
ISRA

Belladonna is happy the next morning, content in a way I have never seen her. As though her long night healed something, and now she is whole.

I should be happy for her, and yet all I feel is a hollow ache beneath my breastbone.

She returned late last night, with Rosemary. They crept into the apartment, whispering. I watched through a crack in my door as they disappeared into Belladonna's room, only for Rosemary to emerge sometime later and sneak away.

I have not slept. Restless and alone, I have paced the corridors of this hallowed Hall, uncertain about why I was so troubled, knowing I could not rest until I figured it out.

I am no wiser now, as we sit together in the living area, Flora on the floor between us with some wooden blocks Grandmother Dove had carved for her. Belladonna is reading a book and soft jazz is playing on the gramophone. A smile curls her lips and I sip my cup of nectar and stare out at the world beyond the glass.

Flora laughs, the sound shrill and piercing, and I turn to see the girl toddle toward me, her nubby antennae bobbing with each step. I see Manab in her, the older she grows. I see him in the lines of her face, in her smile.

"Tanta," she says. *Aunt.*

Aunt, I am.

I cradled her in my arms when she took her first breath, and I have sung her to a soft sleep more times than I can count. I have held her when she cried and protected her when there was danger.

Now, that word feels like a wedge and I am on the wrong side of it.

"Isra," Belladonna asks. "What's wrong?"

I shake my head. Whatever is building inside me requires definition, and I can give it none. I am just a storm, a vast expanse of rain and all that wind.

"I am feeling so many things, Belladonna."

"If you need me to leave you alone, I will. However, if—"

I close my eyes and the words surge forth. "I am glad you are finding your way back to Rosemary. I love to see you happy."

And yet, now, something has changed and I feel as though I am on the outside, left on uncertain ground.

I offer her this truth: "I am alone, Belladonna, and full of want."

"Do you think you do not have me?" Belladonna's voice is soft, the words carefully chosen. "We are family, Isra."

Family.

I would be something more than family to her.

My head spins. My heart aches. These thoughts are heavy and I am lost within them. Suddenly, being in the Hall with Belladonna near is... too much. I need to sort out my soul, and I need space for that.

Belladonna's eyes are full of clouds when I face her. "I need to think," I tell her. "I will talk to you, but I need... I need time first."

"Okay," she says, the word slow, each letter stretched. "I will be here, Isra. Always."

I sense we are speaking of more than just this moment. I grab onto that lifeline and nod. "Thank you."

"Will you at least tell me where you are going, so I won't worry?"

Of course, worrying her is the last thing I want. "I'm going to

Divine Forest's arbor. I need to visit with him anyway."

"I'm glad you are there for him, caretaking at his last." Belladonna reaches out, loops her pinkie finger through mine. "Return when you are ready and I will be here."

Bending low, I kiss Flora's soft crown and then dash out the door. A moment later, I am in an automobile, and not long after that, I am in Divine Forest's arbor, surrounded by pine trees and whispering wind.

The forest breathes around me and I sit on a luminous blue mushroom cap beneath a towering redwood tree and watch as children stream out of a school tree to play in the yard just beyond. Across the way, a woman with a rat's tail beats a rug with a broom. Further still, a young boy with a ladybug's carapace plays marbles in the dirt while his father changes a lightbulb nearby.

The denizens who call this place home are already transitioning away from Divine Forest's care and doing it well enough. There has been no infighting like there was in Dawnland. Counsels have been created to govern, and such things like rubbish collection and repair work have already been arranged.

These small factors that were not a consideration before, when Divine Forest was in his strength, are so vitally important now. The Divine are giving over their Creations, but we must tend them.

Even here, however, I am not necessary, and that hollow emptiness yawns somewhere beneath my breastbone.

I do not fit.

Will I spend my life eternally looking for home, for somewhere to belong? Perhaps I should find someone willing to take me back to Dawnland. Perhaps it is time for me to uproot myself, to say I tried and go home to my brothers, come what may. At least we will face it together.

"Isra," Divine Forest's voice breaks through my thoughts. "I am glad you have come today. Walk with me."

I start. How long has he been standing there, watching my torment? When I turn to face him, I start again, for he is older now. So much older. His bark-skin looks mortal and wrinkled through. As

I watch, one of the leaves that line his crown falls and a tuft of gray hair appears where it had been. His hands, when he motions me to follow him, tremble with palsy.

I would be honored to love you into the last, and beyond. I had spoken those words to him not long ago and I had meant them. This is my purpose. This is my reason. Beyond Belladonna, beyond Flora, beyond this strange, unfamiliar world, I am here to help this man find peace in his final days, and that...

Matters.

He does not speak as he leads me through his arbor. The path clears before us, and those we pass bow their heads in reverence as Divine Forest approaches.

Something is different about him today, and it goes beyond his newly advanced age. "Will you come with me to my tree, Isra? I find myself drawn there more often of late."

Vulnerability, I realize, is what has changed in him. It breaks my heart, that he would have to ask for such a thing. That my companionship is not yet a given.

"Of course," I say.

He walks beside me through his arbor. We take a different path today, this one twining between towering oak trees, beside a burbling river. There are expansive city parks on either side, full of children and families enjoying the day.

Soon, Forest's tree looms before me, hulking and familiar. It steals my breath. I wonder if I will ever be able to look upon it and not be torn in twain by this ache for home.

Right now, if I was in Dawnland, I would be with my brothers. We would be inside the World Tree, eating lunch: cups of nectar, fruit, flowers.

"I miss my brothers," I whisper.

"I know," Forest says as he guides us to his favorite rock and perches upon it. His tree casts us in comfortable shadow. Moss hangs like lace from its lowest branches. "I would say loss gets easier with time, but it doesn't. It just changes."

The way he says this speaks of history, and I wonder who all he has lost in his long, long life.

"I have always come here to feel closer to my sister." He stares ahead, eyes unfocused. "When I rest, I ask you to lay me down here. This... will be where I finally sleep."

I see it all again, unfolding in the dark behind my eyes:

Falcon laying on her bed. Falcon closing her eyes. Falcon sleeping.

My world ending. Ending. Ending.

"Will it be soon?" I ask. Strange, to speak so frankly of such matters.

He hesitates, and I watch him weigh his words. Sunlight spills through the canopy illuminating us in a pool of melted honey and the branches of Forest's tree bend and sway.

"There is not so much of me left anymore, Isra. I have spent nearly all of myself on my Creation and I grow tired. I think, very soon, I will be ready to rest."

Divine Falcon, "I am so tired, Isra."

The past and the present merge and suddenly, I cannot breathe.

I am spinning. I am spiraling.

This is plucked-wing. This is freefall.

Oh, sweet agony.

"I will lay you down," I tell the god beside me. "I will lay you on a bed of your own design. I will sit beside you, Divine Forest, until sleep finally takes you."

"I recognize your sacrifice, Isra. I see the pain in your eyes. I know that being here wounds you." He pauses. "I do not deserve such devotion. Thank you."

"You deserve all this and more."

I should have said as much to Divine Falcon at the end. Perhaps she can hear me now, through her brother.

Forest sighs and then shrugs, as though he is done with such weighty matters.

"You came here today because you were upset."

"I am extremely upset." I smile to take the sting out of my words. "This is not easy for me."

"You weren't upset about me. Not when you first arrived. I could tell that much."

Belladonna. Rosemary. These issues seem so small and inconsequential in comparison to what is happening here.

"It doesn't matter."

"Will you tell me?"

"You want to hear about my petty qualms, Forest?" I cock an eyebrow at him and my wings flare wide, catching the wind, lifting me a few inches off the stone. "Here, when we speak of eternal rest."

"They are not petty qualms, Isra." He reaches out and clasps my hand with his own.

His skin is parchment thin and wrinkled. Days ago, touching him had been like touching a tree, and now... now he is all bent old man with leaves falling from his crown. What must it be like to be so mortal? To feel aches and pains, to tremble, to age?

Is he afraid?

I... I am terrified.

"I am in love with Belladonna," I admit. "I love her, and I love Flora, and Belladonna loves Rosemary, and I—"

My cheeks flush. Of all the things for me to worry about, this is the least among them and yet somehow it feels my greatest concern.

Forest squeezes my hand. "Love is a circle, Isra, not a line. It does not flow in only one direction."

A bluejay calls from somewhere overhead. Moisture fills the air and I know a storm is brewing. It will rain tonight. Lightning and thunder. A fractured sky fit to match my fractured soul.

"Will you tell me about my sister's resting place?" Forest asks, leaning his head back against the stone, his eyes closed.

"Forest, I—"

"Only tell me as much as you are able. I will not push you to re-open wounds."

His acceptance eases the grip around my throat.

"Would you like to hear of the World Tree, Forest? How grand it once was, when the Monarch Roost was at the height of its power?"

Forest smiles. "I would love nothing more."

NOW
ROSEMARY

Mother is resting in her window seat and Dream sits across from her, her pad of paper propped on her knee while she looks out the window and draws. She has changed recently, as the Divine fade ever more around us. The last night we went dancing was the last time I saw her truly smile. Now, her eyes are full of worry and sorrow and her silences are punctuated often with soft sighs.

Her father is out there, I know, in a Creation of his own, fading and far away. She will likely go to him soon. Ferriers leave every day, to points unknown. She will only have to go to the dock and tell someone which Creation she is heading toward. Plenty will have merchants lining up with goods, eager to sell.

I am reading to Mother when Dream ducks out and appears a moment later with Isra. I had missed the knocking.

"Oh," Mother breathes when she beholds Isra's monarch wings, "what a splendid creature you are."

I watch a blush creep across the white spots on Isra's cheekbones.

She looks different than when I last saw her. Now, she wears a pair of trousers that seems to have been pulled from Belladonna's trunk and a halter top, something that looks to have come with her from Dawnland, as orange as her wings. I wonder if it means something, that she has adorned herself thus: half from one place, half from another. Split across the center.

Isra's butterfly eyes focus on Mother, and I watch first curiosity, then understanding, then sorrow crash across her face in waves.

Mother stands, reaches for Isra's hand.

She is so much older now. Ancient and bent with it. Her hair is long and thin and her face is lined by furrows. It is as though proximity to our fading is impacting her, too.

"I had a dream once," Mother says, leaning forward, her voice pitched to a loud whisper, "that I had a daughter who grew flowers for hair. Can you believe that? She was beautiful, and sad, and I think she would have loved you very much, had she been real."

Isra's face crumples and I look away. Her realization is too much to bear.

Dream slips past us and sits on the window seat across from Mother, her pad of paper perched on her knees. Her moon-bright eyes twinkle. "Tell me what your dream daughter looked like and I will see if I can draw her."

"What?" Mother says, all bright-eyed innocence. "I didn't know you could draw."

Isra touches my arm and I let her lead me out of the room, down the hall, and then into the entryway. My wheelchair makes scarcely a sound as it whispers over the carpet. We are silent, the two of us, and somehow that silence feels so loud.

Her shoulders are stiff but her eyes are troubled when they find mine.

She is a storm, this butterfly. There is a hurricane trapped beneath her onyx skin.

I brace when she opens her mouth to speak, uncertain what she will address first: her reason for coming here, or my mother.

Isra clutches a paper in her hand and holds it aloft. "Belladonna wants to set up a meeting with her crew to discuss Oleander's offer. She would like to inform them of a time and place, but only two of them had telephones and the rest she needs to run messages to. I thought I could do this for her and I was hoping you could help me."

I... of course I will help her. It would be a relief to be out of this apartment and all it holds, for even a moment.

I nod and she offers up her list. There are five names on it. Two are crossed off and one is circled.

"I called these two," she points to the crossed-out names. "The circled one lives in Divine Forest's arbor. I will see her when I visit Divine Forest later."

"I did not realize you were so close," I say, studying the other two names. One is my cousin, Shadow. I'd known he was a ferrier, but I had not realized he'd worked on Belladonna's crew. He will likely be in Muse's office now, which is not far.

"He's asked me to be his caretaker, Rosemary."

Oh. This pain.

I understand her hurricane now. I recognize her torment.

"My cousin," I say, pointing at Shadow's name. "I know where he will likely be and it is not far."

Isra nods and opens the door, holds it while I wheel through. Outside, the corridor is silent and rather than being on the first floor like we usually are, we are now on the second. Even the Hall is changing. It does not shift nearly as often as it used to, and when it does, the change comes slower.

We are quiet as we make our progress toward the lift at the end of the hall, a contraption I have never had to use until recently. Now, as my body ages and my pain increases, I use it every day. I hate the way it rattles and clanks.

I feel Isra glancing at me and I see, out of the corner of my eye, her hands flutter and her mouth open and shut. Her wings twitch and I know she is preparing herself for... something. The real reason for her finding me today.

"I had hoped we could discuss something," she finally manages as we wait before the lift. Her voice trembles and I dislike her unease, the fact that she feels it around me.

"I know you love her, Isra, and I know she loves you."

"Are you angry?" she whispers.

Am I angry? She asks this and then hunches and opens her wings wide as though to hide beneath them. Does she think I will shout at her? Hate her? Be consumed by jealousy? "I am glad she found you, Isra. It eases me to know she had someone beside her to help her through her days. You make her happy and that makes me happy."

My vines grow a riot and love, love, love blooms within me.

The lift arrives and we ride it down in silence.

"You've made a family together," I say once the door opens. "Do you think I have not noticed? The two of you and that glorious child."

And I...

Something cold pierces my heart. How I long to be part of something young and tender and thriving.

Instead, I feel as though I am surrounded by ruins.

"I don't begrudge you your love, Isra. Belladonna knows her soul." I pause. It's hard to speak of these matters, especially with someone I don't know. Suddenly I wish my hip did not hurt so desperately so I could stand up and pace the way I want to. "I love her and I always will, but I will only be in as much of her life as she allows and I will not push for more. I have no desire to diminish whatever you have with her, or whatever may grow of your feelings."

I feel like I am saying goodbye. Isra will tell me that there will be no more carrying on with Belladonna and I... I will leave. I will turn around and I will ensure I stay well clear of their path. It will stick me through, but I will do it if it means Belladonna will be happy.

Instead, Isra's fingertips on my shoulder are soft and timid. "I should like to get to know you, Rosemary. Can we start there?"

Can we start there?

Oh, sweet, keening relief. From falling so far to soaring so high. It is heady, this sensation. I do not know what might happen, but there is an open doorway and beyond is where possibility dwells.

Our eyes meet. There is a certain sweet intimacy in this moment. I examine her soul and she searches mine.

Our eyes meet.

It is as simple and complex as that.

"Should we?" Isra asks, gesturing forward, a blush creeping across her cheeks, staining the white of them with colors of sunset. I nod, and we continue along our way.

"What is Belladonna busy doing today?" I turn a corner and lead her deeper into Father Luna's wing.

"I—" Isra hesitates. "Because you love her and mean her well, Rosemary, I will tell you this in confidence.

"Belladonna's mother has cancer. Belladonna has been visiting her. She didn't... she didn't strictly ask me to do this"—Isra waves the list in the air—"but I wanted to do something to ease the ache. Give her one less thing to consider."

It takes a moment for me to work through all Isra had said. Belladonna's mother has cancer? Why had she not told me?

"Is she—"

Isra reaches down, weaves her fingers through mine, and squeezes.

"Belladonna is fine, she's just worried. Her mother's prognosis is good."

Relief hits me like cool water on a hot summer day.

We arrive at Muse's door, where I know my cousin, Divine Shadow, will likely be playing a game of cards, or taking music lessons, or... whatever it is they do together when he is not ferrying.

Muse's office is nearly as familiar to me as my father's own for all the time I have spent here over the years. For a moment, I am not here now, but a lifetime ago. A child seeing splendor for the first time. An intimidating god and his overwhelming kindness.

I have not been here in too long, distracted by other things. I regret that now, as we near the end.

The door opens and Muse appears, older now. So much older. His spine is bent and his skin sags. The moons in his eyes are faint and far away. The music that surrounds him can hardly be heard.

Not yet!

I want to scream.

Not yet. You said you'd never leave me. You said we belonged to each other. You promised I would never be alone and yet...

And yet...

Isra sees who she is looking for. There are no cards or instruments arrayed around them today. No, Shadow is upset, and this room smells like a funeral.

Muse reaches out and cups my cheek with one trembling, liver-spotted hand.

His touch is so soft, and it breaks me. I press my face against his palm. His smile, when it comes, is feather-soft.

"Nothing ever ends, Rosemary." His voice quivers. My cousin, behind Muse, wipes away a tear. "It only changes shape."

"Divine Falcon," Isra breathes.

Muse winks. For a heartbeat, I see some of his old self shine through. "I knew her well, before."

And then, it hits me. The moment falls on me like a mountainside. Like a tidal wave. I am oceanic.

I know what I walked in on.

My cousin was saying goodbye.

That's... that's what this was.

He was saying goodbye.

"Not yet," Muse whispers, following the tide of my thoughts. "Soon, but not yet."

"No," I breathe.

"Rosemary."

"Muse, I beg you. Please. Stay a little longer."

"Rosemary—"

"A moment, an hour." A breath would feel like eternity.

A sob hitches in my throat. Isra's hands on my shoulders, grounding me when I feel untethered.

"Linger in the doorway, uncle. Do not... do not just leave."

Do I not love you fiercely enough? Cannot you see how desperately I need you—you—to light my nights? Do you not remember the moment when I was young and upset. You took me into Father Luna's Observatory and held me while I sobbed. You whispered, low in my ear, "Let me show you how darkness turns into light." You chased away my sorrow with stars. Do you not see how you have always illuminated my midnight? This night will be everlasting without you to guide me through. My lighthouse. My safe harbor. My north star.

Muse, Muse. What is the world without its favorite song?

"There is not much of me left, Rosemary. Very soon, I will Create my final song and then... then I will become the music."

Peaceful, peaceful is his mien.

Childlike rage claws its way up my throat. The words are torn from me, impotent and furious. "Everyone leaves, Muse."

He kneels—the act takes an age—and tilts my chin so our eyes meet. Magnolia blossoms along my vines. Muse plucks one and offers it to me.

Acceptance.

"Soon," he pulls me into his embrace and then whispers low in my ear, "but not yet."

THEN
ROSEMARY

I spent three days in Muse's temple, resting, eating, and being cared for. I had never known such luxury. I slept in a spare bed kept in a room down the hall from Lavender's. During the days, she'd hand me a rag and show me where to dust, or give me other small jobs that were both easy to do and easy to lose myself in. Her company was pleasant. She'd tell stories as we worked, of fantastical plays and salacious things actors did when the audience was not watching.

It was Muse's visits that I lived for. He would come during his off hours. We would choose a different art gallery to sit in each night. I would listen while he wove stories around me, about Creation and Chaos, about the Divine and their accomplishments. He would tell me of artists and their work and painted pictures with words I had never heard before.

Being with Divine Muse was like being in a dream.

On the third day, Lavender bade me sit in the foyer and fold playbills for the night's performance while she went out into Meadowsweet to buy me shoes and a new pair of gloves. I had told her I was well enough without these extras, but she seemed to enjoy having a child to dote on, so I let her go about it.

I took to the task of folding willingly and found solace in the silence. Hours passed in a blink, and it was afternoon by the time I looked up to see mountains of folded playbills stacked all around. The theater stretched, empty and warm. My life felt so blissfully far away.

I stretched, easing the muscles in my hip, and flinched as the bells on the front doors chimed. A moment later, blood hummed, recognizing its own. Dread played my spine like the keys of a piano and I pushed myself back against the wall, drew my knees up to my chin, and made myself small.

How does a child prepare to face a god?

I felt his presence long before I saw him, a certain growing pressure as he drew near. Pressing my forehead against my knees, I closed my eyes. I did not want to have to see his disappointment as he regarded me.

His footsteps echoed across the room.

"I am sorry," I said, breaking the quiet. Oh, how my voice trembled.

"For what?" he asked, sitting beside me. "Will you not look at me, Rosemary?"

I hesitated and then nodded, lifting my head and opening my eyes. Divine Aether sat beside me, legs crossed. His gaze was tender.

I found a playbill, folded it, and set it aside.

"I am sorry for my limp. For how strange I am." I hesitated. "You cannot..." Nettle sprouted along my scalp. "I do not wish to bring you shame."

I was drowning.

Why had no one taught me how to swim?

"Beautiful daughter." He cradled my chin with a finger and turned my face so our gazes could meet. "Whatever makes you think I would not love you?"

"I am broken, Divine One." I thought of my bad leg and a wolf howled somewhere in my soul. Its long, mournful cry shivered through me. "I am not worthy."

He wiped away my tears with the pads of his thumbs. "Quiet, my heart. Be gentle with yourself. Believe me when I say, there is no part of you that should not be."

His words set off an earthquake in my soul. Mountains moved and the ocean of my heart surged, high tide and churned by storms.

I picked up a playbill, folded it, set it aside.

"I didn't know Willow was pregnant," Aether said. "God Forge felt the call to Create and I was sent to help him bind himself to Chaos. Willow and I discussed it." He hesitated. "I thought I understood time. I was certain I had been gone but a moment. Now I have returned to find a whole new life waiting for me. I have a daughter and Willow is unwell. Her family is... where is her family, Rosemary?"

"Her family has never been part of our lives, sir."

He flinched as though struck. "Her father was a hard man. I thought I had returned soon enough to spare her that trauma."

"She thought you forgot her."

"I could never forget her. I need you to know that." Stars spun from Aether's palms.

"I don't know how to do this," he finally said, meeting my gaze and holding it. I could no more look away than I could stop breathing. The universes in his eyes spiraled and danced, but slower now, as though to a somber song.

"I should like to get to know you, sir. If it would not be too embarrassing to have me around. I can care for Mother and I will... I will be quiet and out of the way. No one need know that I am yours."

"I am not ashamed of you, Rosemary." The pride in his eyes told the truth of that statement. Then, as though whispering a prayer, "May I hug you?"

Hesitation. Would I risk letting him even this close?

"Yes," I breathed.

He let out a sigh that sounded a lot like relief and shifted toward me. The smell of ozone washed over me. Then came his arms, hesitating on my shoulders before he pulled me to his side.

I sank into him and let myself be held.

For a moment, the world hung silent and still. Then, I felt it. A slight tremor cracking the bedrock of his soul. An earthquake, barely felt but no less powerful for it. I pressed my ear against Divine Aether's chest and listened to his shuddering breath. His arms clenched around me, not painful, but tight. I heard him sniffle.

He held me as though he could not exist a moment more without holding me. As though his next breath depended upon me being in his arms.

Home, I knew then, was not a place, but a steadily thumping heart.

"Rosemary," he murmured against my ear, "watch." I sat back and wiped my eyes. Night spun from Aether's midnight hair, and though it was daylight outside, the theater grew dark, and darker still, until the walls faded and I was surrounded by the eternally spinning cosmos.

Divine Aether let his mortal mask fall and opened himself to me, letting me spy the fullness of his nature.

It will ever be impossible for me to describe that moment, for here I was being offered the marrow of existence. Perhaps my father is not one of the Most High, but he is close enough, and he held nothing back. Dipping my toes into time's currents, I felt the universe stretch and splay about me. I experienced the agony of Creation and felt the weight of his unending days. I watched through Divine Aether's eyes while Father Luna broke off one of his own ribs and, with Aether's help, formed the moon. I stood beside him while Father Luna plucked hair from his crown and blew it like dandelion spores into the vault of the heavens to create stars.

My father was young when this happened, a boy if such terms matter, more helper than anything else. All soul, undiluted and filled with the need to Create. Aether chased after Father Luna, helping him scatter the pieces of himself to create dark, shadows, dreams, and...

Then, a span of forever later, his brothers began appearing, fully formed and blazing with Divinity. "Let us go forth," Father Luna said, "and Create for us a land..."

Then, later, as the Divine helped the Most High bind themselves to portions of Chaos to force from it Creation. And later still, as Meadowsweet sprouted like flowers in a landscape of nothing.

Time sped, faster and faster, a dizzying whirl of events, a slide of passions and disappointments, the slow souring of novelty then—

Stop.

An image of my mother. The light was low, but she was smiling and her amber eyes dazzled. She spun and the beads on her flapper dress shimmered. He did not know he had a heart until it started aching.

Mother faded, and the stars receded until we were back in God Muse's temple. I pulled away so I could look into my father's eyes.

"We are very new to each other. It will take us time, I think, to become close," he whispered, running his hand through my vines. Thyme tipped with tiny white flowers laced through my vines. Sweet perfume filled the air.

This was my father's first and greatest mercy, and it is the moment I decided to love him. He did not force it from me, nor was I obligated to feel such a thing. He was opening a door and offering me a way in, while still giving me the opportunity to flee. And he was giving us time, the passing of however long for this to happen.

"I would give you more than just the world," he whispered against my crown. "I would give you all of Creation."

NOW
BELLADONNA

I do not like being here.

Mother's room is large and unchanging. Stepping into it is like stepping back in time. On the wall is the same framed picture of an oak tree I remember from my childhood. A square table sits beside the window, where it always has. The same blue vase with golden lilies adorning its side sits on the table's surface. Even the wallpaper, white with small pink roses, is exactly as I remember it.

I used to stand in this very spot as a child and rest my palms on the round ends of her bedposts as I spoke with Mother about this or that. She would eye me from the mirror over her dressing table and I would clutch that knob and brace, waiting to find out what she would focus on next: my smile, my posture, my social connections.

How much does it cost her, to keep this room so untouched by time? There are signs of newness everywhere. This comforter with the pink roses is the same. Mother had it made, just before my father left. She had ordered it to match her wallpaper and had been so pleased with the finished product. I study it and realize that like the wallpaper, it too is unfaded. Is it possible she has these items specially tailored for her, so each time they appear worn she but has another made?

Mother's woman, Daisy, let me in, eyes wide as though surprised I had deigned to show up. I wonder if she will ever get used to me. I wonder if I want her to get used to me.

Now I stand here, studying Mother asleep in that big bed. She lets out a soft snore and I know it is time.

I am not here for Mother alone. Not truly. There are things I want from my room, but I have been waiting for an opportunity to gather them, a moment when she would not be watching. I do not want her to examine what is important to me.

Mother looks so small. So feeble. She has seemed a giant all my life, this woman who could but say the word and destroy me.

I blink and truly see her for the first time. She is neither giant nor god, but so very, tragically mortal.

As a child, I had been terrified of storms. She used to sit beside my bed and read me stories with her voice pitched just right. I would fall asleep warm and safe under her watchful eye.

Not everything was bad.

That is also why I am here. Out of the memory of those good times.

Still, if I want to get what I came here for, I must act now. There is a bell on the table beside Mother that she can use if she stirs. She has warned me, however, that she sleeps well for a few days after her treatments.

I creep to the doorway, hesitating there to listen. After a thunderous heartbeat, I hear Daisy downstairs. It sounds like she is sweeping rugs, the steady *swoosh, swoosh* echoing through these cavernous halls.

I don't want her to catch me. I have a right to be here, in my childhood home, but rather that I want this moment to be mine and mine alone, personal and private, silent so I can savor it.

So I flit through the hallways, creeping shadow to shadow like a wraith.

In my childhood, the halls of this house felt so very small, perhaps because my mother's presence loomed so large. There was nowhere I could go to get away from her.

Now, however, it strikes me how big this house truly is, the corridors so wide, and so many stairs. I must climb another flight to get to my room, which is at the end of a long, narrow hallway. Soon enough, I am standing before that familiar white door with that familiar brass knob.

I turn it and then hesitate before entering, for I am not sure what will be worse: if everything has stayed the same, or if it has all changed. Still, Mother has kept her room so well preserved, I imagine she must have done the same for mine. This house feels more museum than anything else, and curators do not let their exhibits collect dust.

It is the smell that hits me first: of mildew and long forgotten, old things. I feel along the wall where the light switch is and flip it. For a moment, the lightbulbs buzz and hum, and then yellow lamps flicker, casting ghostly illumination along walls, warring with the sunlight outside. Then, a heartbeat later, they come on; all except the lamp near the far window, but that one always was fussy.

My heart breaks as I take in my old room and understand what I am seeing. Mother did not preserve so much as forget.

This bedroom was an oasis to me. Mother had relegated me to the third floor when I was sixteen, explaining that walking more stairs each day would keep me trim. I had been upset until I realized that the third floor was further away from the noise of the city, and more, Mother rarely climbed so high. I could do what I wanted.

I had painted the walls yellow and the trim around my three windows white. My curtains were fine lace to allow in the light. In the corner was a small table beside a plush pink chair where I would sit and look out the window at the streets below.

I had bought large pillows in all colors of the rainbow and strewn them around my room for pops of color and creature comforts. To my left is a closed door that leads to my dressing room. It will be full of clothes from an earlier time, relics of the past. Each of them tailored to hug the curve of my body, and yet none of them truly fit.

I think of Isra. *I don't fit, Belladonna.*

I swallow hard and close my eyes.

Almost everything is exactly as I left it and it is all covered in seventeen years' worth of dust and cobwebs.

I remember waking up in the small hours and tossing off my comforter. That comforter has stayed how I left it: folded over, the imprint of my body still visible. The book I had been reading is open on my end table, the bookmark where I had left it.

The pillows on my floor have been left where they lay, so faded I can barely make out their colors. Spiderwebs stretch between the two windows framing my bed.

A stuffed bear sits in my window. Once it had been soft and brown with button eyes and a black nose, shiny from how often I had kissed it. I had wanted to gift that bear to Flora, but now I see that it is beyond recovery. The seams are frayed, and the dust is so severe, I am reluctant to touch it.

Mother knew what that toy meant to me. Perhaps I should have taken it with me when I left, but it also would not have been hard for her to remove it from the window, keep it somewhere safer from the elements, should I return.

My heart beats a violent tattoo. The bear is only one of the things I came here for.

I turn to face my father's bookshelf.

As I was told it, my father had taken to ferrying because he so loved collecting. He would wander from Creation to Creation, filling his ferry with books and then bringing them home. I had spent countless nights as a child, studying their spines, wondering what manners of creatures wrote them and imagining the worlds that existed beyond Meadowsweet's horizon.

Father Terra had Created this bookshelf to preserve my father's collection and gifted it to me shortly after I inherited his books, many of which are hundreds of years old. It is a gorgeous contraption fashioned of one piece of flawless wood with two doors that, when shut, lock the books away from the elements and keep them preserved. This is all I have of the man I barely remember.

I never left the doors of my bookshelf open.

And the doors are open now. The books have been pulled off their shelves and thrown in a discard pile on the floor, left there.

Tears burn my eyes, blur my vision.

I can picture Mother standing in my doorway after I left, examining my room and deciding which part of it could hurt me the most, should I ever return.

This is deliberate, a fatal blow, and I put a hand to my heart as though to staunch the blood.

My father's books lie in a pile now: open, closed, pages bent, missing, torn, tattered. Perhaps some of these could be repaired, but it would cost.

I want to cry. I want to scream. I kneel before these relics and touch a loose page of ancient paper, watch it crumble.

Mother could not have found a better way to hurt me.

I compose myself and bury my emotions deep. She does not deserve my pain.

There is one last thing I need to check before I can leave this place.

My writing desk is beside my bookshelf, an ancient thing I'd inherited from my mother, and she from hers. I notice, with relief, that this has been left as untouched as the rest of my room. The second drawer where I stuck Rosemary's letters is still ajar. It groans in the silence as I pull it open the rest of the way and look inside. A stack of papers, folded and tied with a ribbon, sits within, exactly as I had left it.

The victory feels hollow.

I grab the letters, feel the solid weight of them in my hand. I owe them to Rosemary and I am glad that at least this much still remains.

When I was a young, the Narrows was whispered about amongst children at night, stories we told to scare each other. "Go to the Narrows," we'd dare, "and become unmade."

That is how my room feels as I study it. Fading. Going back to Chaos.

I don't know what I expected, in truth, but something more than dust and cobwebs. Something more than sabotage.

I lean against the wall and thumb through my letters and collect snippets of thought:

ROSEMARY,
I regret to inform you that...

ROSEMARY,
My mother has...

ROSEMARY,
Do not ever doubt how much I love you.

THE BELL DOWNSTAIRS chimes and I tuck the papers under my arm, glance around my room one last time, and leave, flipping off the lights before I close the door behind me.

I no longer creep around the hallways. I have no more secrets.

Mother is sitting in bed when I get to her room. "Water," she croaks.

I pour a glass from her ewer and hand it to her, sloshing water over the rim with my trembling hands. The room is quiet, punctuated by Mother's soft sigh as she sinks back into her bed. "You're still here," she says.

"I said I would be."

She toys with her comforter, fingers tracing those pale pink roses.

"I have been thinking." Her voice is husky and trembles just so. She sounds sick, and yet I cannot help but see that she does not look terribly ill. Her skin is not wan, her hands do not tremble; her eyes are not bloodshot or exhausted, but calculating and cold.

I will always doubt this woman. I will always doubt that what I see is real. Is she sick? Or is she exaggerating her symptoms to gain my sympathy?

"You have been thinking," I press.

"Your daughter." Another hesitation. "Flora."

Every part of me clenches: from soul to muscle.

"Even if she is strange, Belladonna, it need not be the end of the world. Divine Rain's arbor is full of winged creatures, and Divine Forest's arbor... we could pair her with the child of an established family in either of those..."

The world screeches to a halt. Already she is trying to wed my daughter off. My daughter, who still toddles about. My daughter, whom she has never met.

My.

Daughter.

I breathe deep and turn to go.

"Belladonna?"

"I will never let you anywhere near my daughter," I hiss over my shoulder.

"Are you leaving?"

I stride to the door.

I am. And I will only return with movers.

"Belladonna, wait. I only want—"

"It is always about what you want!" I shout. I spin and see her half out of bed already, preparing to fling herself at me. "You were at the heart of everything that drove me away from Meadowsweet."

She flinches.

"I keep returning here hoping you'll be different. Maybe this time you will love me as a mother should and maybe I won't disappoint you." I run my thumb along Rosemary's letters again. I think of her arbor, her great sacrifice. "I have a life to return to, Mother, full of people who love me."

"Belladonna—" Mother says, but I am already halfway down the stairs.

Daisy watches me leave with wide eyes.

NOW
ISRA

The sun is soft, penetrating the canopy in a misty haze. It reminds me of Dawnland and for a moment, I smell orchids and milkweed and water. The earth is verdant and rich with promise, and the trees that arch over my head have been here eternities and shiver with stories.

Someone clears their throat, and I open my eyes to see a short woman to my right. Her mousy tail twitches and her round black eyes focus on me.

"Isra," she says. "I'm pleased to finally meet you in person."

I remember Belladonna, when I hung up the phone and told her who had called. Her brow had furrowed, her voice somber. "Will you want to go alone, Isra, or... I can go with you, if you'd like? For support?"

"No. I think Divine Forest will want to do this alone."

Then I had come here with all haste.

Now, I look around and see how different the forest is today. The mood is somber, the air is heavy. Not even birds chirp in the canopy. The pathways are lined with people pressed shoulder to shoulder. Great white banners hang from the tops of the trees and stretch to the forest floor.

The woman clasps my hand in hers, a matronly gesture that comforts me despite the fact that she is a stranger. Her palm is furry and soft and warm. "Divine Forest said he was tired. He wants you to help lay him down."

I take in the arbor again.

This is how we should have sent Divine Falcon to her slumber, with banners and pathways lined with kindred. With this quiet reverence and solemn dignity. Not the way we did. Not in the dark with bombs exploding and all that smothering terror.

I wonder if Forest chose me, in part, because he knew I would need this. My brothers would have appreciated the opportunity to do it right. Though with Chaos becoming more stable, capable for mortals to travel, I know I will see them again. We are not so separated as we once had been.

"I would have your name, if you please."

She hesitates, then shakes her head. "I'm not here for me. I'm here for the arbor. Right now, I am all of us."

I nod, humbled.

With a wave of her hand, she leads me forward, down a path lined by the descendants of Divine Forest's original Creations. I wonder if he thought this was how everything would end when he bound himself to this part of Chaos. I wonder if his Creation has ever surprised him.

It surprises me, to see that all of this came from one man. What a soul it must be, to allow such beauty.

The forest unfolds around me, wide and tall and sprawling, and so silent, all I hear are my footsteps and wind sighing in the trees. The heady scent of loam surrounds me. I know this place. I recognize these smells. I am not a stranger here.

I am...

Almost home.

The path leads me through the heart of the arbor, past quiet, closed shops, silent schools, and empty shopping centers, down to where the path ends and the glade Divine Forest showed me not so long ago begins.

I see him, a bent shape sitting on his favorite stone, staring at his tree.

"We love him," the woman beside me says. Her eyes are sad and her hand trembles on my arm. "He has done well by us. Let him know... let him know we'll take care of what he's Created."

I turn and look over her shoulder, at all of Forest's arbor arrayed behind her. Love, I realize, is what I feel in the air, tinged by both grief and hope.

The woman leaves and I am alone.

I remember, suddenly, when Divine Falcon fell. I had been alone with her outside, despite the char, despite the bombings. She had wanted to enjoy the morning light. I had been worried about how unsteady she had been of late. Still, we went, taking a turn in the sun, and I stayed close beside her to give her something to lean upon, should she need it.

I thought she'd tripped at first, over a root or rubble. It was not until I bent to help her and she had whispered, "I am so tired, Isra," that I had understood.

She had not tripped.

She had fallen.

I am so tired, Isra.

I stood there then, alone with the magnitude of what had just happened. Of what was about to happen.

I'd called my brothers and we had faced it together. Now, I am alone. I wish Belladonna was here beside me. I would feel stronger with her at my back. Or Rosemary, and one of her flowers. Perhaps a bloom that would give me courage.

Instead, Divine Forest sits ahead of me, wrinkled and aged, and he is waiting. I hardly know this man, and yet here I am, to usher him through this final, most intimate moment.

I approach him carefully, sacredly, making no secret about my progress. My wings bend the grasses, showing the path I tread. This place is peaceful, bathed in soft light and softer mist, with the ocean like a pulse not so far away.

It is only the birth pains of grief that mar this moment.

Divine Forest is ancient. He looks both like an old man and petrified wood. His skin is so wrinkled, I cannot see his eyes, and his head is shiny and bare, age-spotted.

"Isra," he says and his voice, so ancient and frail, drives a spear through my heart. "I am glad you have come."

I edge closer to him. "I had not expected it to be so soon." I feel like I have only been getting to know him, and now it's already nearly over.

His smile is soft and he pats the stone beside him. I sit, uncertain, and flare my wings so the angle does not hurt. Around us, the world waits. I cannot help but feel I am at a threshold, poised between the before and the after.

I think of Divine Falcon, resting on her bed of flowers.

"I can no longer feel my sister, Isra. I woke this morning and knew she... she is now Dawnland."

I knew this was coming. I knew Falcon would fade. I am only surprised it took her this long. Perhaps she held on until she knew we would be safe. Perhaps this means the war is over and my brothers have survived. There is joy in that thought, and yet agony as well. I miss them.

Divine Falcon was everything to me: my reason, my purpose. Who am I now that she is gone?

And my brothers. Oh, how I long to be with them, mourning the way we should.

"I look around and I am satisfied with what I have wrought," Forest says.

I cannot fault him this. What he Created is glorious to behold. In so many ways, I feel like this is what Dawnland could have become, if we had not so torn ourselves apart.

He sighs. "I will not rest yet, but soon. I can feel myself drawing ever nearer to that tree. I will not leave this glade again. Isra, I am ready."

Tears prick my eyes, and yet there is no denying the pride I feel for him, for the regal way he is meeting his fate.

"Nothing ever ends, it only changes shape," I say.

Forest smiles. "My sister used to say that."

"That's where I learned it."

"She had a way with words."

"Are you scared?"

He studies me and I feel the weight of that ancient gaze. "Everything you see cost a piece of me. I am spent, Isra. So much of me is already part of Chaos, Sustaining the things I have Created. I am eager to be whole again." Forest shifts and then whispers, "The unknown is always frightening. Even to the Divine."

Silence holds us close and I find solace in its embrace. For a moment, I do not need to do more than feel. I close my eyes and let the day wash over me, warm and alive and full of pain.

"I was hoping," he says, "that you would help me construct the bed I will lay on. I had not thought it would matter but now... now I find myself fixated."

This was how Divine Falcon was, near her end. She could not think about anything else.

"What kind of bed would you like rest on?" I ask.

It is agony to ask this, to speak of endings in this calm, easy way.

"When I was young and newly formed, after I Created the first tree, I became fascinated by its branches, the way they stretched, the way they moved. I think... I think I long to rest on a bed of woven branches, Isra, collected from my arbor. Will you help?"

My heart sinks. "I don't know how to weave, Divine Forest, but I am certain I can learn."

His smile, when it comes, is soft, and I noticed for the first time a small pile of thin branches resting at his feet. "I took up weaving long, long ago. I had thought it an idle hobby. I wonder if, even then, part of me was preparing for this end."

It is haunting to think of that, so I force my mind to the sticks at his feet. I grab two, each about as long as my arm. Forest smiles and I hand him two others. His fingers are knobby, knotted things, and he cannot grasp them well. After an apologetic grimace, he rests them on his lap. "I will walk you through it," he says.

We spend hours like that, heads bent together while he showed me how to weave, and then corrected my attempts. It would not all be branches, I was glad to learn. The branches would form a wide lattice through which I'd weave soft leaves and ivy, what green and growing things I could find to cradle him. At the end of it, I thought we had a fairly good stretch of bed made, but he just shook his head. "That was good practice. The real work will begin in the morning."

"Do you want me to stay with you?" I ask as the day breathes its last.

"No." Divine Forest tilts his face to the sky. "I think I should like to spend tonight here, in my glade, communing with Father Luna. It has been a very long time since I have prayed."

I nod, though it does not sit easy with me, leaving him alone so near his end. I find the woman who led me here hovering about the edge of the glade and I know she will watch over him tonight.

"Go home," he says to me. "And mend your tattered heart."

As though he can see my sorrow.

I say goodbye, and press my lips against his wrinkled, soft cheek. Gone are his leaves and his bark-like skin. Now, he is all bent old man and it chills me through.

He is so similar to Falcon, I feel as though it is her cheek I am kissing.

"Come back after you've rested," he says. "It will be soon, Isra, and I will want you to sit beside me so I am not alone at the last."

"Of course," I say. As though he should even question it.

Divine Forest has his face turned to the sky. "I wonder," he says, "when I first forgot to look up."

NOW
ROSEMARY

Belladonna arrived at my apartment earlier this night, with Isra in tow. "We need to talk," she had said. "The three of us. And there is something I want to show you." Her eyes had been bright and wild, intoxicating in a way that only Belladonna can be.

Now, we sit on a rented raft sailing down the placid waterway that bisects Divine Rain's arbor. Belladonna navigates for she has sailed a ferry and if anyone knows how to steer, it will be her. Isra is at the back with an oar, and I sit between them.

We pass houses both on stilts and floating on the water. Boardwalks and suspended bridges connect everything. The waterways are lined with small boats and rafts and the air is alive with sound. Yellow light pierces the dark from open windows, and overhead are all those stars.

Divine Rain has always had a fascination with bugs, and so here he has an arbor Created to foster different kinds of insect life. The water is still and warm and murky, and yet it never brings disease. Houses are illuminated not with lightbulbs, like the rest of the city, but with captured fireflies, Created by Divine Rain so they might cast light for generations. They live in ornate lanterns handed down from parent to child, a family heirloom. I see them as we slide down the river, towering lanterns and small ones, each uniquely decorated.

We pass a patch of glowing red-capped mushrooms along the shore. A luminescent white dragon fly spits fire that glows but does not burn, briefly illuminating Belladonna's face before flitting off.

"Up ahead," Belladonna says. She sounds excited. "On the right. It won't be long now."

It is the first thing anyone has said since we boarded this raft.

Isra moves her oar from one side of the raft to the other, timing the switch perfectly with Belladonna. They move well together, as though they have practiced such an action often, and they probably have. Isra did survive a journey through Chaos. Likely she spent time at the oars, if she was able.

A small dock looms out of the mist on my right, an orange firefly lantern casting a pale glow. Belladonna calls something over her shoulder, a word I cannot understand, and Isra replies. The raft turns and a few moments later, Belladonna jumps onto the dock and ties the raft to a pier.

She holds a hand out to Isra next. The butterfly woman alights, half flying to the dock. "We need to be above the water to see it, Rosemary. Do you mind?"

"No." I shake my head. Not long ago, this would not have been so hard. Now, I grow a bit older each day and my body is less forgiving. "But I will need help up."

I am ashamed to admit I cannot even do this much anymore without assistance. Every day I can do a bit less.

I shift to the edge of the raft. My hip sings its agony and nerves fire along my spine. My vision goes black and I clench my hands around my leg to hold it still, keep it from twitching as my muscles pulse along with my heartbeat.

Hands reach out and grab my own and soon, between the three of us, I am on the dock. I kick my legs over the edge and dig my knuckle into my hip.

I am glad I came, despite the pain.

"I used to come here before I left," Belladonna says, lowering the hood over the lantern so we are cast in perfect night. She sits between me and Isra. "I'd sit beside the river and think."

I can picture her here, alone with her thoughts.

Divine Rain's arbor is magnificent, it is true, but there is nothing special about this dock. This stretch of river is dark, an inky smear reflecting the sky. There are not many houses around us, and the sounds of bullfrogs and crickets is loud enough to make my head ring.

Belladonna sits between Isra and I. Her glow is so faint, I have to focus to see it. The woman appearing before me is full of mortality and when she smiles, I feel like a bird in flight. "Watch," she whispers. "You'll understand why I brought you here."

At first, I don't see anything: a river, nothing more. "It's coming," Belladonna says.

"What is coming?" Isra whispers.

"Hush!" She is positively humming with anticipation. Leaning forward, she grasps the edge of the dock. Something in the air shifts. The bullfrogs go quiet, and then the crickets too.

It is the light I see first. Like stars but underwater, in the distance and growing closer. A wave comes next, and then another one, bigger this time. Belladonna clasps my hand. Her fingers squeeze so hard it nearly hurts and her eyes are focused on the river.

And then, it happens: the water is filled by a thousand, thousand shooting stars. So many of them, they illuminate the dark, casting the riverbanks silver. It reminds me of Father Luna's Sacred Observatory, like stardust.

"What are those things?" I ask as yet more stream by.

"They are starfish," Belladonna whispers, her lips caressing the shell of my ear. "Every night schools of them swim through these waters."

It is magnificent, as though Divine Rain has captured a bit of the night sky and somehow made it even more glorious. The starfish swirl and dance beneath the water; a few leap into the air. It is impossible not to feel joy when watching them.

A dragon fly spins around my head. This one is purple with a long, sensuous tail. It perches on my finger, painting my hand with an amethyst glow. She preens her wings for a moment, then belches her fire and flies away.

The last starfish swim by.

"There will be more," Belladonna says. "They do this all night."

She moves to lift the hood off the lantern, but Isra stills her with a touch. I agree. I am also enjoying the dark.

Silence stretches. The bullfrogs take up their songs again. A few more starfish swim by. A blue dragon fly flutters near Isra's shoulder.

"I saw my mother today," Belladonna finally says. She has not let go of my hand, I notice, and when I look, I see she is holding Isra's with her other. "How is it possible to both love and hate someone so profoundly in the same breath?"

I shift, kick out my leg to ease my hip, and then give up and lie back on the hard planks of wood. I groan as my spine snaps, but the flat surface is doing wonders for my back and for the first time in days, the scream beneath my skin fades to a dull roar. A moment later, Belladonna lies on her back beside me. Only Isra stays seated, her wings flared and tilted at an angle that looks uncomfortable as she studies the night.

"She is sick and alone and I am her daughter. I know I should care for her and yet..."

And yet? I want to press. *Speak, Belladonna. Finally, after all this time, let me see the mess of your soul.*

Belladonna sighs. There is so much pain in that sound. "She destroyed my father's books. I used to dream of the places they came from, of visiting them one day. I would look at them each night before bed and feel as though he was near. She knew what they meant to me and she ruined them the moment I left. I thought mothers were supposed to love their daughters."

"They are," Isra says.

"My mother's regard does not feel like love."

I think back to my time in the Narrows, back to the children I'd see with bruises, split lips, swollen eyes. "Family is what you make, Belladonna, not always what you are born into."

A green dragon fly hovers near her face, watching her with wonder.

"I didn't come here to talk about this," Belladonna sighs. "It is time we are honest with each other. There are things I must say to the two of you."

I brace, Isra flutters her wings, and Belladonna plays with the laces on her wingtip shoes.

"May I touch you, Belladonna?" Isra finally asks, the words a whisper. Belladonna nods, and I watch Isra pull her close. Her wings flare wide and for a moment they are both hidden behind a veil of orange and black. I hear their murmurs.

Belladonna extracts herself from Isra's embrace and I sit up. She smiles at me then wraps her arms around our waists. "If we make our own families," she whispers as I lean my cheek against her shoulder, "then I should like to make my family with the two of you."

My heart stutters. Stops. Starts again. I meet Isra's eyes across Belladonna's body. Her smile is soft and her gaze warm. It feels right, to be here now, with the two of them.

Strange, how even now I feel my connection to my arbor diminishing. Even now, I am approaching a certain end, and yet beginnings are all around.

"Belladonna," Isra says, pouring more layers of emotion into each letter than I knew possible. Love, I know, is in how Isra cradles that name.

Belladonna presses her fingers against Isra's lips, the touch so gentle I swear I can feel it as well. "My heart is putting down roots," she whispers. "I'll learn your smile. You'll memorize my laugh. We won't put labels on it. We will pretend we aren't falling like leaves in autumn."

Isra closes her eyes and hums something low in her throat. Behind Belladonna's back, I feel her fingers twine with my own. Starfish illuminate the black.

"I should like to hold this feeling in my arms forever," Belladonna says, turning her focus to me, "but not everything can be touched."

"Name one thing that cannot be," I reply, grinning up at her.

She hesitates. "What of love?"

If love was tangible, it would be her mouth.

"And happiness?" she presses.

I weave my fingers through hers. "I will take you to the garden where happiness grows."

"Rosemary," she breathes.

Even the stars shiver.

THEN
ROSEMARY

He was nervous as we drove the short distance from Divine Muse's temple to the Hall of the Gods. Divine Aether did not seem to know what to do with himself, so I watched as we left Divine Muse's sacred space and his mortality waxed and then waned as we drew near the Hall of the Gods. Watched as he twitched and fidgeted through his years.

Outside, clouds obscured the sun and rain turned the world into pools and reflections. The ocean hung heavy in the air, the scent of sea and salt thick. Down in the Narrows, I would mostly smell shit and rotting fish. Here, the world was clear of that, and for the first time I could truly savor the scent.

Petrichor, I later learned. Sometimes at night, I roll the word around in my mouth. Feel the shape of it. Let the letters hang like fat drops of dew in the garden growing between my ribs.

The city was grand, something I always knew but had never truly savored until this moment, when, safe for the first time, I could finally sit back and take in my surroundings. And what surroundings they were. Each arbor was Created by one of the Divine; their temples stood proudly for the tithe. One arbor we passed was rolling farmland and cabins. The next was a forest, so thick it was impossible to see through the foliage. I thought if I squinted hard enough, I could spy the houses nestled into those branches.

"That arbor's god is one of Father Terra's sons. Divine Forest, I believe. Which reminds me... Rosemary, I have asked Father Terra if he would be willing to fashion you a more durable cane. He said he would love to, but he should like to meet you first." My breath froze and I suddenly felt warm. Divine Aether held his hands up in surrender. "I told him you may not be ready yet. A lot has changed, and I think you may need time to... rest... before you meet more of the Most High."

"Was he angry?" I whispered, head low, back bent. If Divine Aether had already come to harm on my behalf...

Just because Most High Father Luna was kind did not mean his brother would be.

Though the stories painted him as the gentlest among the Most High. I took some comfort in that.

"Father Terra smiled and gave me..." His eyes went wide and he patted the pocket of his suit coat, then pulled out a large white magnolia blossom. It had not withered in Divine Aether's pocket, still as fresh as it had been before it had been plucked.

"He gave this to you?" I asked, taking the bloom from my father's trembling, age-spotted hands. We turned a bend and the age spots receded a little. I watched as they dissipated more with each breath we drew nearer to the Hall.

"Does it mean something?" he asked, staring at the flower as though it was a puzzle.

"Magnolia symbolizes acceptance. Do you think that is why he gave this to me? Does Father Terra... Does he know the language of flowers?" For that is how I had always thought of it. Symbolism to some, but to me, it felt more like each flower's language, and I was but the vehicle which gave them voice. To think there was someone else who spoke thus was a heady prospect indeed.

"He is of the earth itself, Rosemary. Of course he knows." Now, Divine Aether studied me as though I was the puzzle, but I paid him no mind, for I beheld a bloom from Father Terra's Sacred Garden, and the Most High himself had picked it for me.

Father Terra did not know me and already he accepted me.

A tear pricked my eye, slipped down my cheek. When I looked up, we were circling the long drive before the Hall of the Gods and my father was once again youthful.

It was raining when the automobile stopped, the clouds thick and the air heavy. Divine Aether stepped out of the cab, reached toward the heavens, and plucked a nebula from the black, draping it around his shoulders like a cape. It was beautiful, with swirling bands of teal, emerald, and indigo emanating soft ethereal light. He wrapped a corner around me and tucked me well against his side, warm and safe from the chill of the wind. Then, he helped me battle my way up the stairs and when we reached the top, he pulled his heavenly cloak free and smiled at me. "You have stardust in your hair."

Divine Ones stopped when we entered the Hall of the Gods, for likely I had been whispered about, and with Divine Aether newly returned and with his lost wife in tow, likely he was an object of conversation as well.

I shied away from his hold, tried to put distance between us, a buffer so he would not have to be seen with me, but his hand clamped onto my shoulder firmly, rooting me in place. He stared down the length of the Hall, meeting the gazes of all who gathered there. "This is my daughter," he said, as though introducing me to a dear friend. Then, smiling down at me, he murmured, "Come along, Rosemary. Let me show you your new home."

Whispers spread around us like wildfire as gods gathered, watching us pass. My vines grew long, hiding my face in shadow, and I retreated behind the forest of my hair, letting my father guide me forward, my leg only dragging slightly.

"Ah," Aether said after we'd turned a corner, down a quieter, narrower hallway, "the Hall has shifted, likely so you walk less. This is the Hall of the Moon. At night, the soft light turns this space silver. It is as though living among the stars themselves." He sounded positively enchanted by it, but I could see it well enough in my mind. The carpet we tread on was silver and plush, and the walls were painted a white with just a hint of gray. Large windows were evenly spaced, but higher than windows normally would be, to catch the moonlight, I realized. Yes, I could see that this hall would be a thing of beauty when the moon was full and the night ripe with it.

"Tell me, Rosemary, do stairs pain you?" He slowed then and studied me. The stars in his eyes spun, dazzling and bright. His hair was more like smoke now, wisps of night spinning and dissipating with his every motion. His skin gleamed as though lit by galaxies and was black as the space between stars.

"Yes," I whispered, my cheeks flushing.

"I only ask because my apartment was always on the second floor, but when I returned, the Hall had moved it to the first floor. Now I understand. It knew your need and answered it."

"I'm sorry, sir." For I assumed he preferred the second floor.

Divine Aether shrugged. "Oddly enough, the balcony is still on the second floor, and that view of Father Terra's rose garden is why I cherished it so." He winked at me. "The Hall does this. It rearranges to fit the needs of those who dwell there. Divine Muse will walk this very hall and find it on the second floor. Like reality, my heart, it is perception."

He looked over my shoulder and then motioned down the hall a few feet, where a small nook surrounded by glass-paned windows looked out at a garden beyond. Strangely enough, I realized, I was looking down at the rose garden from above, though I had traversed no steps.

There was a bench and it was open for us. I sat, and Divine Aether sat beside me. "I should like to ask you a favor, Rosemary, before you see your mother."

"Is something wrong?"

Terror filled me. Cold as winter. It clamped its crone's hand around my throat and squeezed.

How easily all of this could vanish.

"No, nothing like that. Only, the doctor came. Willow has something they call pneumonia. She will survive it, and heal, but she needs medication three times a day and I..."

He folded his hands in his lap, and if he had been anyone else I would have said he was, perhaps, embarrassed. Gray swirls of color, like storm clouds obscuring moonlight, gathered on his cheekbones and I wondered if this was how he blushed.

"I cannot tell time. I have no notion of one day and the next, even years or lifetimes." I read the story his bent spine and slumped shoulders told me. Dejection needs no words to tell its tale. "I cannot give Willow her medication. She needs it three times a day and I do not even know what a day is."

He hesitated and held his hands out before him. A cloud of gossamer darkness spun in his palms, dotted with small planets still burning hot from the fires of Creation, and there, a nebula, red ribboned through with clouds of indigo. A moment later, he whispered, "I may be Divine, Rosemary, but I cannot even do something so simple. I have not felt helpless in a very long time."

I looked out the window, watched rain bead on the glass and followed the drops with my fingertips.

What would it be like to live, only to fall?

This was another door, I realized. A way I could connect with this man beside me, secure time with him, get to know him. How desperately I had longed to be seen, known, loved. Now, I had someone willing to offer all three. I had but to accept his precious gift.

"It is not such a large challenge," I said.

"It seems... monumental." I have never heard a sigh as exhausted as the one following those words. "I do not think it is within my nature to understand such things."

This made it harder, but not impossible, for while he was beyond time, I was not.

"I can come to you," I offer, "three times a day, every day, and tell you when to give it to her. Remind you of the moments when you are most needed."

He was quiet for so long following those words, I began to worry I said the wrong thing.

"Perhaps..." I hesitated. "We might even be able to track the days together, by counting sunsets."

"Do you think it will be so simple as that?" he asked. Such hope filled him now, the clouds on his cheeks parted and his face glowed with moonlight.

No, it would not be so simple as that. Nothing was ever as simple as sunsets, but his naïveté charmed me. This god had the universe at his fingertips and yet could not do something as simple as tell time.

Suddenly, he did not seem so frightening.

He focused on the cosmos spiraling above his cupped palms. His fingers twitched, and starlight illuminated the black. Then, he held it up to his lips and blew. Together, we watched it drift higher and become larger and dimmer as it floated away.

"It has been a long time since I last observed Mother Sol's artwork," he said.

To hear her described thus surprised me, for I had heard many things about Mother Sol, but few of them were kind. All know that Mother Sol burns.

But, thinking about the sunset, I realized he was right. If the sky was a canvas, the sunsets were Mother Sol's moments of whimsy. Perhaps I need not be so afraid of her, either.

"Yes, Rosemary. We will begin, you and I, by counting sunsets." He held his hand out to me, and I shook it, sealing our deal.

Divinity throbbed between us, a tether fine as spider's silk and just as strong.

I suppose that is how my father and I truly began.

NOW
BELLADONNA

Isra is up before Flora this morning. I can hear the *tap tap* of motion in our otherwise quiet apartment. I listen to the sounds of life coming from the other side of my bedroom door and find comfort in them before I pull myself out of bed and don my robe.

It strikes me then, that this is the first time I have ever taken comfort from sound and I know what that means.

We are, all of us, changing.

A moment later, I am peering in on Flora in her bed. She is lying on her side, her thumb in her mouth, all tangled in her blankets. Her eyes are closed, lashes long and fluttering. I run my fingers through her soft hair. Emotion rises within me, so strong for a moment I cannot breathe through it.

What is this I feel? It cannot be love, for love is too tame a word for this lion clawing at my ribs. The shape is all wrong. The vowels too soft, the consonants too hard. What I am feeling can only be described by the difference between a pebble and a mountain. A tender, curving wave and an ocean.

It is violent and all-consuming.

It is not love. It is not so soft as that.

"Belladonna?" Isra's voice is soft. I turn to see her standing in the hall and go to her, shutting Flora's door behind me. We make our way to the living room so our voices do not carry.

The scent of coffee fills the space and exhaustion presses on me. I drag myself to the kitchen and pour a mug, then lace it with cream.

Isra is waiting when I am done. She stands on the balcony, her arms folded across her chest, wings flared wide. There is a look on her face that I have never seen before. I sip my coffee and wait.

"I will leave today, to Divine Forest's arbor, and I do not know when I will be back," she whispers.

"I know," I say. It hurts. Divine Forest has always been kind to me, his arbor a place I loved to visit on the rare occasions I made it that far. Now, everything will be different. His arbor will still be there, but not the man who Created it. "How is he doing?"

I long to rest my hand on her shoulder. To touch her and bring her comfort, but I feel I need more time to wake up and fortify myself before I so shatter my quiet.

Isra sighs. "Divine Falcon—" Her breath hitches and I cannot stand this distance anymore, so I steady myself and then wrap an arm around her waist and pull her against me. Her wings open behind us, offering us privacy. Isra sighs and rests her head on my shoulder.

My heart trembles and trips to feel her skin against mine, the scent of her. To be so close to summer I might hold it in my arms.

"Divine Falcon often spoke of fulfillment. *I am fulfilled, Isra,* she would say. *I have served my purpose.* She always seemed so easy with it, so content. Atheed, Manab, and I would weep over her, mourning her before she was even gone, and she... It was as though she could not understand our sorrow. *Nothing ever ends, it only changes shape.* She would say those words over and over, until I grew so tired of hearing them."

Isra rarely speaks of her last days with Divine Falcon. Often starting stories and then never completing them, as though that time is so weighed by emotion she cannot find the way to describe what it was like. Now, her voice is smooth and steady and I cling to each of her pain-limned words.

"It was all made so much worse by the war. We could not even send her off the way she deserved. She spent an eternity Creating Dawnland and we had to lay her down secretly, quietly, with no fanfare and no thanks. Bombs going off all around. She fell asleep to the destruction of the very thing she sacrificed herself to Create. That... that is what keeps me up at night. What must it have been like, to know it could so easily be destroyed?"

I do not know what to say to her, so I press my lips against her brow, close my eyes, and hold tight. She shifts and I feel her wings beat the air. Her antennae tickle my cheek, soft as fingertips.

"Divine Forest reminds me of his sister. He is... content, Belladonna. Fulfilled. His arbor is quiet, and respectful, and waiting." She hesitates. "I feel like I am getting to do this right, finally. I am laying down Forest the way I should have laid down Falcon."

But it's hard.

She doesn't have to say as much. I can see it written all over her.

"I wanted to hate you for bringing me here," Isra finally whispers.

I feel her breath puff over my skin as her lips form the words. Sunlight splits the horizon and suddenly the world is all shades of amber and coral. Birds call from nearby trees and I am struck breathless, for how can so much pain exist in the midst of such beauty?

"I am tired of all this misery. My soul aches to feel joy again, to celebrate, to remember that life is not only loss after loss after loss."

"We will have to celebrate," I murmur against her crown, tucking a piece of hair behind her pointed ear. "After this is over, we will have to celebrate their lives, their Creations, and the fact that we made it through."

"I worry," she says after a beat, "about Rosemary."

My heart throbs. I worry about Rosemary, too. For so many reasons.

Isra extracts herself from my embrace. Our eyes meet and she stiffens her shoulders as though marching into battle and then presses her lips against mine, a touch as soft as a butterfly's wings. I feel it in every inch of me. This woman stirs my blood. "I will be back," she says, her eyes wide and watery and soft. "After."

And then she is gone, and I am alone.

I grasp the railing and feel the cool marble beneath my fingers, the way it refuses to bend, refuses to move.

I cannot follow her. I must stay here.

I must be like stone.

Flora wakes, toddles from her room, and rests her hand on my leg. She stares through the posts of the railing at the garden beyond, silent and small and stalwart. It reminds me of how we used to stand on the ferry, side by side like this, watching Chaos seethe all around.

"I love you," I say to my daughter. My heart beats her name.

Flora smiles at me.

I take her inside and feed her a breakfast of berries and oatmeal before she informs me she is still hungry, and I know it is time to take her to the milkweed grove, to satiate that part of her appetite as well.

It is there, in a pool of sunlight, that Divine Shadow finds me. He enters the glade silently, as though afraid to disturb our peace, but I sense him all the same.

Shadow is a hulking figure, hired on to be the enforcer for my crew; he is slow to anger but once he finds his fire, it is hard to put out. His loyalty is unmatched, and his quiet, thoughtful nature has always been a comfort. Now, however, he looks older, and his skin does not alter its hue nearly so much as it once did.

"I heard about the new milkweed grove and thought you might be here." He rests his gaze on Flora. "She's getting big. I feel like it was only yesterday that you were bringing her into the world."

Flora has leaves sticking out of her mouth and her antennae bob as she roughly pulls a flower from a stalk and waves it in the air, babbling all the while.

There is a stone in the center of this place, and Shadow takes a seat. I cannot help but wonder why he is here. I have called a meeting with the crew, but it is not scheduled for some days.

"Do you ever think about it?" he finally asks.

"About what?"

"Dawnland." His eyes find mine, heavy and full of fathomless emotion.

I live with Isra, how could I not think about Dawnland? Still, I nod and watch as he twines his fingers together.

"Sometimes, it's all I can think about. I left Meadowsweet because I was immortal, with an eternity ahead of me to waste away. I had nothing to do and no reason to stay. No arbor or Creation to bind me. I wanted adventure, and so I went in search of it. Now I'm back and everything has changed. More years than I expected have passed, and Grandfather Rain and Uncle Muse are..." His voice chokes off on a sob. "I wish I could go back there, sometimes. Back to the rainforest before war, before I understood what it meant to end."

I don't speak. There is nothing to say. Everything he feels, I feel as well.

"I didn't come here to say this," he says.

"Why did you come here, then?"

"I'm uh.. I'm submitting my resignation from your crew, Belladonna. I... I've lost so much time being away and now, with everything..." He gestures at the Hall of the Gods. "Maybe someday I will want to ferry again, but not... not now."

It hits me, then, a wave of misery. One part of my life is ending. I hear a door slam shut in my soul. I was young once, and full of ideas for adventure. Now I am older and only long for stability.

And then the wave recedes and I realize...

I had not put it into words. I had not given the thought voice, though it has been living inside me all this time. I had not allowed myself to contemplate it, but Shadow's words unlock truth and I can deny it no more.

I don't want to ferry, either. I have lost too much time and I do not want to lose more.

"I don't want to ferry anymore either, Shadow."

He lifts his head and our eyes meet. In his gaze, I see the fullness of his understanding.

Shadow sighs. "Did you know it would be this hard?"

I shake my head, though I do not know if he's talking about the fading, returning to Meadowsweet, or leaving Dawnland. Perhaps all of it.

"Belladonna," he says after a moment, "do you think we could... spend time together? Get a drink sometime? Something?"

Companionship is what he is asking for, a moment to be with someone who understands what it is to return after a lifetime away.

Nothing ever ends. It just changes shape.

"I would like that," I say.

Flora toddles to Shadow, rests a hand on his knee. I watch as her touch fills him with peace. His muscles unclench and uncoil.

"This child," he says, studying my daughter, "is a gift, Belladonna."

"I know," I reply.

NOW

ISRA

I know I am done weaving his bed before I finish tying it off. It is less something I see and more something I feel, a certain shift in the air. My fingers hesitate, halfway through my row. Divine Forest's hand trembles on my shoulder, his touch light. "Thank you," he says with his soft, soft voice.

My breath hitches. This is harder than I thought it would be.

Divine Forest has not spoken much. The longer I am here, the quieter he becomes. Every now and again, he stands and shuffles forward a few feet, drawing ever nearer to his tree, and I watch his progress as I work. Mist clings to my wings like jewels. About an hour ago, I moved my weaving to a rocky outcrop near where he is currently sitting, so close to his resting place I can see the whorls on the emerald door from where I sit.

With his last bit of Divinity, Forest has summoned a root from the soil and sits upon it. He is so much smaller now, and not just in size. His presence has grown insubstantial, the edges of him fading.

It reminds me so much of Divine Falcon, at the last.

I look upon my handiwork with pride. The fabric is tight and the sticks are bent in a way to cradle his body. It looks like a hammock, all soft green and warm brown. A place where he will rest cradled by his Creation.

My fingers are all blistered and sore, though it has not been so difficult as I suspected. The arbor was busy overnight, collecting sticks and leaves worthy of Divine Forest's resting. They divided themselves into groups, some taking the task of foraging, others peeling off bark and sanding, still others softening the leaves so they will be soft as cotton against his tender skin.

Weaving leaves is not so different than braiding flowers.

I bend the last leaf into place and tie it off, but the tie snaps and slices my finger. I watch as a drop of crimson falls, marring the green of Forest's bed. For a moment, I sit in horrified silence. I have destroyed his resting place with my carelessness.

But more...

Forest offers a spare leaf to use as a rag. "Will you leave your blood, Isra? Or will you wipe it away entirely?"

Such simple questions, and yet Forest knows what he is about. I have not bled in Meadowsweet yet. I think of my brothers and my trunk. Once my blood soaks into the weave, part of me will always be in Meadowsweet. Part of me will always be *here*.

Is that what I want?

I reach for the leaf Forest is offering. Hesitate.

Is not part of me already in Meadowsweet?

Belladonna, golden as the new day.

Flora and her dimples.

Rosemary and her flowers.

"Home," Forest says, his voice a low murmur, "can be in more than one place. It can be with more than one person." It must be their years that give the Divine such an uncanny understanding of a person's soul.

I watch my blood sink into those leaves and wait for part of myself to cry out for Dawnland, but it does not come. For the first time since I woke on Belladonna's ferry, woozy from Manab's medication, I feel... found. Like I am finally somewhere I belong.

My heart is putting down roots, Belladonna had said in Divine Rain's arbor.

I feel that now. My heart is putting down roots. Part of me will always be in Meadowsweet. Suddenly, this place feels a little less strange, and I not so lost in it.

Home can be in more than one place.

Pressure releases and I realize, with shocking clarity, that I am not giving up Dawnland by living in Meadowsweet. I do not love my brothers any less for finding love here. Manab may have done me wrong, may have manipulated and hurt me and Belladonna both, but now that I am here... I can see he was only trying to give me more. That does not mean I forgive him, but I am beginning to understand the shape of how he loved me.

A ragged wound in my soul begins, at last, to heal. It will leave scar tissue in its wake, a memory I will always feel.

"Will you tell me of my sister? What did she enjoy?" Divine Forest's voice sounds like the last gasp of autumn before the first winter storm.

"She loved reading," I say. "There were books in the World Tree, a vast library of tomes she had collected from other Creations when ferriers came through, and some she wrote about her life. So many of them, I never read them all." The library was magnificent, a huge hollow carved from the World Tree, lined with branches that Divine Falcon had Created to function as shelves, always growing as she needed more space. Orchids lined the walls, the fragrance both heady and soft.

When we were young, before pupation, Divine Falcon would take us there. We would array ourselves around her feet and she would read stories from times long, long ago.

We did not yet understand how life could hurt.

Ten of us hatched. Six of us survived pupation. Three of us were alive when I left. Am I the only one now?

That thought fills me with suffocating loneliness.

To be the last.

No. I refuse to believe it.

Divine Forest shifts, gets comfortable on his root. "I have missed her every moment, and yet it is strange, Isra. I feel closer to her than I have in years, as though she is but a breath away." He pauses. Looks around. Behind us, his arbor is arrayed in shades of white. The air is hushed in a way I have never before heard. There is a reverence here that I can feel with every part of me.

The residents of his arbor have kept their distance, but I can feel them behind us, lining the pathways and the trees, watching and waiting to see what comes next. "I feel their love every time they use one of my prayers, and every time they tread their feet upon my soil. I look upon them as my children. I cannot imagine what they make of my arbor, when I at last gift them this place. Do you think they will care for this piece of me, Isra? Do you think they will love me as much as I have loved them?" Forest hesitates. "Have I done right by them?"

I take my time to answer. "Your arbor is full of happy, well-fed, healthy residents. The trees in your forest are tall and stalwart. All of Meadowsweet is bedecked in white to celebrate your accomplishments." I turn, look him in the eye. "You have done right by them, Forest. You have done right by all of us."

A breeze rustles the grasses and a cloud of swallowtail butterflies alight. Their wings look like stolen bits of sunshine.

Forest smiles. It is soft, that smile, and satisfied.

"I always wondered, what it would feel like to be at this moment. If I would be afraid, or perhaps regret."

"And do you?"

Forest plucks a blade of grass and studies it.

"I am tired, Isra, and I am ready."

Divine Falcon's voice echoes through my mind.

"I have never been inside that tree," Forest says after a moment. "I Created it from Falcon's design. I know where the rooms are inside the trunk, the stairs. I know where I want to lie down, but I have never seen it."

"Why not?"

"At first, it was because I was afraid being there would make me miss Falcon too much. Now, I realize that might be where I find her." He braces himself to stand and I hop to my feet and hold out an arm to him. He grips me with his trembling hands and heaves himself up, groaning as his body unfolds.

"I'm ready, Isra. The time to rest has come."

I see Divine Falcon, stooped and frail at the last. *"I am so tired, Isra."*

I see Forest now, stooped and frail at the last. "I am so tired, Isra," he says.

I hold back a sob, barely.

This moment is an ocean and I am lost within its waves.

"Do not weep for me." Forest brings one trembling hand to my cheek. "This is what I was Created to do. I am content."

A gust of wind off the sea brings salty air and a soft susurration with it. I cock my head to the side. Whispers, I realize, a chorus of them from the arbor at our backs.

Forest turns, each step hard fought for and hard won. I turn with him and behold the wonder of his Creation—for behind us, his arbor is filled, not just with the residents of this place, but with every member of the Divine who is capable of attending, and each of them holds a candle. The pathways are lit with a thousand, thousand points of light, each one burning bright.

"Oh," Forest breathes. His chin wobbles and tears spill down the runnels in his cheeks. "What are they saying?"

I listen until I can make out the words. "Thank you," I reply. "They are saying thank you, Divine Forest."

He studies the glory of what he has Created, from the trees to the soil, and all that is held between the two. Then, he turns to me. "I am ready, Caretaker Isra. It is time to give this Creation to those it is truly meant for."

I can't do this.

I have to do this.

I wipe my eyes, steady my trembling heart.

"You are acting as though this is a death story," Forest says, gentle rebuke in his voice. "Nothing ever ends, Isra. It only changes shape." I savor those words. It is as though Divine Falcon is whispering in my ear. How I miss her.

How can he be so easy with this when it shreds me so?

The walk to his tree feels like it takes an eternity and yet it passes in a blink. Reality mixes and merges.

I am in Dawnland.

I am in Meadowsweet.

Forest grasps the threshold with his free hand and turns. His eyes, as he takes in his arbor, are filled with pride. "I have done well, Isra," he says. "I am pleased with what I have wrought."

Thank you.

Thank you.

Thank you.

The susurration is hypnotic, the sweetest lullaby.

We stand on the threshold of his tree, his resting place. I rest my hand on the knob, prepare myself for what is inside, for what will happen there.

Suddenly, Forest draws in a breath and shouts with strength I did not realize he still had, "All of this is yours now. Make something wonderful of it."

Then he looks at me. "Lay me down, Isra. I am ready to rest."

"I will love you, Divine Forest," I say, repeating my promise to him, "even into the last."

I turn and look over my shoulder.

I catch my breath for there, in the crowd, holding onto each other and watching me with tearful eyes, are Belladonna and Rosemary, draped in white.

I am not alone.

NOW
ROSEMARY

Images of Divine Forest haunt me all the way back to the Hall of the Gods. Neither Belladonna nor I speak on the journey back. All of Meadowsweet has been draped with white, and the streets are silent. The speakeasies have shut their doors. The lanterns on the corners have been festooned with white ribbons. White on white on white.

Belladonna weaves her fingers through mine as our automobile jolts its way toward the Hall, but neither of us speaks. We are riding toward our future, toward our fate. There is no avoiding it. No turning around. No going back. Behind me is sorrow. Ahead of me is sorrow. I am nothing but an ache, a wound, suppurating and raw.

I watched Divine Forest disappear into his tree, to rest, and yet what I saw was my father, my uncle, my grandfather. All the people I have loved. All the people who have been so formative in my life.

I dig my knuckles into my hip to ease the ache, but it doesn't help. Nothing helps anymore.

The Hall of the Gods looms ahead of us, and Isra behind. All I can think of is pain, and all the different kinds of it. Like flowers in spring, it sprouts within me. A garden of it. Thistle and briar and all those thorns. They wrap around me until I am suffocating.

"Belladonna," I whisper as the palatial complex sprawls before us. She turns her attention to me. Her eyes do not glow so much anymore, and I see the woman beneath all her summer. She is beautiful and blonde, with deep laugh lines and gray threaded through the hair near her temples.

I have never seen someone so beautiful.

"Yes, beloved?"

The automobile pulls into the large, circular drive. Even the Hall feels muted now, and the only people milling about are crying.

All of Creation, it feels, is crying.

Belladonna squeezes my fingers. The car stops and the engine cuts off. Our driver gets out and waits a respectful distance away to let us talk.

I have never been good at asking for help. I had to be an adult far too soon, in a world where relying on others was dangerous. Yet if Belladonna can be open and speak her feelings with Isra and me, then should I not do the same?

"I need help," I whisper. I hate how my voice quivers.

"Anything," Belladonna says. There is a furrow between her brows, and I long to rub my thumb over it, to smooth that crease.

"I think I need to see a doctor, for my pain." It fills me with shame, even saying these words, admitting this is a problem I can no longer cope with alone. I am not as strong as I want her to think I am. Part of me is afraid that she will see the truth of my condition and leave. That there will be a day when she looks upon me and realizes I am a burden, or perhaps she will become tired of my pain, my limitations. I do not want to hold her back. Equally I do not want to be left behind.

"A doctor?" Belladonna asks. Her furrow deepens. Her eyes scan my face. I feel her gaze like a touch.

I hesitate. "I... I am scared." I remember my father, all those years ago, when asking me to help him learn the way of time. *It feels monumental,* he'd said. That is how this feels. Monumental. I am admitting something now, a truth about myself that I have not been able to face yet.

Tears blur my vision. I am so tired of crying. "I am in so much pain," I say. "It lives within me."

"Rosemary," she breathes.

"It is more than just physical, Belladonna. I am sad. I am so sad. It is in my heart, in my soul. I live in winter and remember what it was like to be surrounded by summer. To open my eyes and only see light. I want to feel that again, but I don't know how." I draw a breath. "Does this make me weak?"

"Weak?" Belladonna whispers. "Never that." She moves closer to me, wraps me in her arms. I wonder if she realizes how much easier she is with touching now. "Would you like me to go to the doctor with you, Rosemary? I could sit in the waiting room or go in with you."

"You would do this for me?"

She presses her lips against my crown. "Don't you know by now that when I look at you, I only see light."

I lean into her words, wrap them around me.

I remember a time before Belladonna left. "Promise me," she had said after she had found me weeping in my room while my leg twisted, "to no longer hide your pain."

I opened my mouth to speak but she stilled me with an upraised hand.

"If we laugh together, Rosemary, why then do you ache alone?"

Belladonna's hair tickles my nose and I am back in the present. "I am so scared," I admit, "of being alone and in pain. I am scared of drowning in sorrow."

"Never alone," she says.

Our driver pointedly checks his watch and I know it's time to let him have his automobile.

Belladonna helps our driver get my wheelchair. Once I am situated well enough, Belladonna pushes me into Father Terra's garden. She finds a bench beside a clump of daisies.

"I miss Isra," Belladonna whispers as she rests her head against my shoulder.

My heart squeezes, and I realize I miss Isra, too.

"I know," I answer.

We sit in silence as the night stretches around us. I rest my head on Belladonna's shoulder and close my eyes. We need this, I think. A moment of stillness before the unraveling.

"Rosemary?" A new voice this time.

Dream stands before me, a photo frame clutched in her hand. She is so much older now, aging a bit more each time I see her. She looks more like a grandmother than the young cousin I have always considered a friend. Still, I would recognize her anywhere.

I know what this is before she needs to say a word. I have seen *goodbye* in her eyes for weeks.

"My father," she says.

I straighten in my wheelchair. My heart squeezes. Wind rustles nearby flowers.

This endless night.

"I know," I say. "You need to go to him."

"I miss him so much, Rosemary. A ferrier is leaving in the morning, going to my father's Creation. If I can make it before—" Her voice hitches. "If I can lay him down…"

She sounds like she is apologizing for this, or perhaps convincing herself she is making the right decision. Dream has never left Meadowsweet.

"I don't know if I will ever see you again," she says.

It is strange, how quick the realization settles on me that this goodbye is not just for now, but probably forever. To not see her every day…

I am so scared of being alone. I am so tired of saying goodbye. I long to rid myself of this ache.

Belladonna weaves her fingers through mine. Her touch is steadying, her presence calm.

"You have been my greatest friend," I tell Dream.

She holds the frame she has been clutching out to me and I take it.

"Your mother has often mentioned that she dreamed she had a daughter, Rosemary. I asked her what her dream daughter looks like and then drew her how your mother described her."

With trembling hands, I turn the frame over.

"Wow," Belladonna breathes.

Dream's lines are careful and her shading is masterful. She has used charcoal on this sketch, and the figure seems realistic enough to breathe off the page. That is not what staggers my heart as I study her art, however, for I recognize the face staring back at me. I look into those eyes in the mirror.

"You see?" Dream says. "Your mother loves you, Rosemary, even when she does not know you."

It is then that the tears fall. My mother's love heals me, and Dream breaks me all over again.

"Promise me you will always dream," my cousin says.

"Always," I whisper.

"I love you, Rosemary. Maybe someday we will see each other again."

I press my lips against her cheek, but when I go to speak, a sob is all that I can manage. She extracts herself from my embrace and then backs away slowly. Just before she disappears around a lavender-shrouded bend in the path, she blows me a kiss.

And then she is gone.

Gone and gone and gone.

"Should we go inside?" Belladonna asks.

I nod. I do not want to be alone tonight.

The journey to the Hall takes longer than it needs to, but we are both delaying. Belladonna stops to admire each flower, and I aid in the distraction by pointing out ever more flowers for her to note as we go. By the time we enter the Hall, nearly an hour has passed.

Belladonna walks beside me to the lift that I now need to use to get to my apartment on the second floor. It's small and cramped and makes a horrendous grinding noise as it moves, but it's better than trying to brave the stairs when my pain is high.

The hallway outside my apartment is quiet, and I hesitate at my door, wondering if Belladonna is going to leave me here or if she is planning on following me in. What is the protocol?

I decide to let her decide what she wants to do and push the door open.

Father is sitting with Mother on the couch in this dark room. They are facing the windows Mother so loves, their heads bent together.

"When are we, my darling?" Father asks. He is nearly mortal now. His pate is bald and age-spotted, his eyes are black, starless voids, his hands tremble.

"I was young, standing on a beach at sunset. A jazz band was playing—"

"I remember," my father says. "You were dancing. Never have I seen such a beautiful sight."

They spend hours walking through their history together, as though my father is reliving each one, sipping from this cup of sweetest memory.

I maneuver my wheelchair through the door and in the process, knock over the cane I have resting there. The clatter attracts my parents' attention. Belladonna bends over to pick up my fallen item and my father...

There is something different about him now.

It isn't until he speaks that I realize what it is.

"My heart," he says, "I am so tired. So very, very tired."

THEN
ROSEMARY

Muse found me late one night, several months after I moved into the Hall of the Gods. He had a mischievous glint in his eye and a smile that made the world erupt with birdsong. "Would you like to play a game tonight, niece?"

"A game?" I asked, for Muse so enjoyed games and fun, and I loved the adventure that constantly seemed to swirl around him.

Dream was helping Mother relax and Aether had gone into Meadowsweet to visit his temple and create prayers. I had little to fill my empty hours this night aside from radio shows, and I had listened to my share of those already.

"A game," Muse grinned. "Do you know how to play cards?"

Cards? I had seen them played often enough, but I had never had a chance to play myself.

"It is no matter. Come with me?"

He chuckled and a symphony burst from between his teeth, the music joyful, like bees in lavender.

How could I deny a smile such as that?

He waited for me to stand from the ottoman I had set myself upon to listen to my radio shows, and then again as I braced myself with my cane. My leg was a twisted snarl, and had it been any other day I would have preferred to stay sitting, but the light in Muse's moonlit eyes was infectious, so I followed him. He kept the pace steady and serene, allowing me to set the limits of my ability. He did not offer me his arm or hover about me as I limped but accepted me how I was.

Outside, it was raining, a soft spring storm. Water beaded on the windows, obscuring Father Terra's garden beyond. The world was becoming alive again after a brutal winter, all bright green and beaded with blossoms. The vines around my crown lengthened their coils, hanging loose and languid around my shoulders.

Still, the hall felt too long and my leg too twisted, this day. Before we made it far, I was limping and leaning heavily on my cane, my leg dragging. From my crown grew nettle and blackberry. The private hallway of Father Luna's sons' apartments ended at another hallway, this one wider and full of the Divine. We turned left onto it, passing a mother and girl of about five, both of them luminous as sunlight.

"What is wrong with her?" the girl asked, her voice pitched loud enough for me to hear.

"Hush," her mother replied. "Don't say such things aloud."

No, the word vibrated through my mind like plucked guitar string. *You must only* think *them.*

My cheeks flamed pink and I hid my face behind my vines.

Muse ducked around a corner, and Father Luna's Sacred Observatory opened before us. When I next looked at my uncle, the muscles in his jaw were pulsing and his eyes were bright with fire. I eased myself onto a stone bench and watched as a planet, purple and glowing, spun past the windows.

What's wrong with her?

I clutched my cane, suddenly ashamed that I needed it, hated that I had it. That and my strange gait would always mark me out as other.

"I am broken," I said, wiping tears from my eyes. My leg throbbed in time to my heart, and I dug my knuckles into my hip.

"Broken?" Muse spat the word like it was a curse he could not be rid of fast enough. "What nonsense is this? Of course you are not broken. Just because I have never seen your like, does not make you wrong. The best songs are the ones I have never heard before."

I sniffled, wiped my nose.

Muse's presence was warm and comforting. I could feel Father Luna there somewhere, ephemeral as dreams, spinning his web of darkness on the other side of his Observatory.

"You do not need to be anything other than who you are, Rosemary." He wrapped his arms around me and pulled me close. Simple words, but the acceptance in them stirred up a storm of emotion in my soul. Would I ever get used to how powerfully Muse made me feel?

Before us, a planet, green and blue, spun past, followed by a trail of stars.

"Are we ready?" Father Luna's voice boomed through his Observatory. The light was dappled with the cosmos outside, pools of greens, purples, teals, starbright and silver.

Father Luna appeared before us, a man wrapped in ever-changing shadows. Occasionally, I would catch a glimpse of his eyes in all that night. The dark around him parted and I saw his smile. The planets beyond the glass hummed in response.

"Granddaughter," he said, "I am glad Muse convinced you to come tonight."

Father Luna reached out and took my arm, helped me stand.

"Does this game night happen often?"

"We try to come together occasionally, when we remember," my grandfather said.

Along the windows, I noticed, was a large, round table that looked to be cut from the base of an enormous tree. Around it were four chairs.

"Terra crafted this table for my games," Grandfather said, leading me forward. He pulled out a chair and waited for me to sit and then took the one beside me. This close to the glass, I could smell ozone and the cosmos when they swirled by, painting me with radiant color.

"Is Aether coming?" Muse asked, taking the seat on my other side.

"He's on his way," Luna replied. "I can feel him drawing closer." I could feel him too, that knowing in my blood, a certain shared awareness. A moment later, Aether appeared. His cheeks glowed with moonlight and his eyes were bright.

"My heart," he whispered before pressing a kiss to my cheek and then taking the seat beside Muse. "Are we ready?"

Father Luna reached into his dark and pulled out a deck of cards. I had expected them to perhaps be Divine in nature, glowing or something wondrous like that, but the cards Father Luna held were plain as they came. I could buy this same pack at the corner store for two prayers. He tapped them out of the box with fingers dipped in starlight. A cloud, silver and glowing, rolled slowly up his arm, disappearing beneath his midnight veil.

He shuffled the cards, shuffled again, then cut the deck and began dealing.

"How do we play?" I asked, picking up my cards to inspect my hand.

"Watch, my heart," Aether said. His eyes were twinkling and when he smiled, the dimple in his right cheek glowed like a sliver of moon. "Join in when you understand."

Muse winked at me.

"Ready?" Father Luna asked. Upon his word, the cosmos beyond the glass grew still, hanging motionless in the black.

He slapped a six of stars on the table and the stars sped past again, faster now, then planets. A moon. Aether followed with a ten of suns, then Muse with a two of trees. They played their hand, faster and faster, slamming down cards with little rhyme or reason.

I would see them like that forever, laughing over a game of cards, heads bent while the universe slid by. Painted by rays of luminous light they were.

A moment trapped in amber.

I could find no method to the game. They threw cards down seemingly at random, drew them also at random. They didn't take turns or go in any specific order. They didn't even seem to be playing against each other. I could not fathom what they were about, and so I clutched my hand to my chest and watched in fascination as the three Divine bent their heads and went about their play.

Then, as if by a cue I missed, they stopped.

A small, wooden pot with a matching lid appeared in the center of the table.

"Who won?" Muse asked.

Aether looked at his remaining hands and sighed. "I think you won, Muse." He grabbed the pot and put something in it and covered it with the lid, then handed it to me. "Tell your story, brother." He tapped his nose and whispered loud enough for all to hear, "For Muse, Rosemary. He gets a treasure because he won."

A sprig of laurel grew from my crown and I snapped it off and put it in the pot, then handed it on to Father Luna.

"I remember," Muse said thoughtfully, "when I Created the first song." He met my eyes and smiled.

"In all of Chaos, there was only silence," Aether said. His eyes grew distant, and for a moment, the night around Father Luna churned, and I saw Chaos, seething and silent. "The first I heard your song, Muse, I thought you had lost your mind."

"You came to me," Luna said, his voice a low rumble, "and said, 'Father, what is Muse about? It is so *loud*!'" They laughed, and I laughed with them, though I didn't understand the joke.

"I can still hear it, Rosemary," Muse said, bending close, a twinkle in his eye. "The music of Creation. It is both part of me and apart from me."

"Does it hurt," I asked, "to be so torn?"

"We will not always be," my father said, his voice somber. "Someday we will Create our last and then—"

"Your last?" I said. "How can you speak of last? You are eternal."

"You need to talk to her, Aether, about what *forever* means," Muse said as he removed the lid from his winnings. He held my laurel branch and raised a questioning eyebrow. The moons in his eyes tipped on their sides, smiling.

"Victory," I explained.

Then he reached in again and offered up a star from my father, newly formed and throbbing with light. And then a black wisp from Father Luna.

"A dream," Father Luna explained, his voice tender, "soft and good. Use it when your slumber is most troubled."

"Thank you," Muse said, carefully placing his winnings back in the pot. "I will treasure these gifts."

My father stood and held an arm out to me. "Thank you for the game. I should like to talk to my daughter now."

Luna pressed his lips against my cheek. "Visit me soon, granddaughter."

"I will return tomorrow afternoon, as usual." I loved the way he made my blood hum like the stars beyond the glass.

Aether lead me from the Observatory and out a small door to Father Terra's garden beyond. It was still raining, but he motioned for me to wait while a star appeared before us, summoned into being. With a flick of his fingers, it rolled onto its side and lifted to hover over our heads like a glowing umbrella. Raindrops sizzled as they hit, and then sprayed around us like fireworks. "To the gazebo," he said, pointing a short way away.

The gazebo was a beautiful, understated place lined by trumpet vines and wisteria. Aether motioned for me to sit on the bench and the star floated away to take its place in the court of the sky. He sat beside me, folded his arms and then unfolded them. Moonlit clouds marched across the backs of his hands.

"Rosemary," he finally said, "Muse is right. There are things you need to understand. What you said at the game—"

"You are eternal." I had not thought of what those words truly meant before I thrust them into the world. My father was Divine, and so we would never need to have any long, sad goodbyes.

In my short, tumultuous life, I had finally found someone unchanging. I did not question it.

"It is not so simple as eternal, my heart," my father said.

"Are you saying…" My voice trembled.

Do not make me love you, only to leave.

"Everything I Create costs a bit of my soul, and my soul is not infinite, Rosemary. Someday, we will all Create our last, this body will begin fading, and I will—"

"No." I stood but my leg buckled and I fell back to the bench.

"—join the pieces of my soul I have already offered up."

"No!" I nearly screamed the word. It did not matter that he was speaking of somedays that were likely far off. All I saw was another end.

Love and loss.

Always loss.

Aether wrapped his arms around me, pulled me against his chest, and rocked, a slow, steady rhythm, until I calmed. "My cousin, Divine Falcon, often said that nothing ever ends, it only changes shape. I will not always be wearing this body, Rosemary, but I will always be here. I will be part of everything I have Created. I am part of you."

I clung to him then, curled my fingers in his fine shirt and sobbed.

"It will be a glorious day, when I can bestow all I have Created to those I have Created it for. When I can finally, once again, be whole."

"But you will leave me."

He hesitates. "You were my greatest act of Creation, Rosemary. I am satisfied with what I have wrought." Then, softer, "I will love you, whether I am here to say the words or not."

"But I want to hear you say the words—"

"I love you."

"—always."

I pressed my ear against his chest, listened to the steady beat of his heart as rain fell, a soft drumbeat on the gazebo roof.

Finally, I squeezed my eyes shut. "If this is not to be forever, if I should only have you for now, I..." Aether's fingers wove through my hair.

"There is briar rose blooming between your vines, my heart. What does that mean?"

"Divine love," I answered. Then I sat up and looked him in the eye. "I should like to call you Father, if you—"

He did not wait before throwing his arms around me and holding me close. He buried his nose against my crown and breathed me in.

"Oh, Rosemary," he whispered in my ear, "you are the sweetest bloom."

NOW
BELLADONNA

I arrive at my mother's house at tea time, with four movers. "My room is on the third floor," I say.

"Belladonna?" Mother is in the entryway, watching with wide eyes. "What is this?"

The men disappear upstairs, and it is just us. Mother ushers me into the kitchen. We listen to the sounds of footsteps on stairs, the heavy tread of boots.

"I visited my room," I say when the house finally goes quiet.

Mother sits at the kitchen table with a sigh. She looks better today, though she is still pale. She sips her tea, but I note she does not try to eat.

"Really," she says, arching an eyebrow. Her voice, for all she tries to make it sound rigid and cold, cracks. She picks up her teacup, sips, puts it back down. "When did you do that?"

"Yesterday," I tell her. "While you were sleeping."

She lifts her gaze and we stare at each other across this battlefield the table has become.

"Belladonna—"

"Tell me about your bedroom," I say.

"What?" Her eyes go wide, as though the switch of topic has sent her spinning. "What does my—"

"Ma'am." A mover appears, carrying a small chest, a cupboard I'd used to play kitchen with as a child. I'd wanted it for Flora. "There's black mold on this. Do you want it?"

I glare at Mother. "No, thank you."

He leaves.

"Your room," I say, bringing us back to the conversation at hand. "That quilt is the same one I remember from my childhood, not a stitch has faded. What an extraordinary sum of money it must cost you to keep all of that preserved, or refresh it whenever something fades."

"What are you driving at, Belladonna?" Hard is that voice, and flinty. Daisy enters the room with a tray of food, sees us, and then quickly turns around and leaves. We are alone here, nothing but a table between us and a lifetime of frustration.

"Sorry, ma'am." The mover again. "And this?" He holds up a box of stuffed animals, moth eaten and dusty.

"Keep them, please." I might be able to recover some bits of them. I turn back to Mother. "The moment I left you forgot it existed."

Could she not understand how much that hurt me?

"I didn't know if you were coming back."

"You didn't know if Father was coming back, either, and yet you tend all of his things." I lock eyes with her. "Why do I not warrant the same consideration?"

"Bella—"

"The only thing in my room that was touched in all my time away was Father's bookshelf and the books *you* gave me."

Explain yourself, I want to scream.

"I was angry!" Mother shouts. She does not stand, but stays seated, pulls her robe tighter around herself and glares at the table-top. "I have tried to prepare you for the world, to mold you into a form that would fit into a better life. You insisted on wearing suits and dating women, and then you... left, Belladonna. I put all my energy and effort into making you a daughter your Father will be happy to come home to—"

It is like glass shattering when I hear those words. He has ever been the shadow cast across my days.

"I don't want him to come home."

Mother gasps. "You don't mean that."

"I mean that!" My voice is so loud I flinch from the sound of it. Even the movers pause on the stairs. "I mean every word of that! And even if he did return after all these years, I would not consider him. He left, Mother. He looked at both of us and decided a job ferrying was better than staying here. He *abandoned* us. And you have spent every day since that moment clinging to his memory. He is not even dead and yet you've turned him into a ghost."

"He is my husband." Whispered are those words, so soft I have to strain to make them out.

The movers descend the rest of the way down the stairs and a moment later we hear them on the street, talking as they load the truck.

I am erasing myself from this place.

"I tried to do the best for you," Mother says. "I tried to raise you well, to see you lifted higher in life. I tried to mold you into a better form and give you good prospects—"

I snort. "Mold me into a better form, as though I am clay and you are but shaping me into a proper vessel."

"That is exactly what I'm doing." Her eyes flash in triumph, as though now that I understand, I will see reason. "A woman must be a proper vessel, Belladonna. Now that you have a daughter of your own, surely you understand."

Flora is not a vase or a bauble. She is not a portrait to hang on the wall and talk to at the right moments.

She will never see us as anything more than tools waiting to be used.

"Don't you see?" Mother whispers. "It requires sacrifice, to be a woman in this world."

Sacrifice, she says.

As though she understands a thing about sacrifice.

"I can't do this anymore."

"Do what?"

I gesture between us. "This."

"Belladonna, surely..." She sighs, and it is this sigh that undoes me, for I have heard that sound all my life. That breath of air slipping past her lips, the exhaustion in it. As though she is saying, *Belladonna is just throwing another tantrum, it will be over in a moment.* As though I am a child again. "I know you, daughter. You will return when your ire blows over."

"You don't know me," I say.

"I'm your mother. I know you," she spits.

"You have never known me."

I brace my hands on the tabletop and breathe deep. Emotions roil. I am a tempest-churned sea. I want to scream. I want to rage, to shout. I want her to understand a fraction of what she has put me through.

I was so easily forgotten by the one person who should never forget me.

Finally, I look up. "Your eyes remind me of diamonds, Belladonna," Mother says.

"Because they shine?"

"Because they are hard."

This hurts. No matter my anger, this moment is a wound and I will feel it until the day I die. Mother, sitting in her chair at her kitchen table, in this empty, empty house, which is getting emptier by the moment. She is sick, and older now. Frail in a way I have never seen before.

There were good moments as well as bad. Times she read me stories at night or laughed and told jokes. Times, before life soured her, when she was easy to love.

"Let me in on your life," Mother says.

I shake my head. I can't. I won't. There are so many things I could tell her. Flora's first word was mama and her second was *tanta,* for she loves Isra so, and I am eager for the day when she looks at Rosemary and calls to her as well. When I was in Dawnland, I ran my own successful business along with my crew. I have ferried. I have survived Chaos. I have gone and returned. I can do anything.

But the words do not come, and they will not. She would not understand and I am no longer the girl who hung so much on hope.

Another mover appears, arms laden with moth-eaten, tattered dresses from my closet. "Do you want to keep any of these?" he asks.

"No."

Mother gasps. "Belladonna, they are salvageable. Still good. There are dresses in there that—"

"Grandmother Dove made them for me, Mother, because she accepts me. She loves me, and she wants nothing more for me than my happiness, regardless of how I find it." And even now, Grandmother Dove is preparing herself for her rest. *I am so tired, Belladonna,* she had said to me only this morning. She and her sisters have been in Mother Sol's solarium and I will return there soon, sit with my cousins. We will prepare their beds for their final resting.

"She should have had dresses made. They are more fitting. Really, Belladonna, suits? How will people think of you if you go walking around dressed like a man?"

Even now.

Even now, she says these things to me.

I know, with a finality I have not let myself yet face, that to stay here, in this house, will mean spending a lifetime with her subtle abuse and passing it along to my daughter. It will mean subjecting those I love to it and I... I will not do that. I will not allow her to mold either me or Flora in her image.

Sometimes, to love, you must walk away.

We are on the cusp of a new age. I will not enter it with an anchor weighing me down, holding me in place. I will not spend my life being molded or manipulated, and I certainly will not allow as much for my daughter.

She is my mother, but I do not owe her my soul.

"I have a whole life outside of these walls," I say, "full of people who love me and accept me as I am and who will love Flora, no matter who she becomes. They see us as people, not clay, not ornaments, not stepping stones to a better life. When I sleep at night, I want to wake looking upon tomorrow, not yesterday." I study the movers as they carry my father's bookshelf down the stairs. "I came here because I thought perhaps we could form a relationship between us. Perhaps after all these years, you'd be different and I'd be different and we could finally be parent and child but I see now that is not the case—"

"Belladonna, I'll do better."

"No," I say, "you won't. There is something soft in you, Mother, and it is rotting."

I turn, stride out of the kitchen, my feet ringing hollowly over the floorboards. Mother follows me, trailing some steps behind. She is silent, watching my progress. She does not argue, I notice.

She is content to let me leave.

"I'm sorry," she whispers.

I wait for the movers to slide past me, out the door, and then follow them down the hall. Already their truck is piled high, I notice through the window. Outside, bells start chiming in temples across Meadowsweet. I think of Isra and Rosemary. I think of Forest and Aether.

There are so many places I'd rather be than here. So many people I'd rather be with. Those bells, however, are ringing for Forest, and Isra will need someone to lean on.

"I'm sorry too," I say. I look over my shoulder one last time. Mother is standing in her robe, hugging herself. Her face is pale and her eyes haunted.

I will not come back here, and when our gazes meet, I know she understands as much. This is the end.

"Goodbye, Mother," I say.

I open the door.

And leave.

For the last time.

NOW

ISRA

Divine Forest lays on his bed inside his tree. His presence is a powerful force here, even in his final hours. This room is very much like the one Divine Falcon rests in. There is a window in the far wall, a slit between the vines that allows me to see to the world outside. His arbor is filled, candles chasing away the shadows. The sweet susurration of *thank you* has not ended, but grown ever louder the more he fades.

I am glad it is the last song he will hear, so he might find his rest wrapped in a lullaby of gratitude sung by those he Created all of this for.

This room is smaller than the one in Dawnland, the walls are smooth wood, the floor is polished. There are no adornments and no furnishings. After I laid Forest down, hours ago, I dashed out to borrow a stool. Now, I sit beside his bed and watch as he fades.

He does not speak often. As the hours grow longer, Forest grows quieter and withdraws deeper into himself. I let him have his peace and I take solace in the silence.

"I had a husband once," he finally says. His voice shocks me for how weak it sounds and I look at him to see he has almost entirely faded. He is more ghost than man now. "A mortal by the name of Sparrow. I loved him, Isra. He was the sun that lit my days and the moon that guided me through each night. I thought, Sparrow is why I Created. So I could see his smile."

He pauses and his eyes fill with tears. They slide down the runnels in his cheeks.

"We adopted five children. Fatherhood was a glorious thing. I kissed their scrapes and eased their aches. When they took ill, I sat beside their beds during the long nights. I helped them do their homework. I cooked them dinner. I loved them. I still love them. Sometimes I catch glimpses of them between the trees, or walking the paths beside me."

The silence that hangs in this place grows heavy. I picture Forest, ripe with Divinity, weeping at the bedsides of those whom he most dearly loved. I can imagine how hard it must have been, to watch helplessly while they experienced something he could not understand.

"Time never mattered to me before, a concept so far outside my nature I never considered it. Then, Sparrow grew old and I hungered for each second, each moment, every beat of his heart. I did not know the meaning of war until he died. Suddenly my soul was a battle-ground, festooned with the viscera left by love and hope and I... I was alone in a way I had never been before. It was years, Isra, before I learned to breathe again. And then I sat by the beds of each of my children when it was their turn. I eased them to their final moments, much as you are easing me now."

"I'm sorry," I say. "That must have been so horrible, Forest."

"I have spent lifetimes living in memory. After they died, the world became quieter, darker. Grief, I have learned, is but another face of love."

The past spears me through and Manab's voice echoes through my mind. *"I need to know one of us had the chance to survive."*

Divine Falcon, when I was a child. *"Love is not always warm, Isra. Sometimes it hurts."*

Forest sighs, a peaceful sound, and turns to look at me. "I see you, and I think of Sparrow and my children. I think of the ways a soul can bruise."

"Forest," I breathe.

"Life is not all pain and loss, Isra. No storm lasts forever." He captures my gaze and holds it warm in his own. "Someday, you will learn to breathe again."

A sob tears up my throat. I howl like a wolf in winter.

He lets out a sigh so gentle a feather would not stir at it. "Nothing ever ends..." he murmurs.

"It only changes shape," I finish.

"Will you help care for my Creation, Isra? Will you love me when I change shape?"

"Always," I whisper.

He breathes deep and nods.

"All of this is theirs now. I am satisfied."

His lips curl into a smile soft as clouds. He sighs and his body goes loose, dissipates faster, like smoke in the air. His tree grows around him, first like a hug, and then like a tomb. All I can see now are his eyes through the branches holding him close. They are closed and lined with wrinkles.

I feel the loss of him first in the earth. The tremors start down low, and then grow to a closer shuddering. The land vibrates and the walls of the tree tremble and groan. Then, the world goes silent and still, waiting. One heartbeat, and then two.

The end.

The beginning.

Here I sit, torn between the two.

The door to the tree opens, a groan in the quiet. Then footsteps and Belladonna is there, wrapping me in her soft, sweet arms.

"I can feel him, Isra." She presses her lips against my crown, breathes me in. "All around."

I can too, and I feel Falcon here as well. I wonder if Forest has finally bridged the gap between them. Perhaps, after eternities apart, they are finally together again.

That thought fills my heart with peace.

Nothing ever ends, it only changes shape.

"Look outside," Belladonna whispers into my ear. I cling to her, my life raft, my still water, my safety.

I lift my head, look past Forest's fading body, the roots wrapping around him, through the window in the far wall to the world outside.

It happens all at once, a burst, an explosion of life, verdant and thriving. I feel the tree growing larger, ever larger. Through the window, I watch as the loam becomes fertile and dark. Trees sway in a breeze all their own and flowers bloom, a riot of them. A burst of birds in rainbows of color fill the sky, while the forest is filled with wildlife. Never have I beheld such untamed, reckless beauty.

Bells ring throughout Meadowsweet and Divine Forest's arbor breaks out in shouts, sobs, prayers of thanks, and celebration. The sky rings with their rejoice, their hallelujahs, their cries of mourning.

All of this is theirs now.

I cannot help but think of Dawnland, of the moment Falcon slept. The bombs had been so near, so frequent, if the world had trembled, if it had transformed, I had not noticed.

"Are you okay?" Belladonna asks as the arbor transforms around us, becomes a paradise.

"Manab and Atheed should be here to see this," I say. "To watch the world be reborn."

"Perhaps, someday, we will tell them about it."

We wait like that, until the landscape quiets. I am too overcome to do much more than watch, exhausted in a way that has nothing to do with being tired. I have spent so long torn between the past and the present. Now, perhaps, it is time to look toward the future.

It is time to learn to breathe again.

There is a knock on the front door, and Belladonna answers it. A moment later, twelve people enter the room, all of them draped in white. "We have come to tend our god," the woman who first called me here, what feels like a lifetime ago, says. She is crying, bent by both sorrow and hope. Her whiskers twitch. "Was... was it a peaceful parting?"

They wait with bated breath for my answer.

"He went with dignity," I tell them. "He was ready."

She looks around, studies the walls of his tree. "He asked me, not long ago, to turn this place into a refuge for orphaned children, once he slept."

Tears sting my eyes as I think back to his story about Sparrow and the children they adopted. This tree would be a marvelous place for kids to grow up in, so many hallways and rooms, all that nature. Like the World Tree in Dawnland, this is a haven for imagination.

"It would make a lovely orphanage," Belladonna says. "What a soul Forest has."

Has, she says. Not *had*. Forest is all soul now. Untethered and pure. Whole in a way he has not been since he Created his first tree.

Nothing ever ends.

I think of Dawnland again, of finding refuge here in Meadowsweet, despite it all. Of this new family I have found.

I think of purpose.

And learning to breathe again.

Will you help care for my Creation, Isra? Will you love me when I change shape?

I draw in a breath, meet Belladonna's warm eyes. "If you would have me, I would like to help with that endeavor."

The woman studies me a moment, then smiles. "My name," she says, "is Poppy, and I would be delighted to have your help." Then, the moment is over and she turns her attention to Forest's bed, where he is wrapped beneath the roots of the tree, his eyes visible, but nothing else.

It is time for us to go. For all I was there with Forest at the last, he was not my god, but theirs, and now it is only right for me to leave them alone with their maker.

I will return here, later, after the dust settles. I will love Forest through his arbor, as long as I am able.

"Isra," Belladonna says. Her voice is lined with sorrow. "My grandmother."

The bells are still tolling across Meadowsweet, and I feel rumbles from elsewhere in the city as Chaos calls more of the Divine home.

"And Rosemary," she finishes.

This day will be an agony. A wound that I will feel forever. More scar tissue lining my already tattered heart.

I stand, look at Forest one last time, laying wrapped in the world. "I will love you," I say to his fading body, "and I will help tend your arbor."

Peace suffuses me. From the corner of my eye, I think I see Falcon for a moment, the way she was before. Her smile is soft and her eyes bright. And Forest... there is Forest beside her.

Belladonna weaves her fingers through mine and tugs me out the door, toward the Hall of the Gods.

NOW
ROSEMARY

Here I arrive, at the end of things.

The end of the world.

The end of an age.

The end of me.

Change surrounds me as the Divine take their rest. The very earth vibrates as soil churns and becomes rich; plants push from the loam, exotic and fulsome. The sky shimmers with waves of color, turquoise and amethyst, ruby and jade. Stars appear and then fade and then appear again. For a moment, the moon is close enough to grasp, and then it disappears before reappearing in an entirely different part of the sky.

They are gifting us their Creations. This reality is becoming ours now.

"Rosemary," Muse says. His caretaker, Lavender, sits beside his bed, weeping.

We are all weeping.

"Yes, beloved uncle?"

He is so faint now, barely there. Fading a bit more with each breath.

"Do you remember when we first met? I saw you standing in the Hall, so lost and alone. I thought, that is the child I am meant to love." He pauses, breathes deep. "Have I loved you well, Rosemary?"

I want to hold his hand, but he no longer has hands, and so I lean forward and press my lips against his craggy cheek, feel his soft skin, breathe him in. He will always be part of me, but oh, this hurts.

To no longer have Muse, my star in the dark.

My song in the silence.

Empty halls. Empty rooms. Empty chairs.

"You have brought me to life with your love, Muse."

He smiles.

We are in Father Luna's Sacred Observatory, where all of his sons have gathered in their last. They lie on beds, their families surrounding them. The air is filled with sniffles and sorrow. At the head of the room, on an elevated dais, is Father Luna. He lost his mortal shape hours ago. Now, all I see is a fog of dark, dissipating, ever dissipating.

"I feel," his eyes are warm, "like loving you was the best part of my long, long life."

"Muse," I breathe, "do not leave me. I beg you."

"Can you hear the music, Rosemary?" His voice is filled with wonder. "It is... all around."

"It is beautiful, my brother," my father says from my other side. "You have the most glorious soul."

This... this is too much.

Sobs tear through me, ravage me.

"I go now," my uncle says, "to finally join the song."

Lavender lets out a harsh, horrible cry and I lift my head in time to see Muse close his eyes one last time. His smile speaks of peace. Of good endings and better beginnings.

A hand on my shoulder. "Rosemary," Belladonna whispers. "We're here."

Relief fills me. I am no longer alone.

I ease myself from my wheelchair between my father's and my uncle's beds, let my hip settle, and then throw myself into Belladonna's arms. She holds me close while I come undone, threads her fingers through my vines and hums low in my ear, the way Muse used to when I was upset.

Muse. Oh, Muse.

All I see now are his eyes through the vines that are encircling him. Those kind, kind eyes. They will never look at me with love again.

It began with Divine Forest. One by one, they have fallen asleep since. They came into being together; it is only fitting they leave the same way. Now, only my father and the Most High remain. "You are in the midst of a Creation story," my father used to tell me. "It is a grand thing, to live in a world still being shaped."

It does not feel so grand now.

Father lies on his wedding blanket, near an apple tree. The cosmos beyond the windows are fading, spinning ever further away. For the first time, the lights of Meadowsweet can be seen through the glass.

I have spent most of my life in this hallowed hall, and yet suddenly I feel a stranger here, lost. Adrift. I do not know where I am, but I know it is not where I want to be.

Mother sits on a stone bench beside Father. She held his hand until it dissipated. Now Mother holds herself. Isra goes to her, rubs her back. I should be there, to help, but I can barely help myself right now.

Belladonna holds me. I cling to her. I need her to keep me afloat. I need someone to lean on so I can survive this.

My father becomes ever more insubstantial.

"How are you?" Belladonna asks. She rubs my back and keeps her voice pitched low, as though to a wounded animal. Her eyes are swollen. She lost her grandmother this day, I know, as well as many of her aunts. I should have been there with her, but my whole world is here.

"Your Divinity, Rosemary. How are you? You look... insubstantial."

I feel like one gust of ill-timed wind and I will blow away. But I know what she means. Chaos is pressing in now, coming closer. I can feel its hot breath on my neck, waiting for the right moment to take back its own.

"Will you love me," I whisper, "when this is over? When I am mortal and middle-aged, bent with pain?"

Now she is crying, tears cascading down her cheeks. She cups my face in her hands and presses our foreheads together.

"On purpose," she says. "Always. Forever."

She looks so mortal now, a woman with laugh lines and subtle crow's feet around her eyes. Her skin still shimmers, but she's lost her glow. Her hair is pale yellow and her red-rimmed eyes are the color of sun-warmed honey. She is alive and vital with it. Never have I seen such a beautiful sight.

"Rosemary," my father whispers. Belladonna wraps an arm under my shoulders and helps ease me to the ground beside my father's blanket.

It is hard, being this close to him when he is fading. Facing what he has become, when all I want is who he used to be. I see the shape of him, but little more. His starlit eyes are fire-bright as they stare at me, and his lips curl into an achingly familiar smile.

I would offer up anything to see but one more smile like that.

"My heart," he says, "don't cry. It is but this body that is fading. I will still be here. I am everything I have Created."

Platitudes. I am so tired of platitudes. I don't want platitudes or pretty words.

I want to *feel*.

I want to feel something. Anything.

I want it all to come spilling out of me on a wordless roar until I am left empty and blissfully silent.

"Don't go," I say, as though I can stop this. As though I can reverse fate.

"I can feel it," he says, "all around."

"What can you feel?"

"Creation," he breathes. "All of the pieces of myself I thought I'd lost. I am so close to being whole again."

The relief in his voice is what undoes me, for it is pure, betraying an ache so profound there are no words to define it. What agony would it be, to spend an eternity incomplete?

"I do not know how to do this." I turn to Belladonna, but it is Isra who takes my hand and kneels beside me. Isra who gives me something to hold on to.

"You don't need to know how to do this, Rosemary. There is no right way through tragedy."

"No one," my father murmurs, "has ever dared map the topography of the soul."

My breath hitches. I am reminded of a time when I was young.

"Where do you feel your emotions?" I had asked.

"Whatever do you mean, my heart?"

I pointed at my stomach, where the butterflies dwelled. "My worry lives here."

"I carry it in my ribs," my father replied, a twinkle in his starburst eyes.

Anger burned my sternum, while my father clenched it in his fists. Passion warmed my fingertips; his was cradled by his throat. We circled each other, mapping the landscape of our emotions, until I realized that I was afraid of what would come next. For the only emotion we had not yet touched was love.

What if he did not feel it? What if it was not the same? What if—

Hands crafted of moonlight wrapped around my own. "I love you with every part of myself. There is nothing your light does not touch."

"I will love you," my father whispers, bringing me back to the moment, "even if I am not here to say the words."

I can't do this.

I can't do this.

I have to do this.

The sky suddenly feels like it's falling, and I can't breathe. I can't breathe. I can't... I can't...

A lifetime of memories fills me, one after the other.

The first time I met him in this very Observatory.

The first time he held me.

The first time I called him Father.

The first time I told him I loved him.

I wish I had savored those moments more. I wish I could live them over again.

How do you say goodbye to your whole world?

Father studies the glass ceiling, the stars beyond. "Rosemary," he says my name as though it is a prayer he has spent his life whispering. There is not much left of him.

I will have to go home after this.

It will be empty.

It will be dark.

And cold.

He will never sit in his favorite chair again. He will never study the stars, or play cards, or hold my hand, or laugh with me.

He is leaving me, and this world suddenly feels far too large and the night too long, and I am lost within its folds. Belladonna kneels on my other side. I am braced between her and Isra both. Their arms wrap around me, keep me from falling.

"My heart, the weight of being is too much," my father says.

"No," I say. "A moment more, I beg you. A breath of time. The beat of a heart."

My world hangs on his breath.

"I am gifting you," his eyes focus on me, "all of Creation."

"I love you," I whisper.

His gaze is soft and his smile softer. "There will be better days than this."

And then...

His eyes close.

For the last time.

It happens all at once then. I feel the moment he is lost to me, severed; the thread of Divinity that binds us snaps, and there is nothing but emptiness where my father used to be. The world trembles, groans. Stars shoot across the sky like marbles. Through the windows, I watch as the land rises like an ocean wave, and then falls. Trees spring from the soil, tall as mountains, and then flowers. So many flowers.

A scream claws its way from my throat. I fall on the space where my father fades. Chaos spears my soul, reaches in through the wound, and picks out the last of my Divinity. My connection to my arbor is severed, and I...

It is agony, to be transformed. Agony to lose pieces of myself. Agony to come undone.

"Aether!" Mother howls. "Beloved, do not leave me! Do not leave me! Do not—"

Never have I heard her so undone. She throws herself on the floor beside my father's body, starts clawing at the vines growing around him until her nails break and her fingers bleed, as though if she but digs far enough, she can wrest him from his cradle in the soil.

Isra goes to her, but Mother thrashes and Isra falls, her wings flaring wide to ease the landing. A wolf's howl pierces the air. "Aether, beloved, we did not have enough time."

I feel my vines, looking to pluck a flower and ease her angst, but none are growing. My flowers are gone with my Divinity and Mother... Mother is unraveling.

Belladonna helps me stand and I go to her, wrap her thrashing body in my arms, and hold her through her storm. "I'm here," I whisper. "I'm here. I'm here."

It is all I can say. All I can think.

I am rupture.

I am agony.

Mother stills, and when she finally looks at me, her eyes are wide and full of painful recognition. "Rosemary," she whispers, "I did not know love could hurt like this."

"I will ache with you," I whisper into her hair.

Bittersweet is this moment, the happiness that wounds.

I close my eyes. I can feel him. I can feel all of them. In everything. All around. Then, a whisper on the wind, "Rain is necessary, my heart, for how else will flowers grow?"

THEN ROSEMARY

"Rosemary, are you listening to me?"

I was sixteen. Of course I wasn't listening to him.

"Yes, Father."

We turned a corner, drawing nearer to a ruckus. Ahead, the main hallway was full of the Divine.

"It is as Divine Falcon always said. Nothing ever ends," my father was saying as we pressed forward. "It changes shape. That's what your teacher is trying to tell you. Nothing ends." Father stopped suddenly. "Muse? Muse!"

"Brother!" Muse's smile was wide; he winked at me. "Are these trumpets not incredible?"

"Muse, you cannot bring a jazz band into the Hall of the Gods without warning."

"Oh, come now, brother..."

Laughing, I left them to argue. Off to the side was a bench. I took a seat on the edge of it and kicked out my leg to ease the ache while Muse and my father argued. I could not see the band, but they were loud, the brass echoing throughout the Hall as they played a jaunty tune. A few of the Divine broke off and started dancing.

Before me, a group of teenagers danced. One of them looked at me and chortled. Loneliness squeezed the air from my lungs.

"Your cane," said a girl beside me, "is very beautiful." I had not noticed her there. I turned and my world stopped. Carved from a ray of light was she, blinding and beautiful.

Oh, my soul whispered, *there you are.*

"What is your name?" she asked.

"Rosemary," I said.

Her smile bloomed slowly.

"My name is Belladonna."

Later - Rosemary

"The merchant and the ferriers are arguing again," Belladonna says. We are in the garden. The sun is setting, making the silver in her hair glow. The laugh lines around her mouth are deep. Never have I seen such beauty.

"Still?" Isra asks.

"They will always fight." Belladonna hesitates. "Dawnland sent a missive. They want to negotiate trade."

My heart sinks. They will want her to go, and Isra as well, which means Flora will leave, and I will be... alone.

"I would like Flora to meet her father," Belladonna says.

And Isra would like to see her brothers.

Flora appears a moment later. She presses her lips against Isra's cheek and then hugs Belladonna before sitting on the bench beside my wheelchair. She is a young adult who has survived pupation and attained her majority.

She will always be a little girl to me.

There is a room in my soul I visit to read her bedtime stories, or hold her when she is crying, or kiss her scrapes better. Places where she will always be sweet and small and mine.

"Would you like to meet your father, Flora? Would you like to see Dawnland?" I ask.

Flora doesn't answer at first. She has inherited her mother's penchant for thinking before she speaks, an admirable quality.

The sun dips past the horizon, painting the world gold.

"I think I would like to," Flora finally answers. She reaches up and wraps a finger around one of her antennae, something she's done since she was a toddler. "Will you come with us, Mother Rosemary?"

"I..."

Could I? Could I leave Meadowsweet? Could I... go?

The wind blows and the pine tree to my right sighs. The sound reminds me of my father, and I am filled with the sweetest ache.

In all my years, I have never once thought of leaving.

There had always been my mother to consider, my father, my own bond with Chaos.

But now...

Mother had passed not long after my father faded. Her death had been soft and sweet and she had, finally, known me at the last.

"You are no longer bound here, Rosemary," Belladonna says. "We could go. All of us. Together."

They stare at me, waiting for my answer. "I think I would like that," I finally say as though testing the words. I would like to see what lies beyond the borders of Meadowsweet. It might be fun, to chase the horizon.

Flora smiles, then goes still. Twilight smears the sky purple. "Do you think Manab will like me?"

"Of course he will," Isra says. She has grown comfortable in Meadowsweet, though I know she has never stopped hungering to return to Dawnland. "Manab will not be able to help but love you."

I think of my childhood, of my mother, who said much the same to me once. I remember my own uncertainty, the insecurity that has chased me since that day.

"Rosemary knows a bit about meeting fathers," Belladonna says.

Flora studies me, and I study her. It is as though I am looking back through the years at myself. I remember being that girl and facing the prospect of meeting my father for the first time.

I remember how it frightened me.

"I had forgotten," Flora says. "Mother Rosemary, you have never told me the story of how you met your father. Would you now?"

The question, so innocently asked, pierces me through, and suddenly I am bleeding.

I will love you, Rosemary, whether I am here to say the words or not.

I can feel him, even now. He is in everything I see, every star in the sky, every shadow, every dream. He is everywhere.

He is my every heartbeat.

Oh, this ache. It has never gone away, just changed shape.

"It's okay," Flora says, misreading my silence. "If it's too hard, or you'd rather not—"

I rest a hand on her arm, steady myself, and find my words.

"What I remember first is my mother's sorrow. When I was very young, she was able to hide it..."

AUTHOR'S NOTE

(AGAIN.)

As I was writing this book, my seven-year-old said, "Mom, you should leave a note at the end saying 'And they all bounced away' so it will be funny."

So.

Alternative ending:

And they all bounced away.

GLOSSARY

I used four main books to create the plant and flower symbolism in *The Necessity of Rain*. Most plants had numerous symbolisms attached to them. For any one scene, I tried to pick the plants that had a few emotional ties to the moment itself. I did not use every symbolism for every plant, but just picked and choose what fit the moment.

I tried, very hard, to weave plant symbolism throughout the book, even in the plants that enter the scene in the periphery. Here, I've listed the most important ones.

The vast majority of the plant symbolism came from the book Flowerpedia by Cheralyn Darcey, which is where most of this text is from. It's a fantastic resource which I used *every time* I worked on this book.

I also used:

- Floriography by Jessica Roux
- Culpeper's Complete Herbal by Nicholas Culpepper, edited by Steven Foster,

- The Complete Language of Flowers: A Definitive and Illustrated History by S. Theresa Dietz (Plants marked with * are from this book.)

Flora

Agrimony – Do not worry, inner fears and worry

Aspen – Sensitivity, yin and yang, duality, confidence, divination, attract money, still fears, trust in love, awareness of the divine

Aster – be true to yourself, I wish this had not happened, patience, variety, elegance, afterthought, increase in magical powers

Belladonna – listen to me, be quiet, be still, silence, emotional breakthroughs, negative imbalances shifted

*Blueberries - prayer

Briar rose – simplicity, poetry, sweet words, divine love

*Cabbage – prophet, self-willed

Calendula – I release you, I am grateful, I am sorry, cleansing , protection, contentment, excellence, gratitude, love of nature, grief, sacredness, sorrow, understanding, release

Cedar – I live for thee, psychic powers, healing, purification, money, protection, encourage love, protection from bad dreams

Clary sage – life, purpose, wisdom from experience, elation, ability to see, inner perception, meditation, clarity, euphoria, sleep-induction, anxiety relief

Clover – good luck, fertility, domestic virtue, fortune, luck, long and happy marriage, second sight, protection

*Cucumbers – chastity, criticism

Daisy – let's play, playfulness, protection, happiness, calm, support, peace of mind

Evening primrose – you are safe, emotional warmth, female balance, calm, soothing, light in the darkness, insight, transformation, sweet memories

Foxglove – I believe in you, beware, stateliness, communication, insincerity, magic, confidence, creativity, youth

Grapes – I am devoted to you, independence, freedom, abundance, inner growth, attachment, love, devotion

Holly – I wish you peace, good luck, defense, protection, domestic happiness, cheerfulness, homemaking, balance of mind, peace, am I forgiven?, am I forgotten?, resurrection, recovery

Hyssop – I forgive you, cleanliness, sacrifice, breath, forgiveness, purification, shame, guilt, pardon, repentance

Ivy – I desire you above all else, nothing will separate us, ambition, bonds, elegance, fidelity, friendship, immortality, marriage, tenacity

Jade – good luck, I offer you friendship, strong presence, friendship, prosperity, fatigue, new beginning, optimism, energy, expansion, focused intention

Jasmine – abundance, victory, congratulations, hope

Lace flower (also known as "Queen Anne's Lace") – you are safe, protection, sanctuary, awareness, female energies

Laurel – I change but in death, I admire you but cannot love you, victory, protection from disease, protection from witchcraft, merit, glory

Lavender – cleansing, protection, grace, trust, I admire you

Lilac – let go of the past, let's move on, humility, confidence, vitality, brotherly love, first emotion of love, forsaken memory, space clearing, divination

Lily – I am proud of you, long-lasting relationship, partnership, majesty, truth, honor, pride, mother, maternal, partnership, fertility, union

Magnolia – wisdom, acceptance, strength, female energies, changes, I will always love you

Marigold – vitality, vigor, renewal, life force, magic, irrational expectations, you ask too much of me, honesty, passion, creativity, grief

Meadowsweet – healing, love, divination, peace, happiness, protection from evil, balance, harmony

Milkweed – heartache cure

Moonflower (also known as "Queen of the Night") – power, intuition, dreams, I dream of you

Morning glory – habit breaking, consistency, mortality, love in vain, affection, enthusiasm, vitality, love

*Moss – ennui, maternal love

Mulberry -I will not survive you, sadness, protection, strength, release of emotions, wisdom, warming of feelings

Nettle – pain, clear choices, decision making, health recovery

Oak – strength, pride, steadfastness, great achievement, durability, courage, protection, truth, masculine strength, steadfastness in faith, virtue, protection from lightning, ward off ill health, immortality, heritage, endurance, willpower, devotion to duty, high ideals, fulfillment of commitments

Oleander – caution, respect, calculated risks, lust, notice me

Orchids – love yourself, uniqueness, sensuality, rare beauty, refinement, enchantment, self-love, self- assured, grace

Pansy – I am thinking of our love, love in idleness, remembrance, immunity, loving thoughts

Pine - self-forgiveness, faithfulness, consistency in adversity, courage, pity, immortality, mourning, uprightness, strength of character, earth-to-heaven connection, longevity, vitality, happy old age

Pink roses – chaste love, friendship

Poppy – memory, continuance, sacrifice, revelations, you are always in my memory

Rosemary – I remember you, your presence revives me, psychic awareness, mental strength, accuracy, clarity, remembrance, memory

Rowan – protection from evil, visions, protection, vitality, spiritual strength, reawakening, healing

Sage – purification, longevity, good health, long life, wisdom, cleansing, protection, higher purpose, reflection, inner peace, esteem, domestic virtue

Snowdrop – I am here for you, hope, new beginnings, illumination, self-neglect, inner peace, renewal, solutions

Straw flowers – I am here for you, I will always treasure you, happy memories, unconditional love, eternal happiness

Thistle – independence, austerity, protection from distraction, habit breaking, spiritual desires, courage, inner strength, coping

Thyme – bravery, affection, courage, strength

Weeping willow – melancholy, mourning

Willow – be mine again, forsaken love

Wisteria – enduring love, endurance, love, honor, creative expansion, patience, longevity, fertility

Woodbine – please keep this secret, fraternal love, peace of mind, secrets, material objects, strength, honesty, family strength

Yarrow – friendship, war, elegance banishing, relaxation

Yew – death, longevity, magic, wisdom, knowledge, transcendence, immortality, rebirth, protection

Zinnia – absence, missing you

CREDITS

EDITING
Nathan Hall, Isabelle Wagner

COVER ART
Pen Astridge

CHAPTER HEADERS
Allegra Pescatore

SENSITIVITY READERS
Nathan Hall, Allegra Pescatore, Tina Kelly

BETA READERS
Fiona Mackintosh and Rowena Andrews

Special thank you to my family, especially my kids, who had to deal with me not being terribly present while I was putting the finishing touches on this book.

Thank you! Please read!

Writing *The Necessity of Rain* was an act of love and determination and now, after years of working on it, I can't quite believe that I've made it to the other side.

Books live or die based on visibility. If you enjoyed this story, please take a moment to help others find it by rating and/or writing a short review on Amazon.

Thank you, from the bottom of my heart, for coming on this journey with me.

ABOUT THE AUTHOR

Sarah has been a compulsive reader her whole life. At a young age, she found her reading niche in the fantastic genre of Speculative Fiction. She blames her active imagination for the hobbies that threaten to consume her life. She is a full-time speculative fiction editor, an award-winning author, a semi-pro nature photographer, gardener, world traveler, three-time cancer survivor, and mom to two kids. In her ideal world, she'd do nothing but drink lots of tea and read from a never-ending pile of books.

ALSO BY SARAH CHORN

IF YOU LIKED THE NECESSITY OF RAIN THEN...

Please check out my Wild West-inspired fantasy, Of Honey and Wildfires, which is available on Amazon now.

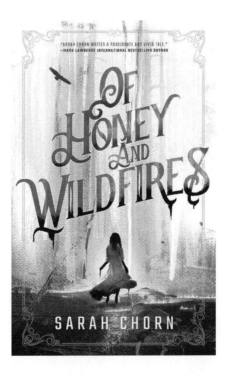

Made in the USA
Middletown, DE
05 July 2025

10139147R00179